A STOLEN MOMENT

"I'm quite content with my life as it is."

"Are you?" His voice was husky in the dark.

Shelby looked at him again. He had turned toward her, and his face was partially in the moonlight, partially in shadow. She didn't know how to answer him. "I . . . I . . . ," she began, but stopped as he touched the side of her face with his fingers. He pushed a stray wisp of hair behind her ear, then ran his fingertips down the edge of her jaw. When he reached her chin, he put his finger under her chin and tipped her face up slightly. "Gill," she whispered.

Her whisper of his name was his undoing. Everything fled out of his mind except an overwhelming desire to know her, to touch her. He bent to kiss her, and found her lips as soft and willing as he had dreamed they would be. *Just kiss her lightly,* he said to himself, *and that's all.* But she pressed into him, and put her arms around his neck, drawing him closer. He felt a surge of desire like none he had ever known. He crushed her to him and kissed her hungrily. . . .

BOOK YOUR PLACE ON OUR WEBSITE AND MAKE THE READING CONNECTION!

We've created a customized website just for our very special readers, where you can get the inside scoop on everything that's going on with Zebra, Pinnacle and Kensington books.

When you come online, you'll have the exciting opportunity to:

- View covers of upcoming books
- Read sample chapters
- Learn about our future publishing schedule (listed by publication month *and author*)
- Find out when your favorite authors will be visiting a city near you
- Search for and order backlist books from our online catalog
- Check out author bios and background information
- Send e-mail to your favorite authors
- Meet the Kensington staff online
- Join us in weekly chats with authors, readers and other guests
- Get writing guidelines
- AND MUCH MORE!

Visit our website at
http://www.zebrabooks.com

THE FIFTH PROPOSAL

Juliette Leigh

Zebra Books
Kensington Publishing Corp.
http://www.zebrabooks.com

ZEBRA BOOKS are published by

Kensington Publishing Corp.
850 Third Avenue
New York, NY 10022

First Printing: July, 1999
10 9 8 7 6 5 4 3 2 1

Printed in the United States of America

One

"Is he dead yet?"

Countess Rimildi moved back two steps, until her back hit the door of the clothes cupboard. She stared, transfixed, at the mound of covers in the middle of the ancient four-poster bed. The clock in the hall began to toll midnight, and she jumped straight up, shrieking.

"Hush, Mama. If he isn't dead, he might hear you," Miss Shelby Falcon whispered loudly, but she didn't turn around to look at her mother. Instead, she walked up to the edge of the bed, leaned over, and tried to see if there was any sign of life. It was difficult to see as the room was pitch-dark everywhere except for the light of one guttering candle that burned on the small table beside the bed.

Shelby pulled gently at the covers to get a better look at her grandfather. She dreaded what she might see, but it had to be done. She glanced around and picked up a half-burned candle and lit it from the guttering stub. The light was better, although still not bright enough to see much. She turned back to look at the bed and pulled slightly on the top quilt.

The covers were stuck, as though held down by a dead weight. "Leave it be, Shelby," her mother whispered hoarsely. "Surely Biddle is somewhere about." She paused. "That is, if poor Biddle isn't dead, too. We shouldn't have come here this late. I knew it. I told you so."

"Hush, Mama," Shelby said and again pulled on the covers. They wouldn't budge, so she jerked hard on them. This time, covers and the body beneath them spun over and almost spilled off the bed.

"Dead? Do you think I'd die in my bed like some common scribbler, woman?" The roar came from the depths of the pillows as Colonel Falcon disentangled himself and sat upright, almost knocking Shelby down. He glared around the room from under bushy eyebrows, his nightcap falling down over one eye. "Are you daft?" He reached out and grabbed the ribbons of Shelby's bonnet, pulling her closer while he fumbled for his spectacles. "Who is this who's wishing me dead?"

"No one's wishing you dead. Never." Shelby put her hands on his and smiled down at him. "It's Shelby, Grandfather." She saw his spectacles on the small table and turned to get them. He pulled her bonnet off by one ribbon. The bonnet fell onto the bed as her hair came loose from its pins and fell, rich auburn around her shoulders. She shoved it back from her face quickly, running her fingers through it. "I've come to see you." She smiled as she picked up the spectacles and put them on his nose.

"You could have said who you were instead of rousing a man out of a warm bed to inquire if he's ready for the coffin-maker." He scowled at her, employing an expression which had in the course of his long and illustrious career brought strong men to the point of trembling. Shelby, however, grinned back at him and straightened his nightcap.

"Just throw that damned thing away," he muttered, jerking it off. He peered around her, looking toward the door. Shelby thought he was looking out into the hall where a single candle burned in its sconce, but he was looking at Countess Rimildi who was shrinking as far as she could into the woodwork. "Who's that over there?" the colonel demanded. "Daisy, is that you?"

"Yes. I . . . Yes." The countess's voice was faint.

"Well, speak up, girl," Colonel Falcon roared. He had been famous throughout the army for his ability to be heard even in the thick of battle. It had even been said that his shouts were louder than the roar of the enemy's cannon.

The countess shuddered delicately. "I've . . . I've brought Shelby to see you as you wished. That is . . . Shelby came right away. Your letter said to make all possible haste." The countess's voice was faint, and she made sure to stay close to the door.

"And it's about time you got here," the colonel growled. "I heard you two was gallivanting all over Italy again last winter." He glared at them over the top of his spectacles. "Husband hunting again, eh, Daisy? You've had your turn. Now you need to find a husband for the little one here. She's turning into an old maid." He turned his glare toward Shelby. "What are you now, girl? Five and twenty?"

"You know I am, Grandfather," Shelby said coolly. She was probably the only person in all of England who didn't fear the notorious Colonel Quilby Falcon, the man who had gone toe to toe with Tippoo Sahib at Mysore, the man who could have saved the American colonies for the Crown if only Cornwallis had heeded his advice in the Carolinas. "Enough of that, Grandfather. Whatever is going on here? We got a letter from a Mr. Gill that informed us you were next door to death and that we should come to Wychwood posthaste. So here we are."

"Where you belong," her grandfather said irascibly.

Shelby ignored him. "Who is this Gill who wrote the letter? Your new solicitor?"

Colonel Falcon sneezed and scowled again as he pushed his spectacles back into place. "Gill? A solicitor?" He laughed. "That's a rich one, girl. No, he's here in the house."

Shelby stared at him. "He's in the house? He's a guest of yours?" she asked blankly.

"Yes, and a good thing. I don't know what I would have done without him since Biddle has gotten so trifling."

"Biddle?" Shelby asked in alarm. "What happened to Biddle? The two of you have been inseparable since he saved your life when Hyder Ali tried to have you killed. Have you turned him off? Think of all the things he's done for you!"

Her grandfather waved his hand vaguely toward the back of the house. "Oh, Biddle is still here. And as sorry as ever." He smiled, remembering the past. "Ah, Shelby, my girl, those were the days. I remember when I was only four and twenty. Young, but I knew how to do things even then. If Biddle and I hadn't persuaded Nizam Ali to cede Madras . . ." He looked at Shelby and frowned. "Have I mentioned that before?"

"Yes, indeed." Shelby smiled at him. He had probably mentioned that particular episode at least four or five times a week every time she had been at Wychwood, even from the earliest years she could remember. They had sat for hours and looked at the large case where Colonel Falcon kept the Jewels of Ali that Nizam Ali had given him in appreciation. Trifles, Nizam Ali had called them, according to her grandfather, but they were certainly not that. There was a diadem, along with two bracelets and a necklace. They were finely crafted of lacy gold and set with colored gemstones, mainly emeralds and rubies. The stones were cabochons, and most of them were very large.

"I suppose I have mentioned it a time or two," Colonel Falcon said. "As I recall, you spent years wanting to wear the Jewels of Ali. When you were ten, you imagined yourself an Indian princess." He gave her a strange look. "Tell me, girl, what would you say if I gave them to you?"

"To me?" Shelby felt her jaw drop, and she heard her mother gasp in the background. "I always thought they would go to Crawford. Isn't he the heir?"

"Well, he's already got the family house and everything that's entailed, but the jewels are mine to do with as I please, as is Wychwood and what money I have. Mind you, I'm not promising the jewels to you, but I'm thinking that way. After all, you are my only granddaughter." He sat up straighter. "I need to get these things settled."

With a jolt, Shelby looked at her grandfather again and realized that he did look older and smaller, almost frail. He had always been a big man, but now he didn't appear much larger than average. Sitting there on the edge of the enormous four-poster, Quilby Falcon looked every one of his seventy years. "The jewels aren't important to me, Grandfather, but you are. I know that telling me about the jewels can't be the only reason you had this person write to me so I would hurry to Wychwood. Are you seriously ill?"

He nodded. "Of course. Haven't I been telling you that for years?"

Shelby chuckled. "Yes, at the same time you've been riding for miles every morning. Still, I was worried when I got your letter last winter when I was in Florence."

"Consorting with those Italians." Colonel Falcon shook his head. "You always want an Italian on your side in a fight—they're fearless. But I can't say they make good husbands." He glanced at Countess Rimildi. "That right, Daisy?"

"Carlo was a wonderful husband," the countess said shakily. "Of course, he could never be like Bates, but . . ." She let her voice trail off.

Colonel Falcon sighed. "Bates was like his mother—frail and gentle. He wasn't like me at all. I think it was ordained that he die young because I don't think he could have coped with life. You know that." He shook his head and glanced up at Shelby. "How you and Bates could have had a girl like Shelby is beyond me. She's just like me."

Shelby laughed. She had heard this many times before. "Well, Grandfather, that may be true to an extent. If I am like you, I'm going to be just as blunt as you always are." She took his hand in hers. "You wrote me in Florence that you'd had several accidents. I remember that you called them minor, but I wasn't so sure that they were. Tell me plainly, Grandfather, why did you have this Mr. Gill write me in London and tell me that you were dying? Is that true? If you had written the letter yourself, I wouldn't have thought you were near death, but, since you had to have someone else write it for you, I feared the worst."

"Of course it's true," he growled. "Can't you see I'm dying?"

Shelby held the candle close to his face and peered at him. "You look fine to me. Perhaps in need of a shave, but otherwise just as usual." She put the candle back down on the table by the bed as she tried to take a moment to compose herself. She had not told him the truth. In reality, he looked older. The fire was still in his eyes, but he was thinner, and his cheeks were sunken.

She took a deep breath, forced a smile onto her face, and looked around. "By the by, Grandfather, where is everyone? Mama and I just arrived to find no one to answer the door. We had to let ourselves inside, and all our baggage is still out in the carriage."

"A terrible trip," Countess Rimildi said wearily. "I wanted to wait for a few days until we got ready, but nothing would do Shelby but to come immediately. We were packed and on the road less than three hours after that man's letter arrived." The countess grimaced. "I ache all over. I do believe I'm coming down with the vapors." She put a hand to her head in her most elegant manner and swayed slightly.

"Then sit down, Daisy." Colonel Falcon scowled at her. "I never could stand these weak women standing around swearing they were sick. Most of them have buried five or six husbands."

"Oooooh!" Countess Rimildi wailed and put her hand over her mouth. "An unkind cut," she said faintly.

"Don't take it personally, Daisy. God knows Bates wasn't strong, but that wasn't your fault. As for your other two—or was it three?—husbands, I know nothing. Carlo and whoever."

He frowned and pinned her with a look. "Just don't give me any talk about vapors or being sickly. You could walk from here to Hyderabad and never get winded."

Countess Rimildi sat down in the only chair in the room and glared at him, but her look was wasted. He had turned his attention back to Shelby. "No one downstairs?" he asked in amazement. "And the door open? The country could rob me blind. I'll have Biddle's hide for this. He's probably stuck back in his room with a bottle of blue ruin and Dick Turpin."

"The door wasn't open, just unlocked. But there was no one to greet us," Countess Rimildi said faintly. "And to think we rushed here as fast as we could, even going so far as to arrive here in the dead of night. We could have stayed in an inn and traveled easily as civilized people do." She glanced around as though something were going to pounce on her at any moment. "I don't even know if I'll be up to returning tomorrow."

Colonel Falcon ignored her. "If Biddle's drunk again, then there's nobody except . . . ," he muttered, reaching for the bellpull. He gave it a furious yank and the clang could be heard throughout the house. "Gill! Gill, I say!" he bellowed, as though the clanging of the bell were not enough.

"Grandfather, just let me do whatever you want." Shelby was scandalized. "You certainly can't ask a guest to go running around to find Biddle."

"Gill won't mind. Besides, if Biddle's in his cups, he's not lost—he's probably snoring in his bed." Colonel Falcon looked toward the door. "Gill!" he bellowed again.

"Whether he minds or not, he's a guest," Shelby said, frowning at him with the same auburn eyebrows the colonel had. "We Falcons don't ask guests to do things."

"The boy's been in the army," Colonel Falcon said, waving his hand vaguely toward the door. "I know he's accustomed to lending a hand and won't mind a whit."

"How do you know that? He might—"

"How do I know?" Colonel Falcon interrupted her. "How

do I know? Girl, have you forgotten what a fine judge of character I am? Besides, Gill used to be an aide to Wellesley himself, and we all know how demanding that man is." The colonel paused, then shook his head. "Gill!" he bellowed again.

"Really, Grandfather, I don't think . . ." Shelby had an image of a middle-aged gentleman being forced to jump at the colonel's beck and call. "Grandfather, we shouldn't—"

"Gill!" Colonel Falcon bellowed again, almost shaking the bedclothes.

"I'm right here." The voice was soft, low, and firm. It didn't sound at all as Shelby had imagined it would. Instead, it was confident and husky, with a touch of something else—danger, perhaps. Shelby whirled around, but could see only a vague outline in the gloom. "Sorry, Colonel. Biddle, ah, needed some slight attention, and Dick Turpin was most insistent on going out." There was a touch of laughter underneath the words.

The man walked across the room and into the small pool of light from the candle. His hair was black, his clothes were black, and his shadow loomed large and black against the far wall. He stood there, black from toe to head, looking for all the world like the devil incarnate. Before she could stop herself, Shelby shuddered and took an involuntary step backward until the backs of her legs and body hit the edge of the bed. In the background, she could hear her mother gasp.

Shelby had to steel herself to keep from cringing; then she forced herself to stand taller. She made herself look at the man, right into his eyes. Gill looked at her coolly and didn't move a muscle.

"Oh, I really am coming down with the vapors," Countess Rimildi wailed, staggering to her feet. "Shelby, help . . ." She swooned gracefully onto the floor beside Gill's feet. Gill looked down curiously at the large woman piled next to his boots and didn't move. Then he looked at Shelby. "Is she ill?"

"Just another of Daisy's demmed tricks," Colonel Falcon

said, tossing back the covers and swinging his legs over the edge of the bed. "Help me up, would you?"

Gill strolled over to the edge of the bed and put his hand on the colonel's arm, pulling him to his feet. The colonel didn't seem to notice that Gill was not gentle. Shelby stood in shock for a moment, staring at them, then rushed to her mother's side. "If you please, leave Grandfather and come help me with Mama," she said to Gill as she gently patted her mother's hands. "We need to get her off the floor." She remembered that he was a houseguest. "That is, if you don't mind."

"I'd be delighted." Gill strode over to them, put his hand underneath the countess's arm, and hauled her to her feet. The countess swayed a moment, fluttered her eyes open, and screamed. "Unhand me, you . . . you . . . ! Help! Turn me loose!" Gill quickly let her go, and she flopped down to the floor again. He stood quietly as the countess pulled herself to her feet. Shelby held her mother and helped her to the chair. "Ooooh," the countess wailed. "That long, miserable carriage trip and now this. I can't take any more. I can't!"

Shelby turned and glared at Gill. "My mother is in great distress and you presume to shove her around like a . . . like a . . . like a sack of laundry."

He gave her a level look. "I merely followed instructions."

"She didn't mean that. Have you no sensibility?"

"It rather depends on the situation. On occasion, I've been lauded for my extreme sensibility." Gill smiled at her, and she got the distinct impression that he was mocking her.

"And on the other occasions?" Shelby asked coldly as the countess fluttered her eyelids and began to moan prettily.

Colonel Falcon chuckled as he tottered over to them, his nightshirt flapping around his bare legs. "A man after my own heart, Gill is," he said. "Daisy, stop that sniveling." He wandered over to the clothespress and threw it open, banging the doors. "I might as well get up and have a snack. Gill, do you see my dressing gown anywhere in here? One of the great curses of growing old is that you can never find anything. Not even with these demmed spectacles." He banged the doors as he rummaged around.

Gill coughed discreetly. "I do believe you're confined to bed, Colonel."

"Nonsense. I'm feeling much better. Besides, with all this caterwauling Daisy's doing, the whole house will be awake anyway. We could hunt everyone up, go down, and get reacquainted." He paused a moment and scowled. "I wonder if they're back yet."

"They haven't returned unless they've come in during the last few minutes while I've been occupied here." Gill watched the colonel rummage in the clothespress. "I see you're determined," he finally said, turning toward the foot of the bed, where he picked up the colonel's dressing gown, and held it out to him. The colonel took it and put it on while Gill watched dispassionately.

"They?" the countess said faintly, swaying in her chair. "Did you say *they?* You didn't ask just Shelby to come?"

"Ah, yes, *they.* No, everyone is here, Daisy, but don't you worry. I intend to take care of Shelby." Colonel Falcon shuffled back over to the bed and reached for the guttering candle. "We have a regular party here to see me pass into the great beyond. The two of you and four others are here already. For some reason, Rose is coming tomorrow, but thanks be to the saints, she's not bringing Hettie along." He paused and made a face.

"Hettie isn't coming?" Countess Rimildi was all interest. "Did she say why?"

Colonel Falcon shook his head. "No, but I got the idea that Hettie may have a fish on the string back in town. Crawford said she was staying to see a Mr. Weatherby."

The countess gasped. "Willard Weatherby?"

"Who knows?" Colonel Falcon waved the question away. "All I can say is that she's there and the rest of them are here—or will be soon."

"The whole family?" Shelby looked at her grandfather with concern. His illness must be serious if he had called in the entire assortment. Before this, he had usually written to her that he was, as he put it, going to go to his reward soon; then he asked her to visit. It had happened a dozen times before, and she had always come, not because she believed for an instant that he was close to death, but because she liked to spend time with him. But she had never before received a letter written by another person about the colonel. She was concerned.

"Grandfather," she said in a small voice, "shouldn't you get back into bed?" She cast a glance at Gill, who was standing there impassively. "I'll go get Biddle for you if you wish."

Colonel Falcon leaned down and rummaged under the bed-coverings, unearthing a bottle of whiskey and a glass. With the whiskey in one hand and the flickering candle in the other, he strode across the room. "Nonsense. If Biddle's in his cups, he certainly won't want to join us. Let's go down and have a touch of refreshment ourselves. Those other hellions should be back shortly if they don't decide to stay out all night. All four boys have been here all of a day, and they're already bored beyond words."

Shelby grabbed at his sleeve. "You did say the four of them are here?" She paused a second and made herself swallow. "Crawford's here?"

"Yes, yes, he's here, along with the rest of that sorry crew."

"Hayward? Bentley? Pearce?"

"The lot of 'em." He turned and glanced down at the countess who had sagged into her chair and was fanning herself. "Get that heft up from there, Daisy, and let's go down and grab a bite. Nothing like a little snack to give you a good night's sleep." He went out the door and headed down the stairs, leaving the three of them in the dark. The countess jumped up, grabbing Shelby's arm. "You know the way out, Shelby. Do help me."

Shelby had lived in the old maze of rooms and halls that was Wychwood when she was small, and she knew every cranny, every turn in the house. She knew and loved the place, and had even helped plan several of the gardens. She began to lead her mother toward the door.

At that moment, there was a tremendous crash and a great deal of cursing. Gill sprang to life and shoved Shelby aside as he dashed through the door. She left the countess and ran out behind him, stopping at the top of the steps. Gill was already at the bottom, bent over the prostrate form of her grandfather. Colonel Falcon wasn't moving.

"Is he . . . is he . . . ?" Shelby couldn't bring herself to say the words that had come so easily to her mother.

"No," Gill said briefly, "although his dressing gown seems to be somewhat charred from where he landed on his candle. Thank goodness, it was almost out anyway." Gill moved aside and gently sat the colonel upright, picking up his spectacles and placing them on his nose. Colonel Falcon blinked his eyes and looked up at Gill. "Again?" he muttered as Shelby came down the stairs.

Gill shook his head as though to warn the colonel not to speak. He glanced back up toward Shelby, then down at the colonel. "I think you're fine," he said to Colonel Falcon. "I don't know who put that rug at the top of the stairs, but I'll move it." He stood and started up the stairs.

When he moved, Shelby caught a glimpse of something out of the corner of her eye. She turned to look. "The curtains!" she screamed, grabbing Gill by the sleeve with one hand as she pointed with the other.

The colonel's bottle of whiskey had rolled across the floor, crashing into the small table by the door and knocking it over. The candle on the table had slid into the puddle of whiskey on the worn rug the colonel had brought back from India. The carpet was now blazing merrily, and the flames were getting dangerously close to the heavy curtains that draped the side windows in the hall.

Gill shoved Shelby aside. "Grab the colonel and get him out of here!" he yelled over his shoulder as he jerked the curtains from the windows and shoved them through the nearest doorway. He stomped at the carpet, trying to extinguish the flames while Shelby pulled and tugged at her grandfather.

"Leave me be, girl," Colonel Falcon said, swatting away her hand. "I want to see this."

In the background, Shelby could hear her mother screaming at the top of the stairs. "Hush, Mama," she yelled, not bothering to look up at the countess. She was too busy trying to get the colonel to move. He wouldn't budge.

"Just look at that," the colonel said with admiration. "Burning like the flames of hell! Stomp that one over there, boy!" He chortled and pointed as he stood up, almost dancing in the hall.

Shelby glanced back at the entry. Gill was clearly losing the battle. He stopped and pulled off his coat, revealing a snowy white shirt that was plastered to his body with sweat. He started swatting the flames with his coat, cursing fluently all the while. It was quite obvious that he had learned well that part of army life.

Colonel Falcon chortled again and sat down on the second step to watch. "Good show, boy!" he yelled again. "Watch that other corner!"

To Shelby's horror, the fire had spread to the other corner of the hall and was threatening the curtains there. She gave up on her grandfather and ran to help Gill. She had left her shawl upstairs, so had nothing to use to beat the flames. In a moment of inspiration, she grabbed the edge of the carpet and began trying to roll it up from the edge of the stairs toward the door. Gill saw what she was doing and jerked the door open. The flames spurted up as the breeze hit them, but Gill ignored them and grabbed the far corner of the carpet. The carpet was heavier than it looked, and had been nailed down here and there to hold it firmly in place. Shelby couldn't get some of it pulled from the floor, but Gill jerked hard on the edge and it finally came loose. The two of them rolled the carpet up as best they could and began dragging it through the door. In just a few moments, they had the carpet outside on the gravel where it blazed up in a shower of sparks.

"Don't get too close," he said, touching her arm and pulling her away from the blazing carpet. "A spark could ignite your gown."

Shelby turned away from the burning mess and took a breath of the cool night air. Then she looked up at Gill and their eyes met. He was drenched in sweat, and his face was streaked with soot. His white shirt was smudged, and sweat plastered it to his body where it clung like a second skin. His black hair, long enough to almost reach his shoulders, had curled with dampness and was stuck with sweat to the planes of his cheeks and jaw. The flames from the still-burning carpet outlined his features against the dark, causing shadows to move across his face. His shadow loomed behind him against the wall of the house, larger than ever possible in life. He exuded pure, raw maleness tinged with danger.

Shelby's breath caught in her throat, and she involuntarily stepped back. Gill was looking at her in a strange way. *His hooded look seems almost predatory,* she thought with a shudder. She took another step back, but he reached out and caught her arm. "Careful," he said. "You'll back into the fire." Shelby tried to speak, but couldn't. Mercifully she was saved from having to answer by a shout from the doorway of the house.

Colonel Falcon was standing in the doorway, waving yet another bottle of whiskey, his dressing gown flapping in the night breeze. "Good show! Come on in and celebrate, you two! Damme, what a deathwatch this is turning into! I haven't had this much entertainment in years!"

Two

Shelby slowly turned and looked at her grandfather. She felt dazed, and it took her a moment to realize where she was. As if she were in a dream, she turned to look back at Gill standing there in the faint spill of light from the house, his shirt clinging to a muscular body, outlining it in white-silver. She shivered hard. Gill stepped over to her.

"You'll get a chill in the night air, Miss Falcon," he said softly, taking her elbow. "I believe we should go inside." He looked back down at the smoldering heap of what was left of the hall carpet. "I'll send Luke or Thomas out to take care of this." He nudged her elbow and Shelby began to move toward the house. The move wasn't abrupt, but Shelby was aware of the strength of the man and found his nearness was disturbing.

"Good work, boy." Colonel Falcon chortled as they passed him. Gill released Shelby's elbow once they were inside and turned back, extending his hand to the colonel. *He's very helpful, very efficient,* Shelby thought to herself as she watched Gill help the colonel and then close the door softly behind them. *But there's something . . . something just not quite right.*

Servants from all over the house had gathered and were standing in the front hall, gaping out at the commotion. "Everything is fine," Colonel Falcon growled. "Just go back to bed."

"Luke, Thomas," Gill said quietly to the two footmen standing by the door, "make sure the carpet has burned itself out, and then bury the remains."

He sounds, Shelby thought to herself, *as though he's the person at home here—the one in charge.* That surprised her. Never had anyone been in charge except Colonel Quilby Falcon. She noted also that, in spite of the smudges of soot covering his face and clothing, Luke and Thomas didn't question Gill's authority. Instead, they both went out immediately.

Gill glanced at the colonel, the countess, and Shelby. "If you would like to step into the drawing room, I'll find the housekeeper and have tea or coffee brought," Gill said, nodding toward the small green drawing room to the left.

"Oh, I could use some coffee," Countess Rimildi wailed. "And something to eat if you have it. I'm completely depleted."

"Eat? Daisy, that's not what you need." Colonel Falcon looked up and down the countess's plump frame. "If anything, you could use a diet. What's that someone told me Byron used to keep from looking like a whale—boiled potatoes and vinegar?" He laughed and held the bottle out toward the countess. "Actually this is what you need. Just a little of this will perk you right up." He waved the whiskey bottle toward her.

"Allow me, Colonel," Gill said smoothly, taking the bottle away. "I'll just take this with me and put it in a proper bottle."

"Good. And bring me back a glass with it. There's never a glass in the drawing room. Biddle hides them from me because he has the maggoty notion that a man can't drink unless he has a glass. I try to tell him it tastes the same from the bottle, but he won't believe me." He sighed. "Worse, he's right. No proper gentleman drinks from the bottle."

"I agree," Gill said, moving to the door. "If you wish, I'll bring glasses and have some tea and coffee brought in. I'll be back in a moment." He glanced down at the bottle and back at the colonel, a wicked gleam in his dark eyes and a touch of a devilish smile on his lips. Shelby could have sworn that the man was enjoying this. In just a moment, however, the gleam was gone and Gill was once more somber and impassive. He nodded slightly to Shelby as he passed her on his way across the hall.

Shelby followed her mother and grandfather to the drawing room as Gill disappeared toward the back of the house. A dark heap in the corner of the hall caught her eye. It was Gill's coat, the one he had used to beat the flames and then had tossed aside. Pausing a moment, Shelby bent down and picked it up. She ran her fingers down the soft black fabric that hadn't been touched by the flames. To her surprise, it was a very soft, fine wool and very well made. It was, of course, burned beyond repair. She held it up and looked at it again, trying to come up with a clue about Gill. Unless she missed her guess badly, the coat was very expensive and had been made by one of the better tailors in London. Even the buttons were heavy and thick, and, unless she was sadly wrong, they were silver. There were no identifying marks on either the coat or buttons that she could see, so all she could do was guess the origin, but there was no mistaking the excellent tailoring.

She folded the coat and put it on the hall bench, then went into the drawing room. Not tonight, but tomorrow, she promised herself, she would find out about this person who was so mysterious. She had never, in all the years she had been at Wychwood, heard her grandfather mention anyone named Gill. Now he was here, and seemed to be making himself right at home. He seemed almost like one of the family. Something was definitely not right.

Colonel Falcon sat in his favorite chair and began regaling them with stories of his clash with Tippoo Sahib. He was still talking when Gill returned, followed by a footman and the housekeeper, Mrs. McKilley, who were carrying tea, coffee, and some small cakes. The bottle of whiskey was there, also, but it was now in a cut-glass container which was considerably fuller than it should have been. Shelby suspected that Gill might have watered the whiskey down. It did appear that Colonel Falcon had already had one glass more than he needed.

Mrs. McKilley put the tray down, and the countess immediately snatched up two small cakes and began nibbling. "Oh, lemon cakes—my very favorite! I do need sustenance. You don't know how famished I am after that terrible carriage ride," she said. "Shelby was so distressed about her grandfather that she refused to stop except for the briefest of necessities. My bones ache in every joint." She finished her cake and reached for another, hesitated, and then took two. "Then to come here and discover all this." She waved her arm around to take in the entire household.

"Put it in a box, Daisy," Colonel Falcon said, reaching for the tumbler and cut-glass bottle. "You know you enjoy a spot of excitement."

"Grandfather, you really shouldn't drink. It's not good for you," Shelby said as the colonel poured the glass full to the top. He didn't put the bottle back on the tray.

He looked at Shelby and laughed as though they shared a secret. "You sound worse than Biddle. I'll tell you exactly what I told him: When a man's dying, he can do as he pleases. Who's to stop him?"

"Exactly. I agree wholeheartedly." The familiar voice that came from the direction of the door sounded just as laughing and lazy as always. Shelby whirled around, almost knocking over the tray of cakes.

"Crawford!" she gasped, then caught herself. "That is, I knew you were here, but . . . well, you weren't here." She paused to get a grip on her thoughts. "I mean, I knew you were coming back."

"Oh, we're all here, just like a row of bad pennies," he said, laughing as he came across the room. Shelby had to make herself breathe normally. She hadn't seen Crawford since he had broken her heart a year and a half ago by announcing his engagement to Aunt Hettie's daughter, Rose. Now she waited for her heart to lurch just at the sight of him walking across the room in that lazy way he had, the candlelight glinting off his blond hair. He looked perfect, dressed in blue that, even in the pale light, brought out the blue of his eyes. Strangely, her heart did nothing. *Perhaps,* she thought, *I'm really over him. Or perhaps I'm just in too much pain to feel it.* Throughout her trip to Italy and back, she had thought her heart hadn't mended at all, had believed perhaps it never would.

Crawford sauntered across the room, perfectly at ease. He sat down beside Shelby and put an arm around her shoulder. "And how's my favorite cousin?" he asked.

Shelby tried to make her voice light, but even to her own ears, she sounded breathless. "Just fine," was all she could manage. "And you?"

"As usual." He moved his arm and shrugged, then reached for some coffee and a lemon cake. "What's that moldering mess on the gravel in front of the door? Luke and Thomas were standing there, looking at it as though they were wishing it would go away by itself." Without waiting for a reply, he glanced at the tray. "Someone needs to ring for more cups and coffee. The others will be here in a moment."

"They're already here," Gill said, glancing out the window. "Although I don't know if they'll be able to get inside without assistance."

"You're probably right." Crawford grinned. "As I said, the footmen are outside, so I'm sure they will see that the others will have any assistance needed." He grinned. "I think Luke and Thomas have had enough practice getting Bentley, Pearce, and Hayward into the house in one condition or the other." Crawford waved a hand in dismissal and looked first at Gill, then at Shelby. "What in the world happened here? You two look as if you've been dragged through the mud."

"Oh, it was terrible," the countess wailed. "First we thought him dead, and then there was that terrible crash when he fell, and there was the fire!"

Crawford looked at the countess in amazement, then looked back at Shelby. "Could *you* tell me what happened?"

"Not much," Colonel Falcon said, pouring himself more whiskey. "Have some of this, Crawford. It's what you need. You're far too stiff, my boy." He halfway got up and shoved the bottle toward Crawford. He paused with his glass in midair as the door crashed open and the sound of drunken singing reached their ears. It was Biddle, in full voice, butchering the lyrics of "To Anacreon in Heaven."

Before Biddle showed himself at the door, however, a blur of reddish brown zoomed across the room and launched itself at the colonel, striking him full on the chest. Off balance, he crashed backward into the chair. It was too much for the chair—whiskey, bottle, colonel, and chair went backward. The colonel stayed in the chair, but his dressing gown fell toward his body as his feet went straight up into the air. "Damnation!" the colonel roared.

"I think I'm going to faint," Countess Rimildi said.

"What's going on here?" someone asked from the door, his speech slurred. Someone else began sneezing and sniffling.

"Dick, damn you, get off me!" the colonel roared. "You're supposed to be with Biddle. What did he do? Get drunk and let you out?" The colonel's bare feet waved in the air. "Gill!" he roared. "Gill, where are you? Lend me a hand, will you? Stop that! You know you're not allowed to do that!" This last was addressed to the dog, which was busy lapping up the whiskey that had spilled all over the colonel's face. "Gill!" he bellowed.

"Right here," Gill said, unperturbed. He put both hands around Dick Turpin, the colonel's dog, and put him on the floor. Dick ran back around the chair and began lapping up the whiskey spilled from the bottle.

"Let me get Dick before he imbibes enough to kill him,"

Shelby said, grabbing Dick firmly around his pudgy midsection.

"He knows he's not allowed to touch whiskey, but he'll do it every time. Nothing will kill that dog," the colonel growled as he reached for Gill's hand. Gill pulled him to his feet. "Dick will probably be around to bury all of us." He peered at the dog affectionately. "Or at least I hope so."

Dick waved his feet in the air as Shelby held him close. He sniffed the open palm she held up to him, then joyously began licking her fingers. "Ah, he still remembers me," she said as Gill righted the chair and sat the colonel back down in it.

"Of course he remembers," the colonel growled. "That dog never forgets anything, especially his favorite people. Actually, he's more intelligent than most of the people around. You can put him down now." He smiled at Dick fondly as Dick looked at him and performed his very best trick. He stood up on his hind legs, sat back on his tail, put his paws in prayer position, and grinned, showing his front teeth. He looked like a rascally vicar. "Wonderful," the colonel said, beaming back at Dick and giving him half of a lemon cake.

"Must we have that animal in here?" someone asked in a thick voice, the question followed by a sneeze. "He's turning into a regular swill. Whiskey's going to be the death of that dog, if someone doesn't . . ."

Crawford interrupted him hastily. "Dick was here before we were, Hayward, and I daresay he'll be here after we're gone."

Hayward muttered something under his breath, then pulled a handkerchief from his pocket and mopped his eyes. "I don't know why I've been sneezing every time I get around him this visit. He hasn't done that to me before."

"Perhaps there's just more of Dick this trip. He does seem to have put on a little weight." Shelby looked at the dog.

"Rather like the rest of us," Crawford said with a laugh. He glanced at the doorway. "Do come in, Pearce, Bentley. Join the family."

The two staggered in, leaving Luke and Thomas by the doorway. "Just sitting here admiring the Jewels of Ali?" Bentley asked, running his words together. "A typical family evening?"

"Actually we hadn't gotten around to that yet." Crawford waited until Shelby poured coffee for Pearce and Bentley. "I'm sure Uncle Quilby will be glad to show them to us."

Colonel Falcon didn't answer him as he was busy feeding Dick Turpin the other half of the lemon cake.

"And how are the fabulous Jewels of Ali? Still with us, I hope," Hayward said. "Have you seen them, Mr. Gill?"

Gill nodded, but said nothing. Colonel Falcon looked sadly into his empty glass, then around at the group. "Might as well say something about the jewels while you're all here," he said.

"You haven't sold them?" Pearce asked.

Colonel Falcon gave him a disgusted look. "Now why would I do a stupid thing like that? I don't need the money. Especially not now. No, a dying man doesn't need a thing except his six feet of dirt." He put on a sorrowful face. "That's all it comes down to, in the end." He waited for reactions, but got none. No one quite knew what to say. "Oh, well." The colonel looked around again and patted a large wooden cabinet that was bolted to the floor next to him. "As for the jewels, they're right here where they've always been, built right into the house." He fumbled with a chain around his neck and found a key. "Here, Shelby girl, see if you can unlock the thing. I can't see the lock anymore."

The wooden cabinet was built onto the floor and was of heavy oak, built carefully with dovetailed joints. There were three locks on the cabinet, one on each side, but the same key opened all three. Shelby carefully opened the locks and lowered the hinged panels of oak that folded down halfway to reveal a heavy metal case. The case had a latch on it that her grandfather had shown her years before. She touched the latch and the metal box unlocked. Shelby lowered metal panels hinged like the oak ones, and there before them, in a heavy glass case, were the fabled Jewels of Ali.

Colonel Falcon moved a candle so that it stood behind the glass case, illuminating the jewels. The cabochon stones glowed dull red and green against the gold of their settings. There was the occasional flash of amethyst and the dull sheen of pearls as well. The intricate workings of gold from a time long past nestled on a bed of rich black velvet. The room was silent as they all looked.

"Now get the bottom," Colonel Falcon said, peering through the glass. "Might as well get them out and pass them around while everyone's here."

Shelby looked at him, shocked. The locked metal band that held the heavy glass in place had only been removed two or three times during her life. "Are you sure, Grandfather?"

He scowled at her. "Why wouldn't I be sure?" He stepped back and looked around at all of them. Then, to Shelby's surprise, he looked at Gill and nodded almost imperceptibly. Gill nodded back. "On second thought," the colonel said, "we don't need to look at the things. I just wanted them open so I could make an announcement." He paused dramatically, reached for the half-empty bottle, poured himself another glass of whiskey, and held it high. "A toast to Shelby Falcon, the new owner of the Jewels of Ali."

There was a stunned silence in the room. Shelby felt her jaw drop, and hastily remembered to close her mouth. She could feel a slight shift in the general level of tension in the room, and it didn't appear to be a pleasant one. "Well, well," Crawford said, breaking the silence. "Do allow me to congratulate you, Shelby. This should make you a very rich woman, indeed."

"I thought they were to be divided equally. Mother said that was what was in your will. She said you told her they would be divided among us." Pearce stared at the colonel.

"Decided against that." Colonel Falcon reached for the whiskey bottle, but Gill had quietly moved it out of reach.

Pearce gave Shelby a stony look. "Equally. That's what you've always planned to do. Counting Shelby, there's five of us."

Colonel Falcon waved the objection away as Dick finished searching for crumbs on the floor and hopped up on his lap. "I've decided to change my will. You boys can take care of yourselves, and your families have provided for each of you to an extent. You're all involved in this and that, I hear, so you don't need any of the jewels. If I divvied them up equally, the only way it could be done would be to sell them and divide the money. I'll not be selling a single piece." He turned to Shelby. "And you won't either, girl. No matter how much you need money. Those jewels will stay right in the family."

Shelby nodded automatically. She was still too stunned to speak.

"Well, Shelby," Bentley said, "at least the emeralds will match your eyes, and I suppose the gold and amethysts are supposed to flatter auburn coloring. As for the rubies . . . I can't say whether or not you fit that old belief. Are you able to wear rubies, Shelby?" His tone was sarcastic. "If not, you can always . . ." He was cut short by Gill grabbing his shirt front and hauling him to his feet.

"Falcon," Gill said slowly, his face a blank mask, "I believe you probably want to go to bed before you say anything else about your cousin. Perhaps in the morning, after you've had time to think about this, you may want to extend an apology."

"What business is it of yours?" Bentley asked, shoving Gill.

"None, other than I refuse to have a lady, any lady, disparaged in my presence." Gill looked at him and did not move. "Do you prefer to apologize now?"

As a reply, Bentley swung his fist at Gill's chin in his best imitation of Gentleman Jackson. Gill moved deftly, stepping to the side and bringing his fist up to connect with Bentley's jaw. Bentley dropped like a tree.

Gill turned to the company. "My apologies. I certainly didn't mean for that to happen."

"Good show," Colonel Falcon said approvingly. "He deserved that. Bentley always says too much when he's in his cups." He sighed. "Actually, Bentley always says too much. He'll probably apologize in the morning and never have a clue what he's said or done." He looked around and sighed contentedly. "I *knew* this would be an entertaining family gathering."

"Bentley did deserve that." Crawford grimaced slightly. "I apologize on his behalf, Shelby, and ask that you forget what he said. He's had too much to drink."

"Never could hold his liquor," Colonel Falcon said. "Close up your jewels, Shelby, and give me the key. I'll let you open the glass tomorrow and examine them. Haven't gotten my will changed yet, but I'll do that sometime this week. Then they'll be all yours. You might even want to wear them around for a while. Get used to them."

"I couldn't. I just—"

"Nonsense. I want to see you wear them. The last person I saw wearing them was an Indian ranee. Beautiful woman. Have I told you that story?"

"I believe we've heard it," Crawford said. He pulled on the bell rope, and Luke and Thomas appeared at the door immediately. They had obviously been listening. "Take Mr. Falcon up to his room and put him to bed," Crawford told them as he glanced at Bentley's prostrate form on the floor.

"You can come back and get the other one as soon as you get that one tucked in," he said, pointing to Pearce, who had fallen asleep in his chair and was snoring gently.

"As you say, sir." Luke and Thomas tried unsuccessfully to hide their grins as they carted Bentley out the door.

Colonel Falcon reached around for another glass and

couldn't find one, but did manage to reach the whiskey bottle. "Hand me that cup, Daisy. Don't you want a little of this?" He sloshed the inch or so of whiskey that remained in the bottle.

Countess Rimildi glared at him and began fanning herself. "I do believe I'll just retire to my chamber. I'm planning to return to London as soon as possible, so I need my rest." She stood and looked at Shelby. "Are you coming?" she asked, then got up and wobbled to the door. "I do wish you'd come up now, dear. I would like to speak with you."

"I'm coming, Mama. I do want to see that Mrs. McKilley has had our trunks sent up."

"Oohh, I forgot about that. Knowing this house, I daresay they haven't." The countess looked stricken. "I daresay that chambers haven't even been prepared for us. Oh, this place!" She put her hands to her face and burst into tears just as Luke and Thomas returned for Pearce.

Colonel Falcon took the last gulp of whiskey. "Put it in a box, Daisy. You need to move over so they can get by you with Pearce." He looked around at Crawford and Hayward. "Anything else to say?"

"I'll check on Bentley," Hayward said shortly as he left.

Crawford stood and paused in front of Shelby, then gave her a small smile. "Congratulations. As soon as word of this makes the rounds, you'll have to fight off every eligible bachelor in London." He touched the end of her nose with his fingertip just the way he had done when she was ten. Then he grinned at her and walked out in that lazy way he had, the candlelight glinting off his blond hair.

Colonel Falcon looked at the countess, who was sobbing, then at Gill, standing impassively, covered with soot. The colonel looked at Shelby and then stood, tucking Dick Turpin under his arm. His nightdress flapped around his ankles as he headed for the door. "Stay up as long as you like. I'm going to bed.

Gill, would you mind seeing if Biddle has made it back to bed or if he's on the floor somewhere? I don't hear him."

He paused at the door and looked back at them, grinning wickedly. Dick Turpin imitated his grin. "Damme," said the colonel. "What fun! I just love these family reunions."

Three

Mrs. McKilley had indeed readied chambers for them, but the countess wanted to change hers. "I can't believe that you've put my things in the blue chamber. Blue does tend to make my skin look muddy. I *always* stay in the red room when I'm here," she insisted.

"Mr. Gill is in the red room," Mrs. McKilley said.

The countess resorted to vapors and tears. "I can't believe anyone would turn out family and put a stranger in my room."

"Mama," Shelby said, trying to be patient, "do sleep in the room beside mine and leave Mr. Gill in the red room. After all, you did say you planned to return to London as soon as possible."

"I certainly don't mind changing," Gill said. He had caught the last part of the conversation as he walked up the stairs. "Countess Rimildi is absolutely correct—the needs of family certainly take precedence. I'll have my man pack my things and move. It won't take long."

The countess recovered immediately, and Mrs. McKilley quickly sent for fresh linens before someone else requested a change. "Our luggage, Shelby. We must have our luggage immediately!" Mrs. McKilley took one look at the countess and ran out into the hall. Luke and Thomas came up the stairs, carrying Pearce. Mrs. McKilley had them put Pearce carefully down at the side of the hall while they moved the countess's luggage. Pearce slept through it all.

Shelby was starting to enter her usual room when an exotic-looking young man came from the red room, carrying several white shirts. Shelby looked at him in surprise, but he went on by her into the room next door. "Foreigner," Mrs. McKilley whispered. "And a strange one he is, too." She leaned toward Shelby and lowered her voice another notch. "He's supposed to be Mr. Gill's man, but he doesn't act that way. Independent, he is. He eats fish for breakfast some days. If that ain't odd, what is?" She stepped back and reassumed her usual manner. "I noted as how you didn't have a maid with you, and I took the liberty of sending for one. She should be here to help you unpack."

"That's most kind of you, Mrs. McKilley. Mama and I usually share her maid when we travel, but this time I was in such a hurry to get here that I didn't wait to bring along anyone else."

"So Madiston is still with your mother?"

"Yes. However, she was visiting her sister for a few days, and I simply couldn't wait until she returned. I assured Mama that someone would be here who could act as her maid for a few days. I simply couldn't delay. I wanted to get here as fast as I could."

Mrs. McKilley pursed her thin lips. "Good thing as you're here. There's been some strange things going on."

Shelby started to question her, but stopped as another wail issued from the countess in the red room. "It's that man, I'd say. That foreigner must have scared her. I don't hold with foreigners," Mrs. McKilley said, bustling out the door.

Shelby closed the door behind her and slid onto the nearest chair, letting all the sounds of moving fade into the background. After a few minutes, the door opened and a young girl stepped inside. "Mrs. McKilley sent me," the girl announced, looking around with huge eyes. "She said you would tell me what you needed."

"What I need," Shelby said, looking up, "is a bath and a change of scene."

"Right now?" the girl asked, staring at her.

Shelby laughed at the girl's horrified expression. "No, right now I just need the bed turned down and someone to help me get out of this gown." She stood and turned so the back of the gown showed. "Have you been a lady's maid before?"

"No. No, mum. Does it show?"

Shelby stifled a smile. "Not at all. Would you mind telling me your name?"

"Dovey, ma'am. I'm happy to help you. Just let me get this . . ." With that, Dovey tripped over the edge of the small rug on the floor and her elbow swept the top of the dressing table clear. Powder flew everywhere. Dovey grasped for something to keep herself from falling, and that something was the back of Shelby's dress. Dovey fell in a heap as all the buttons ripped off the back of Shelby's dress and Shelby grabbed a bedpost to try to keep upright.

Shelby turned slowly as her dress began to fall off her shoulders. Dovey looked up at her, her head covered with powder, and began to cry. The entire hall was quiet before Shelby had Dovey convinced that she wasn't going to be sent to the dairy to work for the rest of her life. It was past two in the morning before Shelby sank gratefully into her bed. She was asleep before she was able to pull the covers up over her shoulders.

The next morning, it took Shelby a moment to realize where she was. Dovey was sitting in the chair by the little dressing table, waiting patiently. There was still powder on the floor. Dovey looked as if she hadn't slept at all during the night. "Good morning, mum," she said, standing quickly and bobbing. "I wanted to be here in case you needed me."

"A bath, Dovey," Shelby said, sitting up in bed. Every muscle was sore and aching. "Just have Mrs. McKilley send up a bath. Nice and hot."

Dovey bobbed again and was out the door in a flash. Shelby fell back against the pillows and closed her eyes. A bath. A nice breakfast. Bacon, eggs, muffins. Maybe by then she would feel human again. Right now she felt wretched.

She sighed, sat up, and dangled her feet over the edge of the bed. There was a knock at her door. "Come in," she called out, rubbing her eyes with the palms of her hands. "You're certainly prompt, Mrs. McKilley. I thought it would have taken a half-hour at least."

"A half-hour for what?"

Shelby looked up, startled. Crawford was lounging against the door frame. Shelby grabbed for a sheet and wound it around her. Then she felt her hair. It was a tangled mass and was going every which way. "Don't," Crawford said with a smile, coming over and disentangling her fingers from her hair. "You look lovely this morning." He gazed down at her, a look in his eyes that Shelby had never seen there before. "All that lovely auburn hair . . ." His voice trailed off as he picked up a strand of hair and let it fall across her face.

Unnerved by his gesture, Shelby gave a nervous laugh and wriggled farther under the sheet she had wrapped around her. "It's too early for lovely. Don't lie to me, Crawford. We've been around each other too long for that."

He grinned and stepped back. "Would I lie to you?"

"Yes, if you thought it would do you any good."

He sighed and sat down on the chair, propping his arm on the dressing table. "You know me too well, Shelby." He moved his arm and looked horrified. There was powder all over his dark blue coat. "What happened here?"

"Dovey spilled powder." Shelby had to laugh at his expression. "She's bringing up bathwater for me. You'd better leave if you don't want to get scalded. Dovey doesn't seem to be . . . be quite . . ."

"She's always at sixes and sevens?" Crawford stood up, watching as powder settled itself all the way down one finely molded pantleg.

"Exactly. But I have to keep her. She's terrified she'll be sent to the dairy."

Crawford brushed ineffectually at the powder, doing nothing except moving it around and resettling it. "That might not be a bad place for her if . . ." He grinned at Shelby. "No matter. I just wanted to talk to you a moment before everyone else started, but I'll wait. Would you like to go for a short ride today? Pearce brought the phaeton with him. We could take it and go see the old Norman ruins. Remember how we used to love to play there?"

"That would be nice." Shelby smiled back at him, then turned as she heard a noise. There was a great clash of metal. "That must be Dovey."

"I'd best leave in a hurry before I have another coat ruined. Shall we plan to go right after lunch? That will give us most of the afternoon."

"Fine." Shelby had to make herself keep her tone light and her expression blank. Her feelings for Crawford were still too raw for her to allow herself to think about his motives in inviting her.

He left, making it out the door just before Dovey came in, carrying one bucket of water herself and followed by three footmen, one with the bath, two with more water.

Shelby bathed while Dovey selected her clothes and readied them. To Shelby's surprise, Dovey had quite an eye for color and matching. Dovey had decided on a cream dress. She had discovered some flower trim that Shelby had accidentally snatched up and brought. She had once intended to trim a bonnet with it, but had never done it. Dovey nodded and ran for her scissors, needle, and thread. She added the flowers around the neckline, then looped pink and green ribbons between the flowers. The whole effect was quite charming.

Shelby thought about dressing her own hair, but Dovey sat her down and began without even asking. Shelby looked in amazement as Dovey worked, piling Shelby's thick auburn hair into a knot on top of her head and arranging soft waves on the sides. "I thought you had never been a lady's maid before, Dovey. Where did you learn to do this?"

"My mother. She always said I should be a lady's maid. She taught me needlework and had me dress her hair over and over." She hesitated. "Actually, Mrs. McKilley asked her to be your mother's maid while you were here, but Mama traded off with Margaret." She frowned as she tried to explain. "Margaret went to be with your mother, and Mama sent me to you instead of her."

"I see," Shelby said slowly. She understood Dovey much better. "I think we shall get along splendidly, Dovey. I'll tell Mrs. McKilley that I'm quite pleased."

"Oh, will you, mum? Just will you?" She dropped the hairbrush and picked up the powder box and a haresfoot. "My mother taught me about this, too. Shall I, mum?"

Shelby had reservations about the powder and other pots and jars on the dressing table. She had never been very good at the art of transforming herself with cosmetics, although her mother kept her well supplied with every new thing and color that was available. "You'd be lovely if you'd just *enhance*," the countess always said. Shelby had never picked up the art of enhancing.

Not wanting to distress Dovey, Shelby nodded her head. "By all means," she said, hoping for the best.

When Shelby looked into the mirror after Dovey had finished, she was amazed. Her eyes glowed, more green than hazel, her cheeks bloomed with a faint blush, and her lips glistened with a deep rose. She had never looked so nice in her whole life. "Dovey," she breathed, "I hope you never leave me. This is wonderful."

"Oh, mum," Dovey cried, then burst into tears.

* * *

Gill was just coming in the front door as Shelby reached the foot of the stairs. He was again dressed in black, and he had obviously been out riding. There was a touch of color in his face that heightened the bronze of his skin, and a single curl of dark hair fell across his forehead. Instead of looking unkempt, he looked dashing and dangerous. "Miss Falcon, you appear a different person this morning." He gazed at her in frank admiration and Shelby felt herself begin to blush. "A much different person."

"Thank you." Shelby forced herself not to look at him. "I was just going in to breakfast. Have you eaten?"

He shook his head and handed his hat and gloves to Thomas. "No, I always like a ride before breakfast. It's the best time of the day." He smiled and offered her his arm to escort her into the breakfast room. "I've always kept country hours— early to bed and early to rise." He made a face. "That habit alone has successfully kept me out of London society since I've been back." He smiled at her, a slightly reserved smile, but one that hinted of a warm person beneath his veneer of reserve. "That may be why we haven't met previously, Miss Falcon."

"Mama is the social one in the family. I don't travel much in society circles." She smiled. "Much to Mama's annoyance, I might add," she told him, looking at the sideboard where many dishes waited. Mrs. McKilley had outdone herself. Shelby had always been one for breakfast, a habit she had picked up from the colonel. She didn't stint now.

"I see," Gill said with a smile as he looked across the table at her, "that you aren't one of those missish society girls who live on toast and tea."

Shelby looked down at her plate and almost blushed. She had gotten bacon, three fat Cumbrian sausages, eggs, two slices of Mrs. McKilley's famous bread, a muffin, and some mushrooms. "Mama and I didn't really have a chance to eat on our way here last evening."

"I understand. Have some jam. It's blackberry, I believe." He pushed the jam pot toward her. "Tell me, Miss Falcon, were you expecting your grandfather to leave the Jewels of Ali to you?"

Shelby looked at him, shocked at the question. He saw her expression. "I assure you that I'm not asking idly. I have your grandfather's full confidence."

She hesitated, then shrugged. "No, I wasn't expecting it. I had no idea. Even though I'm his only direct heir, I always thought they would go to the boys. Grandfather has always said that Wychwood would be mine, but he planned to leave a legacy to each of the boys. We always thought that would be the Jewels of Ali."

"Let me see," Gill paused. "I have trouble with the relationships in this family. All the boys are your cousins?"

"Yes." Shelby spread blackberry jam on her toast and took a bite. It was delicious. "Hayward and Bentley are my Uncle Howell's sons. Crawford and Pearce are the sons of my Uncle Morris."

"Your uncle Howell and uncle Morris. I thought you were the only direct heir? How can that be?"

Shelby shook her head. "Yes, I am Colonel Falcon's only direct heir. My father, Bates Falcon, was his only child. Howell and Morris are both dead now. They weren't really my uncles, although I've always called them that. They were the sons of Grandfather's brother, Wylie." She looked at him and laughed. "I know what your next question will be, Mr. Gill. Everyone who doesn't know the family well asks it. 'Why all the strange names?' "

Gill had the grace to give her a chagrined smile. "Actually I wondered, although I hesitated to ask."

"It's because of a family tradition dating from the fifteenth century," she explained as she buttered her muffin. Mrs.

McKilley made the most wonderful apple muffins. "The first Falcon was able to obtain a title and riches because two friends saved his life. That Falcon—James was his name—was almost killed during the battle with the Spanish armada. Unfortunately, the two friends who rescued him were both killed saving him, and he swore then that he would honor them by naming his children after them, no matter if his children were male or female. He also swore that every Falcon from that day on would honor a friend in the same way." She looked at Gill and laughed. "So, every one of us since that time has been named with someone's last name. It's become quite a family tradition."

"So you were named for a gentleman named Shelby?"

"No. I was named for a friend of my father's. You may not be aware of it, but my father was a botanist and had a great many connections with others who loved plants. He was particularly impressed with Countess Bramleigh's garden, and asked her to be my godmother. Her name, as you may know, is Matilda Shelby."

"I didn't know that, but I have heard about her gardens. Extensive, from what I've heard." He smiled at her again, more warmly this time, and seemed to relax against the back of his chair.

Shelby looked at him closely. In the daylight, he looked much younger. *Of course,* she thought, *it might also be that he isn't covered with soot this morning.*

"Speaking of gardens, I've noted that the ones here are intriguing," he went on. If he noticed her scrutiny, he ignored it. "Perhaps you could give me a tour."

"You haven't been through them?" Shelby pushed her plate aside. "I thought you had been here for some time, Mr. Gill."

"Yes, but I've been doing other things." He left it at that. "Would you be so kind as to show me the gardens?" He glanced out the window. "This would be a good time if you don't have anything else planned."

Shelby started to refuse, then decided that a tour of the gardens might give her the perfect opportunity to quiz the mysterious Mr. Gill further. There was just something odd about the man, and she was determined to discover what it was. She gave him her best smile. "I'd be delighted, Mr. Gill. Just give me a few minutes to go up and change my shoes. We can look at the gardens around the house this morning, and perhaps tour the others on another day."

Gill was waiting for her by the front door when she came back down. He watched her as she walked down the stairs, and she felt strange. It was almost as if he were assessing her, Shelby felt. However, when she reached the bottom of the stairs, he smiled warmly. "I thought I would stop you here and suggest we go out another door. I believe the burning carpet not only charred this floor"—he nodded toward the area that was being scrubbed vigorously by two maids—"but also got soot all over the front of the house. Mrs. McKilley will have everything cleaned shortly, but I don't think she wants us tracking through there now."

"Fine. We can begin at the side garden." She led the way across the hall and into the green drawing room where the Jewels of Ali were kept. "There are French doors on this side that open onto the garden."

Gill paused momentarily beside the case in which the jewels were stored. Shelby laughed. "I know what you're thinking, Mr. Gill. Grandfather keeps the French doors barred at night, and there are shutters that can be pulled over them and locked. He takes no chances."

"Those are valuable jewels," Gill said, following her out the door.

"Yes." Shelby sighed. "We've begged him to store them in a bank vault somewhere, but he won't. As he has often said, he wants them right here where he can admire them. He feels there's no pleasure in beauty locked away."

Gill looked down at her, a strange expression on his face. "Exactly my sentiments," he said.

They took a short tour of the gardens next to the house, and, when they returned, Shelby didn't feel she knew any more about the mysterious Mr. Gill than she had when they began. He, however, seemed to know a great deal about her, the family, the house, the gardens, and, oddly, the jewels. It was puzzling. The only answer must be that he truly did have the colonel's full confidence.

They went to the front door after they had walked through the side garden, but two maids were busily scrubbing, so they walked back leisurely to the French doors of the drawing room. Gill left Shelby there, saying he wanted to go to the stables to check on his horse. "He stepped on a sharp stone this morning," he explained, "and although it didn't appear to be anything serious, I want to check on it." He paused and smiled at her again, his dark eyes turning a warmer brown. "Thank you for the tour of the side garden, Miss Falcon. I'm going to hold you to your offer of a tour of the rest of the grounds."

"I'd be delighted, Mr. Gill." She looked up at his smile and felt her heart lurch. The man was darkly handsome, but there was something more, the feeling of danger she had sensed last night. She really couldn't put her finger on the feeling, she merely knew that he was not a man to be trifled with. She stepped back without thinking, and he smiled at her again. Feeling foolish, she smiled back as he turned and left. Shelby had to force herself not to look at him as he walked away.

Dick Turpin came running up to her as she came in through the French doors. Pearce was in the room, running his fingers over the case that held the Jewels of Ali. He jumped back when Dick began barking joyously at Shelby.

"Oh, it's you," Pearce said, sitting down. He realized Shelby was still standing, and jumped back up again. "What have you been doing?"

"Showing Mr. Gill the gardens." She took off her bonnet

and sat down. Pearce sat across from her. Dick Turpin leaped across a footstool and landed right in Shelby's lap, doing his best to grin at her. Shelby absently began scratching him under the chin. Dick was positively ecstatic.

"What do you know about Mr. Gill, Pearce?" Shelby asked.

"Not a thing. He was in the house when we got here. I understood that he'd been here some days. The son of one of the colonel's old army friends. Or maybe he's one of the colonel's old army friends." He waved his fingers in dismissal. "It doesn't signify." He leaned forward. "How have you been, Shelby? I haven't seen you anywhere for months."

"I haven't seen you either, Pearce."

"I've been busy." He reached over and began scratching Dick Turpin along the back with one finger. "I'm doing some work that I hope the army will be interested in. It's difficult being the younger son, you know. Father's estate was entailed, so Crawford got what there was of it."

"I know. What have you been doing?"

He looked up, and his face began to take on a rapt look. "Rockets, Shelby. Have you read anything that Congreve has written about rockets?" He didn't wait for her to answer, but went right on. "They're going to revolutionize warfare as we know it, Shelby. Congreve has gotten the army to use them on the Peninsula, and I hear they're being used in the war with the United States. Think of it, Shelby! The man who discovers how to make them better—more efficient at killing people—is going to make a fortune!" His face fell. "Of course, it takes a great deal of money to begin a rocket factory. A great deal." He looked at her intently. "What did you say you've been doing lately?"

"Nothing at all. Just traveling some with Mother. Staying with friends. The usual things."

"So you're not engaged or anything like that?"

"Engaged?"

"To be married." He looked vaguely uncomfortable. "Or you're not about to be engaged to someone."

Shelby shook her head and looked down as Dick Turpin wiggled across her lap. He rolled onto his back and waved all four paws in the air. "Would you look at this animal, Pearce, he's . . ." She broke off as she looked up. Her mouth fell open when she saw Pearce fall to his knees in front of her, his hands folded in front of him as though in prayer. "Pearce, what . . . ?"

"Shelby," he said, taking one of her hands in his. "You know how much I admire you and always have. I can withhold my feelings no longer. Please tell me there is a chance for you to be mine!"

"Be yours?" Shelby was blank.

"Yes, be my wife, Shelby. You'll make me the happiest man in the universe if you'll only say yes."

"Pearce, I—" She stopped as the door flew open.

"Dick," Biddle roared. "Where are you, you lazy hound? As soon as I get my hands on you. . . ." He barged into the room and saw Pearce. "What's this? What are you doing down on the floor there? Have you lost something, too? I can't find that dog and if I don't—"

"Dick's right here, Biddle," Shelby said.

Biddle let out a sigh of relief and sat down beside Shelby. He smiled kindly at Pearce and patted him on the shoulder. "So you found him under the sofa! I can't get down there to look for the little rascal, and he gets under there all the time. He's a smart one, he is." He smiled fondly at Dick Turpin who grinned back at him, showing all of his front teeth. "Rat-catching rapscallion," Biddle grumbled, giving the dog an affectionate pat. Then Biddle looked at Pearce. "Thank you for finding him for me. I just can't get down there—bad joints, you know." He stared at Pearce for a moment. "Do you have bad knees too? Do you need some help getting up?"

"I'm fine," Pearce mumbled, standing and falling back into

his chair. He glowered at Biddle and Dick Turpin. Biddle didn't notice.

"It's good to see you, girl," Biddle said to Shelby. "I was hoping you'd come before your grandfather died."

"Is he truly sick, Biddle?" Shelby asked anxiously.

Biddle's eyes shifted from side to side. "At the rate he's going, I don't think he's going to last long."

Shelby bit her lower lip to keep from crying. "Biddle, what's the matter with him? He looked fine last night. If anything, he seemed to be in better spirits than when I last saw him."

Biddle nodded his head. "It's an act," he said solemnly. "You know how the colonel hates people to think he's weak. He pretends that he's doing fine. Take it from me, he isn't long for this world unless—" He stopped suddenly.

"Unless what, Biddle?"

"Nothing. Just an idea of mine." He looked at Shelby and patted her hand. "I'm just glad you're here. He'll be safe."

"Safe?" Shelby frowned. "Biddle, you're not making any sense."

"Safe from disease, was what I meant." Biddle slowly got to his feet and looked around furtively. "Ah, me, my old bones! I could certainly do with a small dram." He wandered over to the cabinet and checked to see if there was any whiskey there. He turned around, disappointed.

"I believe Grandfather took one bottle, and Mr. Gill spirited the other back toward the kitchen," Shelby said.

Pearce stood up. "If you want to ask about someone, Shelby, you should ask about Gill. Who is he, anyway?" He glared at Biddle.

Biddle looked back at him innocently. "Gill? A fine army man, isn't he? Although I can't say that I'm overly fond of that boy of his. The Indian. What's his name—Ranja?"

"The one who eats fish for breakfast?" Shelby asked as Dick Turpin hopped from her lap and began to sniff around

Biddle's feet. Shelby thought Dick was probably looking for more whiskey.

Biddle laughed. "I see Mrs. McKilley has been complaining again. I don't see a thing wrong with fish for breakfast. I like a good trout now and then myself." He paused and cocked his head to one side, then looked innocent again.

"There you are," Colonel Falcon said, coming into the room. He was dressed to go out. "Come on, Dick," he called, holding out his hands for the dog. Dick ran and jumped right into his arms. "You no-good rat-catcher," Colonel Falcon said fondly, rubbing Dick's nose. "We're going for a small trip, we are." He looked back at the three in the room. "Gill and I are going out for the afternoon. I'll see you tonight. Remember, we have supper early." With that, he turned and stomped out into the hall.

Biddle immediately began opening cabinets to search more thoroughly. Shelby rose, remembering that she needed to get ready to go with Crawford after lunch. "I believe I'll go up to my chamber for a short while before lunch. I'll see you then, Pearce. And you too, Biddle," she added to his back. Biddle had his whole head inside the cabinet.

"Certainly," was Biddle's muffled reply.

Pearce came over to Shelby and took her hand. "Shelby, my declaration didn't work out as I had planned, but I do hope you will consider what I've said to you. As you know, I've always had the highest regard and admiration for you."

Remembering Pearce's total indifference to anything that didn't make noise or blow up over the years, Shelby nodded. She hadn't known whether to take his offer seriously or to laugh as though he were playing a practical joke on her. Now she began to realize that he was serious and started to simply tell him no, but the look in his eyes was pleading. She was reminded of Dick Turpin when he begged. So instead of a brutal no, she resolved to reject his offer as gently as possible. "Thank you, Pearce," she said gravely. "I shall certainly think on it. Perhaps we could discuss this more this evening. I know you want a prompt reply."

She fled before Pearce could say anything else.

Four

Countess Rimildi met Shelby at the top of the stairs. "Oh, there you are, dear. I was just coming to look for you." She stood back and looked at Shelby critically. "Whatever has happened to your hair? It looks quite lovely." She frowned. "Not that it usually doesn't. It's just that . . ." Her words trailed off as she scrutinized Shelby's face. "And your skin! Shelby, have you been practicing with paint at last? I told you, dear, that all you needed was enhancement."

"No, the new maid Mrs. McKilley sent up knows how to do this."

"Ah, a good maid is worth her weight in gold. Now if Madiston were here . . ."

Shelby nodded to keep her from continuing. "True, Mama. I believe Dovey will prove to be another Madiston." Shelby glanced back down the stairs to see Pearce looking up at her longingly. She was afraid he would begin bounding up toward her at any moment. "Mama, would you like to come into my room to talk rather than stand here on the stairs?"

"That would be fine, dear. My room is such a mess. I borrowed your girl—did you say her name was Dovey?—to help with my things. I think I'll leave for London tomorrow if you don't mind. Now that I see the colonel isn't going to die, I think I should return. I just wanted to know if you planned to return with me."

Shelby sat down in a small chair opposite her mother and tried to suppress a grin. "Your urge to return wouldn't have anything to do with Aunt Hettie's pursuit of Mr. Weatherby, would it?"

Countess Rimildi's eyes widened innocently. "Good heavens, Shelby! You do me an injustice. Hettie is certainly welcome to Mr. Weatherby's attentions. As I recall at our last meeting, he complained that he found her endless chatter about Rose to be quite annoying."

"It did appear that he preferred your company." Shelby tried to keep the laughter from her voice.

"I do believe you're right, dear. But, to clarify, he certainly isn't the reason I'm thinking of leaving Wychwood. I just don't believe we're needed here." She leaned forward and lowered her voice. "I think Colonel Falcon is pulling another hoax."

"Do you really think Grandfather is going to be all right? Biddle says that he's not long for this world."

The countess made a face. "Shelby, I don't wish to contradict Biddle, but I do know when someone is dying and when he isn't. Your grandfather is *not* dying. Actually," the countess paused and grimaced slightly, "Colonel Falcon is probably much too ill-tempered to die in a convenient way. When he does die, it will be at a time and place quite inconvenient for anyone."

"Mother!" Shelby gasped.

"Well, it's no secret that I think the man a tyrant. And that horrid dog!" The countess shuddered. "Well-bred people don't keep rat-catching dogs in the house for pets!"

"Dick Turpin is special, Mama. He's not just an ordinary dog."

"If you say so, dear. There was one other thing I wanted to ask about." Countess Rimildi frowned. "What was all that Bentley was saying about rubies? Did you receive another inheritance I know nothing of?"

Shelby sighed. "Bentley was merely being obnoxious, Mama. There's an old saying that only virgins wear rubies."

"Oh." The countess gasped. "Oh! My heavens! And that's why Mr. Gill was so offended. My estimation of the man has certainly risen. How could Bentley say such a thing! You've been chaperoned everywhere, and your reputation is without a blot whatsoever!" She stood and began to pace the floor.

"Pay no attention to Bentley, Mama. As everyone knows, Bentley has always said strange things whenever he wished. As you know, he's. . . ."—Shelby paused and groped for words—"he's always been somewhat odd. And, as Grandfather said, Bentley has never been known to hold his liquor. His comments are even worse when he drinks, and he never thinks about what he says. He will probably apologize when he sees me. He's done it before."

"Accused you of such before?" Countess Rimildi sat down with a thud.

"No, Mama. Merely said things he regretted later. Once, I recall, he told me a particularly juicy bit of gossip about Helena Trentham. He was horrified the next day, and pursued me around London for a week begging me not to tell. Not that I would ever have mentioned it, of course."

"Of course." The countess hesitated. "You don't remember what it was, do you?"

Shelby laughed. "No, Mama. I've quite forgotten. No doubt it was inconsequential."

"No doubt." She bit her lip and frowned. "If Bentley is going to say such things, no matter that they're patently untrue, then I really shouldn't be leaving you here unchaperoned. Someone might get the wrong idea." She stood up again. "That settles it. I'm going to stay with you. I belong with my daughter."

"Mama, really. I've stayed at Wychwood alone for years."

"But now, Shelby, you're five and twenty. You need to protect your reputation. It's up to me to see that my daughter enters marriage unbesmirched in word or deed." She marched toward the door. "No matter what it may cost me in comfort or the pleasures of life, I shall do my duty." She went out, closing the door behind her, calling for Mrs. McKilley and Dovey to unpack her bags.

Ever the martyr, Shelby thought with a grin. Her mother would enjoy the sacrifice of a fortnight or so in London in return for being able to tell everyone, especially Mr. Weatherby, how she had given up all for her daughter. Shelby laughed aloud at the thought.

After lunch, Shelby went down to meet Crawford. Bentley was waiting for her at the bottom of the stairs. "Crawford has gone to bring the phaeton around," he said, hardly daring to meet her eyes. "Shelby, I have to talk to you." He looked up at her with bloodshot eyes.

"I understand, Bentley. There's no need to say anything." She started to walk around him, but he grabbed her arm.

"I'm so sorry," he said earnestly. "I don't know what came over me. I know your reputation is perfect, and I know you would never do anything untoward. I just said the first thing that popped into my mind when everyone was talking about jewels." He looked into her eyes. "Can you forgive me, Shelby? I promise I'll make it up to you. I'll do whatever you want me to do." His expression looked rather like Dick Turpin's once had been after Shelby chastised him for hopping up on the table and eating the roast beef that was to have been for supper.

"I forgive you, Bentley. I've forgotten all about it." She walked to the door where Luke stood impassively, waiting.

"What do you want me to do to make this up to you, Shelby? Tell me. I'll walk across the Sahara. I'll swim the Hellespont. I'll do anything."

"Would it make you feel better if I set you a task?" Shelby

turned as she heard the crunch of the phaeton's wheels on the gravel out front.

"Yes! Just tell me what you want me to do."

Shelby nodded and smiled at him. "All right, I'll think of something. In the meantime, why don't you go to bed and nap this afternoon, then get some fresh air?" She went out the door Luke opened and smiled at Crawford as he stood awaiting her.

Crawford looked over her shoulder at Bentley standing in the doorway. "Did Bentley apologize?"

She nodded. "Yes, you knew he would."

"He always does," he said cheerfully, helping her up onto the high seat. "It was just a question of when." He climbed up beside her. "I've been looking forward to this all day."

"As have I," she answered, ignoring the fact that she really hadn't thought much about either Crawford or the trip. She had been too involved in thinking of ways to discover something about the mysterious Mr. Gill to consider anything else.

The day was lovely, and the Norman ruins as Gothic as ever. The fallen Norman towers were right on the edge of the Wychwood property, close to the village road that led to Fenny Compton. As children, the boys, Shelby, and Rose went there as often as possible, playing everything from pirates to Vikings to Robin Hood among the ruins and rocks. Colonel Falcon knew how much they enjoyed it, and had always kept the surroundings groomed and mowed. Now, as Shelby saw the ruins for the first time since she had gone away to school, she was again captivated. "Do you remember how you made Pearce walk the plank from that stone there?" she asked Crawford, surveying the scene from her perch in the phaeton.

"Do I indeed," he laughed. "That was when Pearce broke his arm, and I caught the very devil at home." He pointed with his whip. "There's the little room where you loved to play Maid Marian while we were pretending to be Robin, Little John, and Friar Tuck." He laughed.

"Yes, I remember," Shelby said wistfully. "Hayward always

wanted to be the Sheriff of Nottingham. He tied us all up once and left."

"I recall that." Crawford jumped down and reached up to help her. "We stayed tied up for hours. Hayward wouldn't tell what had happened, and finally the colonel came looking for us. It was dark, and we were terrified."

"And hungry," Shelby added with a grin.

Crawford put her hand on his arm and covered it with his own. "Let's walk up here and look," he said, guiding her gently.

They browsed around the ruins for a good hour, remembering this and that from their childhood escapades. Finally, they sat on the stone from which Crawford had made Pearce walk the plank. The day was sunny and warm, and Shelby began to perspire. She glanced up at the sun to see that a cloud was beginning to cover it. "I hope Mama never finds out that I've taken off my bonnet, but there's a cloud." She untied the ribbons and removed the bonnet, letting it dangle from her fingers. "It's almost too warm for a bonnet today."

Crawford turned to look at her, his eyes even bluer in the half-shade than they had seemed before. "Your hair looks particularly lovely today," he said, touching a stray tendril that had fallen in front of her ear when she removed her bonnet. "It catches the light like a jewel."

"Rubies?" Shelby made a face.

"Yes, rubies. Pay no attention to Bentley. Everyone knows better."

"I know. I try to ignore Bentley's words, but sometimes . . ."

"Sometimes it's difficult, even when he apologizes." He looked at her and smiled.

Shelby caught her breath at the warmth in his smile and was struck again by how handsome he looked. Still, there had been a question nagging at her for months—she had to ask about Rose. "Crawford, I know Rose broke her engagement to you. I also know it's none of my business as to why, but if you need . . . if you want to talk. . . ." She stopped, unable to go on.

Crawford put his finger under her chin and lifted her face so that she had to look into his eyes. "I'd forgotten how lovely your eyes were," he said, slowly moving his finger along her chin. "I'd remembered them as hazel, but today they look a soft green."

"Don't you want to talk about it? About Rose, I mean?" Shelby was struck by the thought that her voice sounded faint and faraway.

Crawford dropped his hand to his lap and turned back to look in the distance. "About Rose. I may as well make a clean breast of it to you, Shelby. You've always known my secrets." He grinned ruefully.

"You don't have to talk about it if you don't want to. I understand."

He shook his head. "No, even I don't completely understand. On one level I do, but on another . . ." He paused, then continued. "I suppose you know that Father gambled away most of his inheritance. I inherited everything, of course, but that's only the house and land at this point. After our engagement, I was frank with Rose about my finances, and she regretfully told me that she needed to marry a rich man. As you know, after Howell died, Hettie promptly sent Hayward and Bentley off to school, even though they were small. She married Benjamin Meadows thinking he was well to grass; then she had Rose. What you may not know is that after Meadows died, Hettie discovered, to her horror, that he left her and Rose with very little except an old and noble name. There was almost nothing else."

"I thought he left her his legacy. At least that was what Rose told me."

Crawford laughed, a short, bitter sound. "Legacy. If you can call it that. It was a piddling amount, and Rose used it all to finance her entry into society. She's as penniless as I am."

Shelby hesitated a moment, then asked, "When she broke the engagement, did she have any prospects?"

"Not then. Don't forget that she wasn't into society when she broke our engagement. I think this past winter Turnbull offered for her, but I suspect she's holding out for someone richer." He sounded bitter. "There. I've told you the sordid reasons, and you can probably get more out of Rose herself. I think she's arriving today or tomorrow." He grimaced. "She probably thinks she can charm the colonel out of some cash."

"Rose wouldn't do that, Crawford. I know you're unhappy, but . . ."

Crawford looked at her and smiled. "No, I'm not unhappy. If anything, I thank my stars that I found out what a fortune hunter Rose is. I admit I cared very much for her, but that was before." He stood and held out his hand to Shelby. "Right now, this moment, I'm in an enchanted place with a wonderful lady. Look, the sun's back out again. Shall we walk some more?"

They walked behind the ruins where the colonel had begun a garden. Standing back a distance, Shelby noticed that the garden and the ruins resembled a painting. "There's even a towering cloud above everything," she said with a laugh. "Mr. Wordsworth would be pleased."

"He isn't the only one." Crawford turned her around and led her to the shade of a tree. "I don't want that lovely face to get too much sun." He backed her up against the tree trunk and touched her cheek with his fingertips. "Shelby," he said, his voice low and husky.

"Crawford, I . . . ," she whispered back, her heart thudding. *This isn't right,* her mind kept saying to her. *This isn't right.* Still, she didn't move.

"Shelby," he said again. "You've turned into a beautiful woman. Did you know that?"

"No," she mumbled, but could say nothing else because Crawford's lips covered hers.

He kissed her thoroughly, the kiss of a man who had kissed many women; then he moved back slightly and looked at her. Shelby's thoughts were all in a jumble. She wanted very much to say something, but there was nothing she felt she could say. "Crawford, I . . . ," she began, but then was distracted by the sound of a joyous yipping. "Dick Turpin," she said, breathing a sigh of relief as tension slipped from her. "If Dick's here, then Grandfather must be close by."

"If he is, I don't want him to see you with your bonnet off," Crawford said, picking up her bonnet from the ground where it had fallen from her fingers. He put it on her head and tied the ribbons, and looked at her as he straightened the bow. "Perhaps we can continue this very soon?"

"Soon. Yes, of course." Shelby tried not to look into his eyes as she answered. Her feelings and emotions were too confused to sort out. "There's Dick now," she said, seeing the little dog come racing across the lawn. Dick launched himself into the air several feet from her, aiming right for her midsection. She caught him and laughed. Dick looked at her and grinned, waving all four paws in the air. Shelby held the wiggling dog to her and looked up to see Colonel Falcon and Gill coming toward them.

"Thought he was after a rat, the way he took off," Colonel Falcon said, taking Dick under his arm. Dick licked his hand and wriggled loose, jumping onto the ground. He made his way to Gill and jumped up onto his boots. Gill picked the dog up and began scratching him under the chin. Dick closed his eyes in ecstasy.

"I do believe you have a good friend there, Mr. Gill," Shelby said.

"Oh, Dick and I sorted out our differences early on. When I first arrived, he was rather unsure, and it took the better part of a week to win him over. He seems enthusiastic now, however."

"Dick is *always* enthusiastic," Crawford said. "Are the two of you just out riding this afternoon?"

"Merely looking things over," Colonel Falcon said. "I like to make sure that all is in order." He looked back at the cloud towering over the ruins. "I think we'd all better get back to Wychwood. Looks like a storm brewing." He turned back to them. "Did I ever tell you about the time I lived through a cyclone in India? Way back in 1770, or was it '72? It couldn't have been much later because right after '72, I was sent to help Cornwallis in the colonies."

"We've heard," Crawford and Shelby chorused, then laughed as they realized they had spoken together.

"I believe you're right about the coming storm," Gill said. "We'd better get back." He smiled at Crawford. "There won't be any shelter on that phaeton if a downpour comes."

They all rode back together, Gill on one side of the phaeton, Colonel Falcon on the other. Just as they came in sight of the house, the first large drops began to fall. Crawford hurried to the front door and helped Shelby inside just before the storm broke. He looked outside and called for Luke to find someone to take the phaeton to the stables.

"You don't need to do that," Shelby said, peering out the window. "Mr. Gill is taking care of it. He's . . . *Grandfather! Look out!*" She screamed and dashed to the door. Outside in the rain, Colonel Falcon was sitting dizzily on the gravel, looking up, rain streaming all around him. Gill was on the ground, picking himself up. Nearby, a large stone urn that had decorated the railing of the upstairs balcony lay shattered.

"Grandfather, are you all right?" she asked, trying to pull him to his feet. "Are you hurt? I saw Mr. Gill shove you aside or you would have been killed." She put her arms around Colonel Falcon's neck and bit her lip to keep from crying. It was no use. She trembled from the knowledge of what might have been.

Gill got unsteadily to his feet. His head was bleeding where the edge of the urn had grazed him. "Crawford," Shelby called behind her. "See to Mr. Gill while Luke and I get Grandfather inside."

The rain was coming down in buckets while Shelby and Luke helped Colonel Falcon into the house. Crawford and Thomas helped Gill in. His face was bleeding badly. "Put him in the breakfast room and send for hot water and towels," Shelby ordered. "And do it quickly."

All at once Colonel Falcon stopped. "Dick! Where's Dick?" He turned to go back out the door.

Shelby grabbed him. "Stay here, Grandfather. I'll send Luke out to find him."

"He don't like Luke. I've got to go see. He could have been hit by that. . . ." He couldn't go on.

"I'll go," Crawford said.

"He don't like you either," the colonel said. He was shaking by now.

"He likes me," Shelby said. "Call Mrs. McKilley to help with Mr. Gill, call Biddle to get you out of these wet clothes, and I'll go find Dick. He's probably just gone under a bush until the storm passes."

Before anyone could stop her, Shelby ran outside to find Dick Turpin. She called and called, but Dick didn't come. Finally, she made herself go look where the urn had fallen. The shards were scattered everywhere. She got down on her hands and knees, calling for Dick. Finally she heard a whimper under a bench in the side garden. Dick was there, holding up a paw. His leg had been cut by a shard and was bleeding. Shelby picked him up and examined the cut. It didn't appear serious, although Dick was trembling. Shelby thought he was more frightened than hurt. She smoothed his soaked fur and, cradling him to her chest, went into the house through the French doors that opened into the drawing room. Colonel Falcon was there, wrapped in a blanket, sipping a glass of whiskey.

"I thought you were going to get out of those wet clothes," Shelby said, looking at him as she shoved her dripping hair from her face.

"I couldn't until I knew if Dick was all right." He held out his hands for the dog, and Shelby put Dick on his lap.

"He needs a bandage on his leg, but otherwise, he seems the same." She grinned at her grandfather. "What is that you always called him—a *chien barbu?* Instead, he's like a cat, I think. He must have nine lives." She reached for the dog. "He's getting you wet."

Colonel Falcon held on to Dick. "That's all right. I'm going up now for dry clothes, and Biddle can put a bandage on Dick." He stood up. "You could use some dry clothes yourself."

Shelby nodded. "First, I want to check on Mr. Gill." She paused. "I think he saved your life, Grandfather. I was looking out the window and saw him knock you out of the way. If he hadn't, you could have. . . ." She stopped, unable to go on.

"I know, girl, I know." Colonel Falcon patted her hand. "Go see how he is; then come let me know, will you?" Shelby nodded as Biddle came to the door.

Gill was in the breakfast room, and his man, Ranja, was attending to him. He had taken off his coat and was just in his shirt. "Ouch, dammit," he said, as Ranja dabbed at his head with a towel. There was a basin of bloody water beside him.

"Are you all right, Mr. Gill?" Shelby asked hesitantly. She looked around for Crawford and Mrs. McKilley, but no one else was there.

"I'm just fine," Gill answered through clenched teeth as Ranja applied some kind of ointment to his head. He grimaced.

"Are you sure?"

"Yes, Miss Falcon, I'm sure. Now if you don't mind. . . ."

He clenched his teeth again. "I'm going to have a hell of a headache tomorrow." He paused. "Do excuse my language, Miss Falcon. I'm not thinking very well."

"You're thinking perfectly, Mr. Gill. I saw the entire episode, and I want to thank you. If you hadn't knocked Grandfather away, he might have been killed. I want you to know how much—"

Gill interrupted her. "Think nothing of it, Miss Falcon. Anyone would have done it." He looked up at Ranja. "Have you quite finished trying to kill me? May I get up now?"

Ranja grinned at him and said something in a language Shelby did not understand. She assumed it was an Indian dialect. He and Gill seemed to be more friends than master and servant. Ranja moved away with the basin and towels while Gill stood and reached for his coat. It was soaked through.

"I suppose this is another coat ruined," he said with a sigh. "At this rate, I'm going to run out of coats before I leave."

"We'll replace it for you, of course," Shelby said immediately. She cringed at the look he gave her. "If you'll allow us to, of course."

"I appreciate the offer, but it's nothing. That coat was in need of replacement anyway." He shrugged and tossed the coat over the back of chair.

Outside, the rain worsened as thunder began to sound in the west. The room darkened. Shelby turned to the window to watch the fury of the storm. "Mr. Gill," she said hesitantly, "that urn has been on the balcony as long as I can remember and it's never moved. Not in any kind of storm, even those that were worse than this one. What do you think happened?" She turned back to face him.

Gill hesitated, an anxious look flitting across his face. "Perhaps, Miss Falcon," he said smoothly, "it was just time for it to fall. There are Roman ruins that have been standing for centuries, and then suddenly they collapse."

"Perhaps," Shelby answered, not convinced.

"What else could it be?" Gill asked. Ranja came back into the room, and he and Gill spoke again in the strange language. "I'm afraid Ranja is rather insistent that I go up and rest until supper," Gill said ruefully as he picked up his ruined coat. "If you'll excuse me, Miss Falcon."

"Of course, Mr. Gill." Shelby watched him leave, his wet coat slung over one arm. The bandage on his head made his hair look even darker. It was only then that Shelby realized Gill's skin had not seemed so bronzed. There had been a pallor under the sun-bronzed tan of his skin. He must have been hurt more than he had indicated. *Thank goodness he was there to save Grandfather,* she thought as she again looked out at the storm. Outside, the pieces of the urn lay shattered on the gravel and Gill's hat blew against the largest piece, impaling itself against a jagged edge. Shelby shuddered again and turned away. *Something is very wrong here,* she thought to herself. Not for a moment did she believe Gill's suggestion that the urn had just fallen. Why had it happened now? Why almost on top of her grandfather? It seemed almost planned. . . .

As she sat in the darkened room listening to the storm, another thought came to her, and it was worse than any that preceded it: someone was trying to kill Colonel Falcon. Shelby put a hand to her mouth and gasped. "If that is true," she whispered to herself, horrified, "then it has to be someone in this house."

Five

Shelby went up to check on her grandfather. From past experience, she knew he would insist on coming down for supper. She was not going to allow any such thing. If she had to, she would get Biddle to help her lock him in his room.

To her surprise, Biddle opened the door when she knocked. "He's next door," Biddle indicated. "He had the mistress's old room turned into a sitting room right after you left the last time. He's in there."

Shelby walked into the other room, which was surprisingly cozy. She hadn't been in it since her grandmother had died, and she had forgotten how charming it had been. The colonel had had the bed removed, and had put in two large chairs, a desk, and a footstool. There was also a little bed for Dick Turpin. Right now, though, Dick was contentedly sleeping on the colonel's lap as they both sat in one of the big chairs, a small bandage wrapped around his paw. The colonel had his feet propped on the footstool, a quilt covering him from the knees down. Shelby stopped a moment and looked at him. Her heart almost broke—he had always been so vigorous and strong, the one person she had always depended on. But now, sitting there with his eyes closed and a look of worry on his face, he appeared old and broken.

"Grandfather, are you all right?" she asked softly, coming to sit on the footstool beside him.

He opened his eyes and turned to look at her. "I'm fine, girl," he said, but the spark was gone from his voice.

"I want you to eat supper up here on a tray. I know you missed being hurt, but it was still a harrowing experience. You need to rest."

He looked at her with weary eyes. "Dick and I had planned to eat up here, child. Don't worry about me."

"You know I always worry about you." She smiled and patted his hand. She paused a moment to think of the right way to ask her question, but could think of nothing except to ask frankly. "Grandfather," she began, "do you remember that you wrote me about some accidents you had last year when I was in Italy? I think you called them 'minor things,' and you weren't specific, but they were still accidents. What exactly happened?"

He looked at her and frowned. "Are you thinking that they weren't accidents?"

"I didn't say that," Shelby hedged. "I just wanted to know what happened then."

He sighed. "Well, you might as well know. I don't think they were accidents either. Once my horse ran away with me and threw me. When I finally walked back home, there he was. I helped unsaddle him, and found a burr under the saddle. I didn't mention it to anyone at the time, but never decided how it got there." He paused. "Two months later, I was out hunting, and a bullet clipped my ear." He pushed up his hair and showed her the notch in his ear. "If my head had been an inch over, I'd be dead today."

Shelby closed her eyes. It was almost too much to bear. "Those two things within two months of each other?"

"No, there's more. Last month I went to visit some friends in London. While I was there, I went to Crawford's house for supper with all the boys. I came down with a violent case of what the doctor called indigestion, but that wasn't what it was. I've had indigestion before. When I insisted the doctor was wrong, the fool was of the opinion that I might have eaten some poisoned oysters, but no one else at the table got sick and they'd all eaten the same shellfish." He looked at her. "I'm convinced that something was in my supper. You can draw your own conclusions."

"I don't think the urn was an accident," Shelby said dully. He nodded. "I don't either, girl."

"It has to be someone in the house, Grandfather." Shelby could hardly make herself speak the words.

He nodded. "That's what I think. The question I've been asking myself for a year is *who*. A man hates to think someone in his own family wishes him dead."

Shelby shook her head. She couldn't believe anyone in her family could be capable of such behavior. There had to be another explanation. "What about Mr. Gill, Grandfather? What do you know of him? He could be here for that purpose."

"Oh, he's here for a purpose, all right. Right after the oysters, I ran into an old friend of mine—Edward Bates."

"I've heard of him. You named Father after him."

Colonel Falcon nodded. "My best friend when I was younger. I'd trust my life to him. Anyway, I was troubled by all these accidents, and I found myself confiding in him about what had happened. He suggested that his nephew might be of service to me. It seems that Gill ferreted out a plot against Lord Minto in India. He's home now on a medical leave— caught a bad fever when he helped take Java—and Bates thought he might be able to help me."

"So he's protecting you?"

"You might say that."

"But what will happen when he has to return to the army? He looks fit to me, and his medical leave may be rescinded."

Colonel Falcon shook his head. "Perhaps things will have resolved themselves, one way or another."

"Grandfather, are you . . . are you really ill?"

He chuckled. "No more than any seventy-year-old. What

you're asking me is: 'Falcon, are you truly dying? What's the purpose of this farce, of bringing all of the family here together?' "

"That's what I'm asking." She smiled at him. "You always know my mind."

"That's because we're just alike. Now Bates was just like his mother, but you're just like me." He laughed. "Even have my coloring. Bates was blond, like Crawford, if you remember."

"Are you dodging the question, Grandfather? Why are we all here now?"

He took a deep breath. "I'm not supposed to tell anyone because Gill says anyone could be the culprit, but I'll tell you. I know you couldn't be involved, Shelby." He paused as Dick Turpin snored and flopped over onto his other side. "Gill's leave has already been rescinded. He has to go to the Peninsula next month, and he was, like you, afraid of what might happen after he left. He suggested that we get together everyone who has an interest in my possessions to see if we can smoke out the rat."

"So this was Gill's idea?"

"Yes, all but my giving you the jewels. That was something I planned on my own, and I wanted to do it in front of everyone, so they would all know. I've sent for my solicitor, but he's in London and won't be back until the first of next week. I've written out my instructions, and Gill and Biddle witnessed it. Just in case."

Shelby closed her eyes. She couldn't bear it. She made herself look at her grandfather and smile. "There's not going to be any 'just in case,' Grandfather. I agree with Gill. If there's a danger to you, then it has to be uncovered."

"Just don't tell the boys anything about it. They'd be on guard if they knew."

"You think it's one of them?"

He frowned and grimaced. "Who else could it be? I've

thought and thought of every slant, every possibility, and I keep coming up with the same answer. It has to be someone who would profit from my death, and that means someone in the family." He shook his head and stroked Dick Turpin absently. "Things have come to a sad pass with the Falcon family, haven't they, Shelby?"

"Only with one of us, Grandfather. The rest of us are Falcons through and through."

He glanced up as Biddle came in with a tray holding his supper. "Yes, Shelby, but which one of us is the bad one?"

Shelby had no answer.

Not only did Colonel Falcon not come down to supper, Gill didn't either. Shelby fretted that his pallor might have indicated he was getting another bout of the fever he had contracted in Java. She had no idea what she would do if he weren't there to help her protect Grandfather.

The meal was a disaster for Shelby. She sat at the table between her mother and Crawford. Bentley, Hayward, and Pearce said little, and the tension in the room was palpable. Shelby herself ate almost nothing. All she could do was shove food around on her plate while she wondered which cousin was a murderer. Worse, she kept looking at her food and wondering if it was tainted in some way. Could—or worse, *would*—someone poison her food? She wished fervently that she could talk to Gill immediately.

The only person who seemed to enjoy supper was the countess. She ate and chattered, drawing out each of the boys, asking them what they had been doing since she had last seen them. Pearce, of course, talked about his rockets, and mentioned the fact that he hoped to build a factory to manufacture rockets. When the countess asked Crawford what he had been doing, the answer was a surprise to Shelby.

"I've gone into publishing," he said. "Have you by chance seen a copy of *The London Eye?*"

"Oh my, yes!" Countess Rimildi said. "Don't tell me that's your publication! I've enjoyed every issue."

"There have been only two," Hayward said, "and I wonder about another. Crawford, I understand you're as much under the hatches as the rest of us. Heard you spent what money you had and were looking to borrow some. Heard the bank turned you down."

"At least I haven't gambled mine away." Crawford's tone was a sharp one Shelby had never heard him use before. "I heard your losses were so deep that you couldn't even go in the door at most of the clubs in London."

"In the *door* at a club," Bentley chortled. "He can't even go into London. Why do you think he was glad enough to come here? At least his creditors don't know where he is."

"Not for a fortnight or two anyway," Pearce said. "They'll figure it out soon, Hayward. What are you going to do then?"

"I'll come up with something," Hayward said, tossing down his fork. "I always do." He stood to leave. "I think I'll go where the company is more congenial."

Bentley stood as well. "He means that he's going down to the pub and get drunk," Bentley explained. "His credit is still good there. They know the colonel will pay his tab if he leaves without paying what he owes." He glanced at Hayward going out the door. "Wait and I'll go with you," he called. "Coming, Crawford, Pearce?"

Crawford and Pearce looked at each other and then back at Bentley. "I believe I'll stay here tonight," Crawford said. "Pearce? What about you?"

"I have some things . . . some reading to do. A friend sent me a new account of Congreve's rockets and how they were used in Spain. I think I'll stay here and read that."

"Your loss," Bentley said. He went out without a nod to any of them.

Countess Rimildi was shocked. "Those boys know better! I can't believe Hettie would ever allow them to act in such a way. She's always been a stickler for manners."

"I daresay that Hayward is upset with Bentley. Most of the gambling debts are Bentley's. Hayward is standing good for them," Pearce said. "We all know how Bentley is."

"That's no excuse for bad manners," the countess remarked, annoyed.

"Perhaps, Mama," Shelby said, "they feel they don't have to stand on ceremony since we're family."

"Horsefeathers." Countess Rimildi was miffed. "Shall we go to the drawing room? I feel in the mood for cards, and there are four of us."

The countess was the only one in the mood for cards, and won easily. Pearce excused himself as soon as the game was over, pleading that his reading would take a while. Crawford, Shelby, and Countess Rimildi sat for a while, the countess thoroughly bored. "These country hours are beyond anything. To think, I could have been back in London enjoying myself!" She turned to Shelby. "However, I know my duty to my daughter."

Shelby bit back a retort and merely smiled at her mother. After a while, the countess yawned from boredom and decided she would go up to her chamber and read. As soon as she was gone, Crawford walked across the room to the large, wooden case where the jewels were kept and rubbed his fingers across the paneled sides.

"Has it become reality for you that you're the new owner of the jewels?" he asked.

"I still consider them Grandfather's," Shelby told him. "I think I always shall." She paused, trying to think of a way to quiz Crawford about his publishing venture. He had mentioned being short of money twice since she had been here, and that was most unusual for him. He must be way up the River Tick.

Crawford looked up at her, the candlelight glinting off his

blond hair, his blue eyes dark. "Marry me, Shelby," he said softly.

Shelby wasn't sure she had heard him correctly. She had waited for years to hear him say those words to her, and now she couldn't believe them. "What did you say, Crawford?"

He came toward her. "I said marry me, Shelby." He sat beside her and took her hands in his. "You know that our relationship has always been a special one. We've always gotten along better than any two people I know. We could have a good life together."

Shelby stared at him, trying not to burst into tears. He hadn't mentioned caring for her. He hadn't mentioned being in love with her. He hadn't mentioned wanting her. This wasn't the way it had always been in her dreams. This wasn't the way it was supposed to be.

"Crawford, I . . . I . . . This is such a surprise." She looked away. She didn't want to look into his eyes. She had always dreamed of looking at him and seeing love shine from his eyes, but now there was nothing.

"I'm sorry, Shelby. I should have led up to this. I should have courted you and spent months telling you of my feelings. It just seemed right to ask you here at Wychwood since the place has so much meaning for both of us."

Since you know I'm to inherit the jewels. The thought sprang unbidden into her mind. She tried to erase it, but it stayed there. Crawford looked at her expectantly, and she felt she needed to say something, anything. "I need time to think, Crawford. I'm flattered beyond words that you would consider asking me to be your wife, but it's so sudden."

"I understand." He moved toward her and turned her face to his. "In the meantime . . ." He ran his fingertip under her chin and tilted her face up, then kissed her lightly on the lips. "I'll leave you then. Please think of what I've said. If you can find it in your heart to marry me, I don't want to wait."

No, Hayward said you need money now, she thought. *You*

can't afford to wait. She smiled at him, although it hurt terribly. Knowing he would marry her for money and really didn't care for her hurt far more than knowing he really loved Rose. "I'm worried about Grandfather right now, Crawford, and feel I can't decide about anything else. Please give me some time on this."

"I'll give you whatever you wish, sweeting," he said, kissing her lightly on the forehead. "You tell me when you've made up your mind." He stood and smiled at her, handsome as ever.

Shelby stood as well. "I believe I'll retire now, Crawford. It's been a long and trying day. I want to check on Grandfather before I go to bed."

"Then I'll see you in the morning. Sleep well."

Shelby had barely turned the top of the stairs into the hall when she heard the front door close. No doubt Crawford was going to the pub to get drunk with Bentley and Hayward. She stopped and put her head against the cool wall of the hall. She wanted to scream or to cry, but she hurt too much. She could never marry Crawford. No matter that she had dreamed of him since she was a child, she could never marry him. He didn't love her, and he never would.

She stumbled into her room to find Dovey waiting there. "I thought I'd wait and help you get ready for bed, mum," Dovey said. "I have everything ready."

Shelby went to the washbasin and splashed water onto her face. "I want to go check on my grandfather before I retire, Dovey," she said, holding the towel over her face until she felt she could turn around without having her heartache show. "By the way, do you know how Mr. Gill is doing? I was afraid he'd had a recurrence of his fever."

"I'll ask," Dovey said, bounding out of the room before Shelby could stop her.

Shelby sank down in the chair, wondering what was going to go wrong next. She turned to look into the small mirror at the back of the little table. She looked the same. That was a surprise. She certainly didn't feel the same. She felt older and shattered inside. She made herself smile.

Dovey came bounding back inside the room. "I thought I wasn't going to get to find out for you, mum, because that man of Mr. Gill's don't speak much English, I don't think. I knocked on the door, and he was all gibberish. He did point down the stairs, so I went down and searched for Mr. Gill. He was in the library, and I asked him if he had a fever and told him that you wanted to know. He said no, he don't have a fever, mum."

"Thank you, Dovey," Shelby said gravely. She was trying not to break into hysterical laughter. She could only imagine Gill's amazement at Dovey's dashing into the library to ask about a fever. Still, if he was in the library and wasn't ill, she might have an opportunity to talk to him about the things her grandfather had told her. "Do you know whether Mr. Gill is going to be there for a few minutes, Dovey?" She held up a hand to stop the maid. "Don't run down and ask him. Just tell me if he was leaving or if you think he will stay there for a while. I thought I might go down and . . . um, see if he needed anything."

"Oh, he's there for a while, I'd say, mum. He was sitting there reading."

"Good. Why don't you come back in an hour, Dovey? I should be back by then, and you can help me get ready for bed."

Dovey bobbed several times and held the door for Shelby. "I'll see you in an hour then, mum," she said, dashing off down the hall. She ran right past Ranja and didn't even see him. He looked puzzled, and followed her down the back stairs toward the kitchen.

The library was dark except for a branch of candles that stood on a small table beside a comfortable chair in which

Shelby had spent many happy hours reading. Gill was still there, reading. "Do you mind if I disturb you?" she asked.

He put down his book and stifled a yawn. "By all means, disturb me, Miss Falcon" he said. "I'm plowing my way through Xenophon and it's no better the second time than it was the first. I would welcome a disruption." He smiled at her, the shadows outlining his smile. She had never noticed how sensuous his lips were.

She did notice that he was no longer wearing his bandage, but there was a cut on the side of his forehead that ran from just above his eyebrow into his dark hair. "Don't you need a bandage on that cut?" she asked.

He touched his forehead gently. "No, I hate the things. Just as soon as I was certain the bleeding had stopped, I took it off. I always think wounds heal better in the air, anyway." He smoothed the skin around the cut with his fingertips. "It'll be unsightly for a few days, but I don't think there's any permanent harm done." He smiled. "Gave me the very devil of a headache, though."

"You saved Grandfather's life," she said quietly.

"Hardly that, Miss Falcon."

"Yes, you did. I saw the entire thing from the window. If you hadn't pushed him out of the way. . . ." She shuddered.

"Just think of the present, Miss Falcon. He's fine, I'm fine. Accidents do happen."

She sat down in a small chair that was beside him, but realized that she did not want to talk to him without being able to see him. She moved to a chair opposite him so she could face him. "You know it was no accident. Grandfather told me everything," she blurted out.

He frowned. "He did? Everything? And what was that?"

"He told me that your uncle sent you to him. He told me you were here to help him because all these 'accidents' had happened to him. He told me you planned this gathering so you could try to discover who is trying to harm him." Shelby paused, almost out of breath.

Gill sighed and caught his lower lip between his teeth. "He *did* tell you everything, then. Our agreement was that we tell no one."

"Not even me?"

He shook his head. "Not even you, Miss Falcon. After all, until we find the culprit, everyone is suspect."

"I assure you, I would never do anything to harm my grandfather. Other than Mother, he's all the direct family I have."

"There are your cousins. You could be helping any one of them."

"I would never do that!" She leaned forward to emphasize her words. "I assure you, I'm not close enough to any of them to allow Grandfather to be harmed. And don't blame Grandfather for telling me. I went up to see him and told him I had concluded that someone was trying to harm him. Both of us are horrified that someone in the family would do such a thing."

"But that appears to be the case, Miss Falcon." He sighed and stretched his legs out in front of him. He appeared utterly relaxed, but Shelby detected a tenseness in him. "I must ask you to promise me that you won't divulge to anyone what your grandfather told you. Absolutely no one. If our plans for this gathering are known, everything is lost." He looked at her, right into her eyes, and she felt a shiver that had nothing to do with cold. "As your grandfather probably told you, I must leave next month, so I want to solve this before then. He'll be unprotected when I leave."

"I'll watch him," Shelby said quietly. "I don't intend to leave him alone again."

Gill sighed. "I'm sure you intend the best, Miss Falcon, but it's difficult to stay with him every minute. He could get a hundred feet in front of you for instance, and something might happen. A quick knifing, a shot—any method might be used, and you could be standing right there."

Shelby put her face in her hands. "What can we do?"

Gill reached over and touched her hand. "Just what we're doing," he said as she looked at him again. "We need to find out which one of the cousins would profit most. We need to find out which one would have a motive."

"I can help you with that," Shelby said. "I'm the one who would profit most since Grandfather is leaving me the jewels."

"But you didn't know that until last night. These 'accidents' have been going on for months. I gathered last night that the colonel had left legacies for each cousin in his will. The jewels were extra. Was that your understanding?"

Shelby nodded. "Yes. The jewels are quite valuable, of course. Everyone thought Grandfather was going to divide them."

"It was in his original will."

"Yes." Shelby took a deep breath.

"So, unless he changes his will, the arrangement still stands."

"Yes, but he said he had written a will that had been witnessed by you and Biddle."

Gill smiled at her again. "True, but no one knows that except you, the colonel, Biddle, me, and Dick Turpin. And I don't think Dick will tell."

"I won't either." In spite of herself, Shelby found she was smiling.

"That's better, Miss Falcon. Now that you know everything, it's important that you behave just as usual. Perhaps we can pool our knowledge and find our culprit twice as fast."

Shelby smiled at him, delighted. "Wonderful, Mr. Gill. What is the first thing I can tell you that you don't already know?"

"I don't know as much about the cousins as I'd like. I need to know about their finances. I've made inquiries in London, but that information can be unreliable at times."

"I can tell you that Pearce is searching for money to build a factory. He wants to manufacture rockets like Congreve's. He. . . ." She paused, wondering just how much to tell Gill, then decided that her grandfather's life was worth more than anything. "He asked me to marry him last night. I know it was just because he thought I was going to be rich and could finance a factory." She looked down at the floor as she told him. "I don't see how Pearce could be involved. He's always been the gentlest of the lot."

"Note what you're saying about your cousin, Miss Falcon. Gentle? A man who wants to manufacture rockets for warfare?"

Shelby had no answer for that. She took a deep breath. "There was also something of a contention at supper tonight. Crawford needs money for his publishing venture. The others mentioned that Hayward is badly in need of money to save him from his creditors. He has debts, and he's standing good for Bentley's as well."

Gill nodded. "Gambling debts. I've heard about those. He's in deep, I understand." He paused. "What about Bentley? Since his debts have been assumed, does he need money for anything else?"

"I don't know, but I'll try to find out. They'll be more likely to tell me than you." She looked at him and her heart lurched. He seemed dangerous in the shadows and candlelight, but it was a danger she wanted to find out more about. She forced herself to keep her voice even. "I think, as you said, Mr. Gill, we should pool our information. We should meet every night and share what we've learned during the day and perhaps make plans for the next day."

"Done, Miss Falcon!" He held out his hand to her, and she clasped it. It was warm and firm, not at all like that of a man with a fever. "I think this partnership is going to work very well."

"I hope so, Mr. Gill." She noted that they were still clasping hands. "What shall we plan for tomorrow?"

"I plan to stay close to Colonel Falcon because he wants to go to Weeding Lois to see about a horse. I don't think anything will happen, but you never know. I intend to announce at breakfast that he's going there."

"The boys won't be at breakfast," Shelby told him. "All of them except Pearce have gone to the pub, so I expect they'll be sleeping in late. They don't hold their liquor very well."

"I've noticed." Gill's voice was rich with amusement.

Shelby thought a moment, still very aware of her hand in his. She wondered if he even realized he was holding it for an unacceptable amount of time. "I'll spend tomorrow trying to discover more about the finances of each one. I think they may confide in me."

"Fine, Miss Falcon." He smiled briefly, then glanced down to their hands and quickly freed hers. "Perhaps we should retire so we can get in a full day tomorrow. Allow me to escort you up the stairs." He stood, held his arm, and Shelby took it, blowing out the candles. She was in the dark with him, and it sent a frisson of excitement down her spine and did strange things to her chest. She wondered if he had any reaction.

They went out the library door and up the stairs. At the top, he turned and smiled at her. "Until breakfast, Miss Falcon."

She smiled back and went into her room, leaning against the door. Dovey, miraculously, wasn't there. Shelby sat down in the small chair and looked into the mirror again. With a sense of shock, she realized that she hadn't thought of Crawford once since she had entered the library.

Six

Gill awoke the next morning and lay in bed for a few minutes, thinking. He had wondered how to discover more about the cousins, and Shelby's offer of help had been just the way he could unearth what he needed. When Shelby had first begun talking, he had been appalled that the colonel had broken their agreement and had revealed the plan, but, on reflection, he decided it was the right thing to do. Yes, he had been emphatic about telling no one, reiterating to the colonel that everyone was suspect. *And Shelby Falcon?* an inner voice asked him. *Are you letting the fact that she's a beautiful woman blind you?*

He sat up and shook his head. She wasn't involved—he'd wager his life on it. She was too open, too innocent. When she had looked at him with those green eyes, he'd known she could never try to harm anyone. Her conversation last night had proven that she was protective of her grandfather. He *knew* she was innocent, just knew it. She was just as horrified as the colonel that someone in the family would stoop to attempting murder.

Gill grimaced, thinking. He had to be right. He wasn't betting a trifle here. He wasn't even wagering his own life—he was wagering the colonel's.

He rang for Ranja and got up, being as noisy as possible since Crawford's room was right next door. He thought the scene he had witnessed yesterday would stay with him forever. He had left the colonel and gone up to the little rise alone. When he had looked down at the ruins, he had seen Shelby and Crawford. Rather, he had seen Crawford kissing Shelby and Shelby seeming to enjoy the intimacy. The colonel had told him that Shelby had always preferred Crawford and had been devastated when he and Rose became engaged. Before witnessing the scene at the ruins, Gill had no feelings for Crawford one way or the other, but after seeing Shelby with him yesterday, he heartily disliked the man. He deliberately dropped his boots on the floor right next to the wall before he began to dress. They made a very satisfying sound, although his behavior did cause Ranja to look at him strangely.

Shelby was already in the breakfast room, drinking coffee, when Gill came down. He looked at her and smiled. She looked as if nothing had ever happened to her or to the family. Her rich auburn hair was piled on top of her head, and little tendrils framed her face. She was wearing a cream-colored dress again, this time one trimmed in russet ribbons. The effect she had on Gill was extraordinary, and he had to stop himself from grabbing her by the waist and swinging her around. No woman had ever affected him in this way. He made himself give her a slight bow. "Good morning, Miss Falcon. You're up early."

"We did have an engagement for breakfast, I believe." She smiled when she spoke. "I've even ascertained from Mrs. McKilley what you prefer for breakfast."

"You are thorough. And, yes, we did have an appointment. I haven't forgotten." He smiled back and sat down across from her. Mrs. McKilley appeared from nowhere with a maid and served their breakfasts. "Don't forget the blackberry jam," Shelby reminded her. "Both of us are fond of it."

Gill was surprised by his reaction to her phrase "Both of us." He'd been rootless since the deaths of his parents. His

Uncle Bates had been his guardian, but that wasn't the same as a family. It felt good to be included, to be a part of a pair.

"Now, Mr. Gill," Shelby said, getting down to business as soon as Mrs. McKilley left, "have you thought of a way to let my cousins know that you and Grandfather are going to Weeding Lois?"

"No, as I said, I thought I would simply tell them at breakfast." He looked around. "You seem to be correct, Miss Falcon. We appear to be the only early risers here."

"Grandfather is up, I know. He always gets up before seven." She leaned forward, across the breakfast table. "Are you expecting trouble on the way?"

Gill glanced around. "I don't know. Of course, if no one knows we're going, nothing will happen." He glanced around again. "I worry about having a conversation here at the table, Miss Falcon. Anyone could come in at any time. Why don't we just eat breakfast and then take a turn around the garden? We can talk as we walk."

She smiled at him, and Gill felt almost dizzy. "Wonderful idea, Mr. Gill." She began eating a dish of orange sections, slowly slipping each one into her mouth and savoring it, a contented expression on her face. Gill felt really dizzy now. He tried not to watch her, but couldn't stop himself from observing each bit of orange slide slowly from the spoon into her mouth. He took a deep breath. If he didn't think of something else, he was going to attack her right on top of the toast. He searched desperately for a topic of conversation.

"Do you garden, Miss Falcon?" he asked, hoping his voice sounded normal. She had spooned up a large section of orange and was ready to put it in her mouth. It slipped slowly through her lips.

"I love to garden, Mr. Gill," she said, running the tip of her tongue along her lower lip. He thought he had never seen anything so sensuous. He wondered briefly if she could hear his breathing or the pounding of his blood.

"I suppose that's your father's influence. Not everyone has a renowned botanist as a parent. Did you learn a great deal from him?" He busied himself with putting blackberry jam on his toast. If he didn't look directly at her, she couldn't possibly bother him. It was a vain hope.

"Not so much. He died when I was small, and really before he reached the apex of his career. I think he could have done much more, had he only lived." She paused and looked over his shoulder at the garden. "Most of what I know about plants and gardening I learned from Grandfather."

He looked at her in surprise. "The colonel? A gardener? I wouldn't have thought it."

"It's a well-kept secret," Shelby said, looking at him with a smile. "He loves to collect plants and show them off. Of course, he doesn't do a great deal of it himself, as you've seen, but he always tells the gardeners what he wants. He says every garden should be like a painting, and the viewer should be able to stand and enjoy it." She pushed the empty bowl away and began sipping her coffee. "Would you like to see the knot garden this morning, Mr. Gill? When you're ready, of course."

He took a large gulp of coffee to fortify himself. "I'd love to, Miss Falcon. Shall we go now?" He stood, offered her his arm, and they went outside into the morning sun.

"It's going to be warm today," he said. "The grass is already dry."

"Good." Shelby was silent until they were well away from the house. "Now, Mr. Gill," she said in a businesslike tone, "I've decided that the only way to inform the boys about Grandfather's trip to Weeding Lois is for me to tell them. I don't think I should tell them you've gone along. Do you agree?"

"I agree, Miss Falcon. Perhaps if our culprit thinks the colonel is alone, he might be tempted to strike."

Shelby stopped and looked up at him. "Yes, but do you think you can protect Grandfather?"

"I'll do my best, Miss Falcon. That's all I can promise."

She resumed walking. "Then everything will be all right." She paused. "I thought I would try to talk to each cousin today and find out what I can about his financial situation. I'm rather hesitant. . . ." Her voice trailed off.

"You're rather hesitant to share family secrets with me?" he asked.

She nodded. "The Falcons have always been a proud family, sometimes too proud for our own good."

"You may rest assured, Miss Falcon, that I would never divulge any details that weren't absolutely necessary to bring our criminal to justice." He stopped and looked down at her. She had come out without her bonnet, and her hair gleamed with red fires in the morning sun. He tried looking at her eyes, but that was just as bad. She looked up at him with a strange combination of innocence and trust. He didn't dare look at her lips again. He settled for looking over her shoulder at a large bush. "If we're to work together, Miss Falcon, it's necessary that you share everything you know with me."

"And you with me, Mr. Gill? Can you share everything you discover with me? That's only fair, I think."

He paused, then looked into her eyes. "All right, Miss Falcon. I agree that seems fair. Right now, I don't know very much except that your cousins drink far too much, spend far too much, and gamble far too much. Our culprit could be any one of them. I do think it's one of them, and not someone else, because there's no motive I can discover for anyone else to harm the colonel."

"I agree with you on that score, Mr. Gill," she said. "And thank you for sharing what you know." They turned and walked on a moment. "Since I promised to share everything, Mr. Gill, I feel I must tell you of something that occurred last evening. I rely on your discretion."

"Of course."

"I told you that Pearce had offered marriage, but I didn't

tell you that"—she paused a fraction of a second, then blurted it out—"Crawford proposed to me last night."

He was overwhelmed by a flood of raging jealousy, and it was a moment before he could speak. "Oh, and did you accept?" His lips felt wooden.

She shook her head. "No. I asked him to give me time. I have come to realize that he cares nothing for me as a . . . as a wife." Her voice broke slightly. "This is very difficult for me, Mr. Gill. After all, you and I are barely acquainted."

"Yes, but circumstances have forced us into a more intimate acquaintance than most people have after a length of time."

"I realize that. I do feel there is an understanding between us, don't you?" She smiled up at him, and he was totally lost.

"Yes, Miss Falcon," he said, trying to keep his voice level. "There certainly is."

She smiled at him and continued. "As I told you, Hayward said at supper that Crawford needed money for his publishing venture. I believe that's why he offered for me. It was the jewels again." She laughed ruefully. "I'm beginning to regret my ownership of them."

"Just remember that the colonel wanted to give you the most valuable thing he possessed."

She sighed. "He doesn't realize that I'd trade every jewel there just to know that he's safe." She stopped and faced him. "We've finished our tour, Mr. Gill. Perhaps it would be best if we just pretended to be distant when we're with the others."

Gill had an inspiration. "On the contrary, Miss Falcon. Why don't I pretend to have become infatuated with you? That way, we could be together to discuss things and no one would remark it. They would merely think I was trying to engage your affections."

She laughed again, her lips pink and smiling. "Perfect, Mr. Gill. You are devious, aren't you? I would never have thought of that." She glanced through the breakfast-room window. "I do believe Pearce is down for breakfast. I'll leave you now and begin spreading my news about the trip to Weeding Lois."

Gill watched her go inside, knowing a sudden sense of loss. *You're a fool,* he thought to himself. *A complete fool.* Somehow, the thought didn't really bother him. Whistling, he went to hunt up the colonel.

Shelby duly informed Pearce about the colonel's jaunt, and then went off to inquire about Hayward, Bentley, and Crawford. They were, Mrs. McKilley informed her with a disapproving frown, still abed. In Mrs. McKilley's world, people did not stay in bed after seven unless they were ill. Shelby told her that the young men were probably indisposed.

"Indisposed!" Mrs. McKilley snorted. "Begging pardon, but if I didn't come home until three or four o'clock, I couldn't get up at a decent hour either."

"Three or four? Are you sure it was that late?"

"I'm sure. They woke me up when they came in singing, and I couldn't go back to sleep. No sense in such. I've a mind to talk to the colonel about it."

"Perhaps we shouldn't bother Grandfather since he's sick," Shelby suggested.

"Sick!" Mrs. McKilley snorted again and stomped off toward the kitchen.

Shelby missed Bentley, but did manage to see Hayward as he was going out. He looked wretched, worse than Bentley had the previous day. In the morning daylight, Shelby could see the unmistakable signs of dissipation on Hayward's face. "Are you going out?" she asked cheerfully as he went by the drawing-room door. She had been in wait all morning and had run out when she'd seen him.

"Yes." He held his head, and Shelby went over to him, feigning concern.

"I believe you could do with a cup of coffee or tea, Hayward. Do come into the drawing room and let me send for some."

He followed her into the room and waited until she had sent for coffee. "Strong and black," he said to the maid as she left to fetch it.

"Hayward," Shelby began, but he interrupted her.

"Don't read me any sermons, Shelby. I know I drink too much, but I don't intend to stop. When I'm drunk, I don't have to think."

"I wasn't going to read you a sermon, Hayward, but since you've mentioned it, I will tell you that I hate to see you doing this to yourself."

He shrugged. "Since it's to myself, it's no one else's business." He stretched his legs out in front of him and leaned against the sofa's back. "What's going on with our esteemed family? Anything?"

"Oh, nothing much. Grandfather is going to travel over to Weeding Lois today to check on a horse he's thinking of buying. That's the only thing happening that I know of. I didn't want him to go so far alone, but he wouldn't listen to me."

"When does he listen to anyone?" Hayward grumbled.

"He is headstrong—we all know that. But, I think he particularly wanted to buy this horse for the stables, so nothing could stop him."

"Buying a horse?" Hayward opened his eyes wide. "I thought he was dying! What in the name of all hell does he need with a horse if he's going to die?"

Shelby was at a loss for that one, and was saved only by the arrival of the coffee tray. She poured Hayward a cupful of what looked to be black treacle. He took it and downed it, without cream or sugar. "Perfect. Just what I needed," he said, holding out the cup for a refill. "When is he going?"

"Who? Oh, you mean Grandfather. I think he left about an hour ago."

"Alone, did you say? Or did someone go with him? A

groom, perhaps? At his age, he shouldn't be out alone." Hayward's tone was casual. *Almost too casual,* Shelby thought.

She couldn't look at him because she knew he could read the truth in her face. Instead, she busied herself with the coffeepot. "Oh, quite alone. He didn't even take Dick Turpin with him. More coffee?"

"Too bad he didn't take that dog and lose it somewhere along the way. I loathe that creature."

"I think Grandfather would trade all of us for Dick Turpin," she said, laughing.

"I know." Hayward's tone was morose. "To think he went all the way to Brussels to get the thing. A rat-catcher. I'll never know why."

"He had the same kind of dog before, one he picked up in Brussels on his travels, if you recall."

"Yes, a complete street dog. What was that one's name?"

"Rogue William," Shelby said, laughing. "And a rogue he was, if you recall. He, too, was a Griffon d'Écurie."

"A stable dog. Just right for the colonel. Is there more coffee in that pot?" Hayward held out his cup again and then looked at Shelby speculatively as he drank from it. "Shelby, I'd have to say you're quite a regular 'un. You don't go reading the riot act over a man just because he's had a little too much to drink. I like that."

"Thank you, Hayward." She didn't know what else to say.

Hayward put his cup on the tray and leaned toward her, his eyes bloodshot. "Shelby, I know we've had our differences, and perhaps haven't known each other as well as most. I know, too, how you were all broken up when Crawford and Rose announced their engagement."

"That's past history, Hayward." She carefully made her face blank and her tone quiet.

"Is it, Shelby? Is that true?"

She looked right at him. "That's true, Hayward." She couldn't hold the gaze. Instead, she began straightening the creamer and sugar bowl on the tray. Suddenly, it was very important to put everything in order.

He paused a moment, turning the coffee cup around in his fingers. Then he looked at her again. "Then could you consider another one of us? Me, for instance?"

Shelby was so amazed that she dropped the sugar bowl and lumps of sugar scattered across the rug. "You?"

He looked offended. "Well, I'm no great prize, I suppose, but I think we'd do well. I think the colonel would like to see you marry someone in the family."

"Yes, but. . . ." She didn't know what else to say.

"I'm not good enough? You still care for Crawford?"

Shelby shook her head. "No, that's not it at all, Hayward. You've just taken me by surprise, that's all. I had never considered that either of us had any feelings for the other."

"Well, we don't," he said baldly, "but that's no deterrent to marriage. In fact, I think the best marriages I know are purely business arrangements. Both parties understand each other and go their separate ways."

"Hayward, I'm flattered to be asked, I truly am, but I don't think I would want to spend the rest of my life in an arrangement like that."

"So the answer is no?"

"Yes, the answer is no." She looked at him, wondering what else she could say. He didn't look disappointed.

"I thought as much." Hayward stood up. "I have some things to do. Just think about what I've said. If you change your mind, let me know. We could be married in no time at all." He paused and looked down at her. "It's true, you know, Shelby. Love is just a waste of time in a marriage. Just look what happened to Crawford. Fell in love with Rose, got engaged, thought everything was going to be fine. Then Rose finds out he's poor as a churchmouse and cries off. It broke his heart."

"I didn't know all the details. I was in Italy with Mama."

She felt her eyes fill with tears of sympathy. "Did it really hurt him?"

Hayward nodded. "Devastated him at the time. He doesn't let on, but I think it still hurts him. He's always been in love with Rose, you know."

"No," Shelby said slowly, "I didn't know."

"He probably always will be." He bent down to look in her eyes. "Are those tears, Shelby? This is a fine fix, isn't it? Rose hurts Crawford, Crawford hurts you. Nobody wins."

"I'm not hurt, Hayward. I merely feel sorry for Crawford. I didn't know his feelings had been engaged so."

Hayward shrugged. "Well, it's true, love is a pain." He stopped and glanced at her before he went out. "As I said, Shelby, let me know if you change your mind. We could be at Gretna before anyone missed us."

And you could be in possession of the Jewels of Ali, Shelby thought to herself as she looked at the empty doorway. *Never, Hayward. Never.*

At lunch, Shelby managed to tell Crawford about the colonel's trip. His reaction was much the same as Hayward's. "I'm beginning to think all this talk about dying was just a ruse to get us up here," he told her. "He doesn't even seem ill."

"Biddle says he's not long for this world," Shelby said. "I gather it's a rather slow, insidious disease."

"Well, what is it? Is it slow enough to last for years? We can't stay here that long."

Shelby was forced to admit that she didn't know what could be ailing the colonel. "Still, Crawford," she said, "he does look older and paler, don't you think? Both Biddle and Mrs. McKilley seem to think he could go off any minute. Mama thinks . . . well, Mama thinks he could die most inconveniently."

"That's probably true, if I know the colonel. By the way, Shelby, I saw your mother upstairs, and she says once again that she's thinking of returning to London. I think the rustication of Wychwood is wearing on her."

Shelby sighed. "Mama can't stay in one place over a fortnight. She's rambled all over Italy and most of Belgium. She did seem to be settling down in London. I suppose she misses society." She finished her tea. "I'd better go check on her. I haven't talked to her today, and she probably thinks I'm neglecting her." She rose to leave. "And what do you have planned for this afternoon, Crawford?"

"Just some odds and ends," he said. "Enjoy your afternoon." He stopped and was distracted by the crunch of wheels on gravel outside. "Did the colonel take the carriage? I thought you said he was riding over to Weeding Lois."

"He did. I have no idea. . . ." Shelby stopped as Luke threw open the front door. She and Crawford stood there, frozen, as Rose stepped daintily out of a carriage and came up the steps. She was, as usual, a fashion plate, dressed all in baby blue silk trimmed with white lace at the wrists and a white crape ruche at the bottom. Her bonnet was straw, tied with wide blue ribbons, trimmed with blue and yellow flowers, a white gauze ruche at the brim. There was a beautiful stuffed bluebird nestled in the flowers. Her blond hair was arranged artfully to frame her face inside the bonnet's brim. She looked at them and opened her blue eyes wide.

"Hello you two," Rose said, in that breathless, little girl's voice she always used. "Aren't you delighted to see me?"

Seven

Bentley came down the stairs as Rose came inside. "What a surprise!" He grinned at her. "How are you?" he asked. "Have you come to join the wake?"

Shelby turned to him, scandalized. "Bentley! And I thought you were on your best behavior now."

"I am." He looked offended. "Isn't a wake what this is? Grandfather sent for us because he's dying, and we're all here, waiting, just seeing what's in it for us."

With a shock, Shelby realized that this gathering could very possibly turn into a wake. "That's not true, Bentley," she said. "We're not all here to see, as you so elegantly put it, what's in it for us. I'm here to try to help Grandfather. I didn't come here for gain."

Bentley sighed. "Spoken like one who doesn't need to wait around for gain." He grinned at Rose. "You're too late, Rose. Grandfather already gave Shelby the Jewels of Ali. He's going to change his will in favor of her next week when his solicitor returns from London. It's all arranged."

Rose turned to Shelby, her eyes narrow. "You? He gave the jewels to you? Every single one of them?"

Crawford took Rose's elbow and led her toward the drawing room. "Of course Shelby got the jewels, Rose. After all, she is the colonel's only direct heir. Who else should have them?"

Rose tossed her head, blue ribbons flying. "I for one don't

care a jot about the jewels. I came because Mama and I agreed it was the proper thing to do. After all, we may not be related directly, but we are related by marriage, even if distantly." She paused at the drawing room door and looked back at Shelby. "By the by, Shelby, will you see that Mrs. McKilley has my luggage brought in? There's not much—I have only two trunks and some boxes. And will you have her ready the blue bedroom for me? It's my favorite." She turned back and allowed Crawford to escort her into the drawing room.

"It appears," Bentley said with a touch of laughter in his voice, "that you've been promoted to housekeeper's assistant."

Shelby fumed, but sent for Mrs. McKilley.

"Do you think I should put her in the blue chamber? Mr. Gill is in there, and I hate to ask him to move again." Mrs. McKilley waited patiently. "I'll do whatever you say."

Rose's tinkling laugh sounded in the hall. "Put Miss Meadows in the yellow room. I hate to ask Mr. Gill to move again. After all, he's already packed up and changed rooms once."

Mrs. McKilley smiled broadly. It was no secret that Rose hated yellow. "Very good," she said. It was also no secret that Mrs. McKilley didn't look on Rose as one of her favorite people.

Bentley laughed and took Shelby's elbow. "Well done, cuz," he whispered. "Shall we go in and find out Rose's motive?"

"I think I know what it is, Bentley." Shelby sighed as Dick Turpin ran up to her.

"Dick, you've lost your bandage," she said. Dick looked up at her and began his tricks. He rolled over once, waving his paws in the air, then flopped back onto his stomach and covered his eyes with his paws. Then he lifted one paw and looked at her to see if she was suitably impressed. "You're wonderful, Dick," she said, scooping him up and ruffling his fur. She tucked him under her right arm, placed her left arm on Bentley's and the three of them went into the drawing room.

Rose was sitting on the sofa, while Crawford was standing

stiffly by the fireplace. The two were not talking. Shelby and Bentley sat in the chairs opposite Rose, and Shelby put Dick Turpin on her lap. He promptly stretched out, tucked his head between his paws, and stared at Rose.

"I see the colonel still has that horrid animal," Rose said. "I can't imagine what he sees in that hideous dog. I've never seen anything as ugly."

"Are you certain of that, Rose?" Bentley asked with a grin. "That viscount you were chasing at Christmas looked worse than Dick Turpin, I'd wager."

"Leave Digby out of this," Rose snapped.

"Heard he didn't come up to scratch," Bentley said lazily.

Shelby interceded before the two began arguing as they always did. "Grandfather likes Dick Turpin. He says the dog has character."

"Yes, but what kind?" Rose wrinkled her nose. "He'll ruin your gown if you aren't careful. Why don't you relegate him to the stable where he belongs? He's a stable dog, isn't he?"

"Grandfather would relegate us to the stable before he would Dick Turpin," Bentley said with a laugh. "As for dresses, that one you have on must have cost a bundle or I miss my guess. I thought you were like the rest of us, Rose— low on the balsam. Personally, I haven't a farthing and that's why I'm here." He looked at her shrewdly. "Is that why you're here, Rose?"

A trace of red rose slowly up and onto her face. "Of course not, Bentley! I was worried about the colonel and wanted to come. He sent word to Mama that he was dying, and I knew I had to be here. As I told Shelby and Crawford, it's the right thing to do."

"Well, you're too late for anything good. You'll just have to join the waiting with the rest of us." Bentley stretched. "How was your trip?"

Rose tossed her head prettily so that her curls bounced. "Oh, just horrid! I do wish you'd ring for some tea, Shelby, so I could restore myself."

"I'll do it." Crawford went to the bellpull, and waited for the footman. As soon as he had sent for tea, he came over and sat beside Rose. Dick Turpin jumped from Shelby's lap and onto the sofa, where he sat between Rose and Crawford.

"It looks as if you have a chaperone," Bentley said with a chuckle.

"Go away, you dirty animal!" Rose waved her reticule at Dick to try to shoo him off the sofa. Dick thought she was playing with him and began to swat at the ruche of white lace on the bottom of the reticule. She swatted at him again, and the lace caught in his toenail. When Rose saw what had happened, she jerked the reticule over to the other side. Since Dick was still attached to the lace, he came with it, neatly landing right in her lap. "Get this thing off me!" Rose shrieked. She jerked both her arms back almost over her head. She was still holding the reticule, and Dick still had his toenail caught in the lace, so he came up with it. He was eye to eye with her, and he scrabbled for a foothold, finally catching his back feet in the lace that trimmed the bodice of her gown. The lace tore and Dick almost fell until he caught his back toenails in the blue silk. Rose screamed; and Dick, wondering what was going on, did a trick for her. He pulled back his lips and grinned his best.

"Get this brute off me!" Rose shrieked, leaning farther against the back of the sofa and pulling her arms even higher. Dick scrambled again, pulled upward by his toenail, now finding a foothold for his lower feet right on Rose's chin. One front paw was still caught, but he managed to put the other on Rose's forehead. Then he saw the stuffed bluebird.

With a snarl, he lunged and grabbed it in his jaws, shaking his head as hard as he could. Rose began screaming as her bonnet swished from side to side. Crawford and Shelby sprang to her rescue. Bentley didn't move; he was too busy laughing.

Crawford tried to pull Dick away, but Dick wouldn't let go of the bluebird. He growled low in his throat, and jerked on the bluebird, shaking his head, swishing his underbelly in Rose's face. "Get him away!" Rose screamed, finally releasing the reticule as she tried to grab Dick. With a final jerk, Dick managed to tear the bluebird loose from the bonnet, although part of the brim came along with it. He slid back down Rose's face with the bluebird in his mouth, coming to rest right on her chest, his face on a level with hers.

She screamed again, right in his face. Crawford was pulling Dick, but the little dog dug his toenails into Rose's dress and hung on. The stuffed bluebird was nose to nose with Rose. She shrieked.

"Do hush, Rose," Shelby said, knocking Crawford away and putting both hands along Dick's sides. "You're exciting the dog. I'll never get him off if you aren't quiet."

Rose stopped shrieking and subsided into sobs, her body rigid. In just a moment, Dick relaxed and turned to look at Shelby, the bird still in his mouth. "Good dog, Dick," Shelby crooned softly. "Now, let go." She reached for his paws and began to disentangle them. Dick released the bird and watched as it tumbled to the floor. He took a deep breath, and grinned at Shelby as she pulled him away from Rose.

Shelby put Dick on the floor and turned to help Rose. Dick picked up the stuffed bluebird, and trotted out the door with it.

"That horrid animal!" Rose screeched. "Someone should kill that thing! It's evil!"

"Rose, do hush." Shelby helped her to her feet. "Let me take you upstairs where you can wash up and change. I'm sure Dick didn't mean to ruin your dress."

"My dress," Rose sobbed, staggering along beside Shelby. "My beautiful dress." Shelby didn't mention the remains of the lovely bonnet that was now flopping around Rose's face, a huge hole in it where the stuffed bluebird had been sewn. Rose could discover that at a calmer time.

When Shelby came back down the stairs an hour later, Crawford and Bentley were still in the drawing room, talking. "Did you get Rose settled down?" Bentley asked.

"Finally." Shelby looked around. "Where's Dick Turpin? Has he come back?"

"Haven't seen him," Crawford said. "I would think he's probably under Biddle's bed, making mincemeat of that stuffed bird."

Bentley began chuckling to himself, his shoulders shaking. Shelby pinned him with a look. "Bentley, stop that! Dick did a terrible thing, and he should be thoroughly ashamed of himself."

"No doubt he is." Bentley's shoulders were still shaking. "This is one of those episodes that will be talked about in the family for years. I just wish the others had been here to see it." He paused as the front door opened. In just a moment, Colonel Falcon came in, looking as healthy as Shelby had ever seen him. The ride had worked wonders. Gill was right behind him. Shelby caught Gill's eye as Colonel Falcon went over to pour himself a glass of port. Gill shook his head slightly. The bait hadn't worked.

"Wonderful day for a ride," the colonel said. "You two should have gone along. And I saw as fine a piece of horseflesh as I've seen lately. Chestnut, white socks on the front. The price is in negotiation, but I think the owner will come around."

"We had our own entertainment here," Bentley said, and proceeded to relate the adventures of Dick and Rose. When he finished, Colonel Falcon shook his head. "That dog," he said with a note of pride. He put his port down. "I've got to go back to the stables. My horse picked up a stone, and I told Rankin I'd come back to check on him."

"Rankin is still with you?" Crawford said in amazement.

"I haven't seen him this trip and thought he'd retired. He must be ninety."

"And still as hale and hearty as a man of fifty." Colonel Falcon looked at the last half-inch of port in the glass, tossed it off, and headed for the door. "He helped me get the stone out of Red Boy's hoof, and said he'd stay and look after it, but I told him to go on home. It will be a sad day when I can't take care of my own horse." He paused at the door. "Did I ever tell you about the time when Biddle and I were in the colonies. New York, it was. It was a terrible winter, and my horse pulled up lame in the middle of a snowstorm. . . ."

"Yes," everyone chorused, including Gill.

"I thought I'd told that story." Colonel Falcon whistled for Dick Turpin, and waited a moment until the dog came running to him. He held out his arms, and Dick leaped all the way from the bottom step right into the crook of the colonel's arm. Colonel Falcon tucked the dog under one arm and went out the door.

Gill took a chair along with the others, and the conversation was merely desultory for a few minutes. Then Crawford leaned forward. "You look strangely familiar to me, Mr. Gill, but I'm sure that before now I've never been introduced to anyone with your name. Have we met before?"

"Not that I'm aware of," Gill said casually. "I've been in India for several years. I just returned to England a short while ago."

Crawford shook his head. "I could swear we've met somewhere, sometime." He smiled. "And may I ask you a personal question?"

Gill nodded and Crawford went on. "I don't mean to be blunt, but why are you here? You're not one of the family, and from what I can gather, you've been here for a while."

"That's quite easy to explain," Gill said with a laugh. "I contracted a fever while I was in the Orient, and that's why I returned to England. Unfortunately, the dirt of London did nothing to help me recover. My uncle is an acquaintance of the colonel's, and he arranged for me to come here to the country for a while." He smiled again. "The country air and the peace and quiet have worked wonders."

Bentley stood to leave. "No mystery there, Crawford. And as for peace and quiet—there's too much here for me. I'm going over to the village. Do you want to come with me?"

"Go on, and I'll be there in a while." Crawford stood, looking slightly embarrassed. "I thought I'd best check on your sister. Don't you think you should as well?"

"Rose? No, she always lands on her feet, no matter what. She takes after her father; he was the same way. Give her my regards, and I'll see you later." He went out the door whistling. Crawford excused himself and went up the stairs. In just a few minutes, Shelby and Gill heard him come back down and go out the front door.

"So nothing happened on the trip?" Shelby asked, picking up Rose's reticule from where it had fallen on the floor. It had been stuffed with papers which had fallen out. She bent to scoop them up. "Bills, Mr. Gill," she said slowly, as she picked up first one and then the other. "Rose has a whole sheaf of bills here." She tried not to peek, but couldn't help herself. The amounts on the few items she saw amazed her.

She turned to Gill. "These bills are enormous. There's no way Rose can come up with this amount, and I know Aunt Hettie isn't good for it. Crawford told me Rose used everything her father left her to finance her entry into society." Carefully she put the bills together and stuffed them back into the reticule. "So I suppose we can add Rose to our list of those who need funds."

Gill looked around cautiously. "I worry about discussing things in the house, Miss Falcon," he said in a low tone.

Shelby tossed the reticule on the table, turned, and smiled brightly at him. "Would you like to take a turn out in the back garden, Mr. Gill? There's a particularly fine sundial that Grandfather had sent in from Rome. It's not original, but it's a beautiful copy."

Gill offered her his arm, and they went out. "Is that Crawford heading to the stables?" Shelby asked, shielding her eyes. She had forgotten to bring her bonnet again.

"I believe it is." Gill moved aside so Shelby could precede him through a small gate. "This is a charming garden. Don't tell me the colonel designed this one as well."

"No, I did this one. I'm quite proud of it." She shielded her eyes again and looked over the garden. "Why don't we sit over here? I had a bench put here, under the arbor. It's a shady, secluded place."

They sat and Gill related the few particulars of their trip. It was a fine day, the colonel had enjoyed himself tremendously, and absolutely nothing had happened.

"Perhaps, Mr. Gill, we didn't give them enough time to prepare anything. Perhaps we should announce Grandfather's next trip a day or so in advance."

"I think you're right, Miss Falcon. By the by, I did tell your grandfather that you and I had talked. I also mentioned that we were planning to pretend a *tendre* for each other in order to allay suspicion. He quite heartily approved."

Shelby frowned. "I just hope he doesn't overdo any comments on that arrangement. Grandfather has a tendency to get carried away."

"I've noticed." Gill's tone was wry.

Shelby laughed and looked up at him. There was a purple bruise along the edges of the cut on his head, but he looked much better today. The wound appeared to be healing well, and didn't seem to bother him. It did, however, mar the perfection of his face, and Shelby hoped it didn't leave a scar.

"Is something wrong, Miss Falcon?" he said with a smile. "Do tell me that I remembered to shave and brush my hair. Ranja would be embarrassed beyond words if I went out without passing inspection."

"Your grooming is impeccable as usual, Mr. Gill. I was merely looking at the cut on your head."

"A trifle. I've had much worse." He looked around the garden as though debating something with himself. Then he turned to look at her. "I'd be much more comfortable, Miss Falcon, if you didn't call me *Mister* Gill."

"Then what shall I call you? I thought that was your name. You aren't here under false colors are you?"

He squirmed slightly. "Yes and no. Gill is part of my real name, and is what all my friends call me. However, it isn't my last name. When I first came here, the colonel called me Gill, and Mrs. McKilley naturally thought it was my last name. I didn't mind, of course, that she called me Mr. Gill, and when she mentioned my name to the cousins, I thought it might make a rather good cover since I'm accustomed to answering to it. There could also be no possibility of connecting me to the Bates name that way."

Shelby lifted an eyebrow and looked at him directly. Gill thought he had never seen anyone so lovely. The sun filtered through the leaves and highlighted her hair. The cream of her dress emphasized the fairness of her skin, while the russet and green ribbons brought out the colors of her eyes. He stared at her, entranced, thinking thoughts that were not quite proper and that he had no business thinking.

"Mr. Gill? Did you hear me?"

He forced his mind back to reality and laughed lightly. "Yes, Miss Falcon. You asked my name." He grinned ruefully. "I trust you will not laugh when you hear it."

"With all the odd names in our family? Never."

"You were talking about the names in your family, but I think mine may seem as odd." He hesitated. "My full name is Farquhar Wylie Gillenwater Bates."

"And your friends call you Gill?"

He nodded. "Yes, thank heaven, and I would prefer you to call me that as well."

"I suppose that would work." Shelby frowned. "I certainly don't want to call you Mr. Bates. If I call you just Gill, the others might think I'm just calling you by your last name." She smiled up at him. "Very well, Mr. Gill. I'll do that." She was distracted by a yipping at the gate. "There's Dick Turpin. He usually doesn't care much for the garden." She got up and let Dick through the gate, then came back to sit beside Gill. Dick dashed up and danced round them, yipping furiously.

"He's certainly agitated," Gill said, watching as Dick almost turned a flip, trying to jump up and down. "If he were any larger, he'd be a terror."

"I can't remember seeing him this way," Shelby said. She leaned down to pick up the little dog, but he scooted away from her grasp, still yipping and jumping. He ran around in circles, barking and barking; then he stopped, sat down, and whined.

"Does he get out often?" Gill asked. "Perhaps he's frightened."

Shelby shook her head. "No, he isn't out very much. He's usually with Biddle or, as today, gone somewhere with Grandfather. I've just never seen him act this way. Grandfather must have. . . ." She stopped suddenly. "Grandfather," she whispered. "Dick left the house with Grandfather to go to the stables."

"Stay here," Gill ordered, jumping to his feet. He began running, throwing open the gate and leaving it swinging in his haste. He ran toward the stables, Dick Turpin running behind him, his little legs pumping furiously as he tried to keep up.

"Wait for me!" Shelby called, jerking her skirts up to her calves and breaking into a run. Gill was disappearing into the stables by the time she was halfway there.

The building was dark and quiet as Shelby came in the door. The familiar smells of horses and tack were there, but the only sounds were Dick's barking and the breathing of horses. Shelby followed the barking down the corridor. It was dark on this end as the big doors were closed, and she almost missed seeing Gill. He was in the last stall, down on his knees, bent over something on the floor. Dick Turpin was out in the hall, on his belly, his head down on his paws. He was whining.

Shelby stopped and scooped Dick up, cradling him close to her body. She recognized the colonel's boots lying on the ground and made herself walk into the stall. Gill's back obscured her view, but she could see enough to know that something was terribly wrong. Colonel Falcon was facedown on the straw, and he was still.

"Is he . . . is he . . . ?" Shelby couldn't say the word.

Gill moved and turned the colonel over. "There's no mark on the back of his head. Evidently he fell face forward and landed on a pitchfork tine." He rubbed his fingers along the colonel's side. "He's bleeding, and he'll be sore, but I don't think it's a fatal wound." Gill touched the colonel's head and felt gently, then looked at the barn floor. "I think he hit his head on the feed box as he fell."

He turned and looked at her. "I think I should stay here with him. Go get Luke and Thomas to carry him into the house. There should be something we can use—a door, or some such—to carry him without hurting him. He may have a bone broken, and I wouldn't want to risk any more harm." He paused. "Is there a doctor in the village?"

"Yes. I'll send for him." White-lipped, Shelby ran back to the kitchen. Luke and Thomas were dispatched instantly, while Pearce, who was lounging in the library reading about rockets, agreed to fetch the doctor. Shelby screeched at him to hurry. Mrs. McKilley and Biddle dashed up to prepare the colonel's bed.

By the time Shelby started back to the barn, Luke and Thomas were carrying the colonel inside, and she stopped in the back garden to watch them. The colonel, deathly pale, was still unconscious. There was a large purple bruise on his head, and the side of his coat was soaked with blood. "Grandfather!"

Shelby gasped as they went by. Colonel Falcon looked waxen; the only color on his skin came from the drops of blood and the bruise on his face. Shelby held Dick Turpin close to her and buried her face in his fur.

Gill hurried to her as quickly as he could. He hesitated, wondering if she would think him forward, then threw caution to the winds. He put his arms around her and pulled her to him, Dick Turpin between them. "It's all right," he said, holding her close and smoothing her beautiful hair. "It's all right."

"He's not going to die? Are you certain he's going to be all right?" She turned her face up to his, her eyes filled with tears.

"As certain as I can be. His breathing is regular, and his pulse is strong. He'll be fine, I promise."

She looked at him, trust in her eyes, and he was lost, drowning in those tear-filled green eyes. On some level, he knew that he would never be the same again, no matter what happened between them. He didn't think he could ever feel this way about a woman again, ever. He had certainly never felt so before.

"Do you think it was an accident?" she asked, curling her fingers through Dick Turpin's reddish brown fur.

Gill pulled her close again, unwilling to let her go. Dick wriggled between them. "I don't know, Shelby. I just don't know. When he regains consciousness, perhaps he'll be able to tell us something."

"That means we'll have to guard him, doesn't it? If it wasn't an accident, the person who did it may fear identification."

He put his chin on her hair and breathed in her scent. "That's true. Biddle and I will take turns, so we'll make sure he's safe. We'll find the culprit. Don't worry."

She pulled back and looked at him, her eyes full of pain, not even noticing that he had used her first name. "Crawford," she said in disbelief. "Gill, when we went into the garden, I saw Crawford going to the stables."

Eight

In the background, the door at the back of the house slammed shut. "Shelby, what is all this commotion? I saw Luke and Thomas carrying . . ."

Shelby had nestled back in against Gill's chest, comforted and secure. She was just thinking how wonderful this felt, the faint roughness of his coat against her cheek, the feel of his arms around her, the steady beating of his heart, and the scent of the man. She never wanted to move.

"Shelby!" The speaker sounded scandalized.

Shelby reluctantly moved back a step and turned around. "I see you're up and about, Rose. Are you all right?"

Rose's look slid curiously over Shelby and then lit on Gill. Her frankly curious look was instantly replaced with one that Shelby had learned to recognize in her years in London society. It was that of a predator after prey.

"I don't believe we've met," Rose said to Gill, favoring him with her prettiest smile. Her wide blue eyes shone.

Shelby performed the introductions quickly. "Rose, this is Mr. Gill. Gill, my cousin Miss Rose Meadows." She turned to Rose. "Have they taken Grandfather up to his room?"

"I suppose so. I really don't know about the colonel, however. I came to fetch you for your mother."

"My mother!" Shelby leaned back against Gill's chest. "What's happened to my mother?"

"I don't really know what could be wrong or what brought it on. I heard a terrible commotion out in the hall, and when I went to see what it was, your mother told me to run fetch you immediately."

"Grandfather," Shelby said, her heart stopping. "Grandfather must be dead." She closed her eyes and swayed slightly. Gill caught her by her arms and pulled her close to him again.

"Oh, no," Rose said brightly. "That wasn't the problem at all. Your mother seems to be having an attack of the vapors and wants you immediately." She looked at Shelby's pale face. "Is something wrong with the colonel?"

"He's been hurt," Gill said. He turned his attention back to Shelby. "Let me help you inside, Miss Falcon. I must see if the doctor is on his way."

Gill helped Shelby into the house. When they were in the front entry, they heard a horse out front. Shelby flung the door open as Dr. Fish dismounted. "Where's the colonel?" he demanded without preamble. "This had better be serious for me to come on horseback instead of in my carriage."

"It is," Gill said softly. "Shel—Miss Falcon, you go up to your mother, and I'll take the doctor in. I'll come tell you as soon as I know anything."

"Are you family?" Dr. Fish said, giving Gill an inquisitive look.

"No," Gill said, at the same time that Shelby said, "Yes." Dr. Fish looked from one to the other. "Mr. Gill has my complete confidence, and Grandfather's as well, Dr. Fish," Shelby said. "Please treat him as though he were family."

Dr. Fish nodded. As he and Gill went up the stairs and out of sight into the hall above, Shelby hung on to the newel post, her knees too weak to move. "Your mother," Rose reminded. "I'll go up with you, and perhaps you can tell me all about this mysterious Mr. Gill. And about the colonel, of course," she added. She took Shelby's arm, and Shelby made her legs move. Slowly, they went up to see about the countess.

"There you are!" Countess Rimildi cried when they went into her room. The red damask walls and heavy, dark furniture gave it a closed, stuffy look. Shelby had never liked the room, but her mother did. "I could have died here while you were off gallivanting. Oh, 'sharper than a serpent's tooth. . . .' " She frowned. "What's that line about a thankless child?"

"Not now, Mother," Shelby said, taking a damp cloth from Dovey and putting it on the countess's forehead. "Grandfather's been hurt. He, um, fell on a pitchfork in the stables."

Countess Rimildi's eyes widened. "I saw them carry him in, but I thought he had just fainted. That's what someone told me. Mrs. McKilley, I think. Yes, she said he had fainted and hit his head. I immediately went right into the vapors. Shelby, you don't know what this visit is doing to my nerves!"

"Believe me, I'm quite aware of everything that has happened to your nerves, Mama," Shelby said, glancing at the door with worry as she heard the tramping of feet out in the hall. "I need to see what's happening, Mama." She tossed the damp cloth over the countess's face and ran to the door. Crawford was in the hallway, knocking on the colonel's door. Shelby looked at him and absently noted that he had mud on his boots, as well as wisps of grass and straw on his clothes.

"They told me below that the colonel had been hurt," he said, glancing around to Shelby. "I wanted to come see for myself."

"Dr. Fish is in there," Shelby said. "They're going to let us know how he is as soon as they're certain."

"He isn't dead, then?"

Was that regret in Crawford's voice? Shelby couldn't decide. All she knew was that she wasn't going to let Crawford near her grandfather until she knew more. "Would you like to go down with me and have some tea while we wait?" she asked.

Crawford's expression changed slightly as he looked over her shoulder. Rose was standing in the doorway, looking at the two of them. "Thank you, Shelby," Crawford said, smiling down at her. "I'd like that very much. Perhaps we could even have something a touch stronger than tea. I think the situation calls for that."

"What a splendid idea," Rose said. "I believe I'll join you."

"Shelby," the countess called out. "Where are you? I need you."

"Later, Mama," Shelby said, taking Crawford's arm. "I need to go downstairs. Dovey will sit with you for a few minutes."

She could hear her mother still quoting Shakespeare as they went down the stairs. " '. . . sharper than a serpent's tooth . . .' "

"She doesn't know the rest of the quote," Shelby explained. "She just knows that it deals with ungrateful children. It's from *King Lear*."

"I trust she's not comparing you to either Regan or Goneril. You're the perfect Cordelia." Crawford laughed and walked with her into the drawing room. Rose followed them, obviously annoyed.

"With Mother, who knows what she's thinking? Most likely not Regan or Goneril, although I own I always found Cordelia rather insipid." Shelby sat down while Rose rang for tea. In the meantime, Crawford poured the three of them some brandy. "Not exactly my choice, but perhaps what the two of you need," he said, handing each woman a glass.

Rose looked at him over the rim of her glass, her blue eyes open wide. "Well, Crawford, I haven't seen you enough to ask . . . how have you been? It's been a while."

"I've been busy," he said, sitting down across from them.

"Yes, I've seen the copies of *The London Eye*. I haven't seen one lately, though. Are you still attempting it?" Rose leaned forward enough to show just the right amount of cleavage at the neckline of her bodice. She smiled slightly, touching her lips with the tip of her tongue. *Just as she must have practiced in London a thousand times,* Shelby thought to herself.

Crawford carefully kept his eyes on his brandy glass. "I'm getting together a new issue. Publishing is a rather expensive venture. Paper is ruinously expensive, and then there are other costs."

"I heard you were looking for money," Rose said bluntly, sitting up straight again, a curiously satisfied smile on her face. "Have you found an angel yet?"

"No, but I have some very good possibilities." He stared straight at her. "And how are you getting along? Are any fortunes beating a path to your door?"

Rose blushed, then stared right back at him. "No, but I have some very good possibilities."

Shelby jumped to her feet and began to pace. "How can the two of you talk this way when Grandfather may be upstairs dying? Can't you put your past away long enough to be concerned about him?"

"Of course." Crawford paused as a maid brought in tea and some biscuits. He glanced at Rose, who picked up the pot and poured Shelby a cup of tea. She sat back down and sipped the hot liquid gratefully. "I'm sorry," she told them. "I'm more than a little overset."

"Understandable." Crawford took a cup of tea from Rose. Their fingers touched briefly, and he jerked his hand back, almost spilling his tea. "Can you give me any particulars?" he asked, his voice sounding somewhat shaky. "Was he hurt badly?"

Shelby glanced down at Crawford's boots. There was some kind of muck on them; she couldn't decide if it was from the stables or just mud from walking someplace where it had been wet. There were several wisps of hay on his coat. "Gill thinks he's going to be all right, but we won't know for sure until Dr. Fish does his examination."

"Another of the colonel's accidents," Rose murmured. "He's just going to have to have a keeper. Biddle is of no use at all."

She paused and her mouth turned down. "And that horrid dog should be shot."

There was a noise at the door, and Pearce walked in. "Who should be shot? Where is everyone?" he asked all in one breath.

Shelby took a quick look at his boots and clothing. His boots were covered with muck and hay, his clothing had splotches of mud on it, and there was grass in his hair. "Rose thinks Dick Turpin should be shot," Shelby said. "Do you want some tea?"

"She would." Pearce grinned as he sat down. "Bentley told me the story. I wish I'd been here." He smiled sweetly at Rose as she made a face at him. "Yes, I'd like some tea. My throat is really dry. I've been out in the meadow experimenting."

"With what?" Crawford asked. "More rockets?"

Pearce nodded. "I've been reading more about Congreve's work, and I think I've found a way to improve on it. If I can just get my experiments to work, and get the ear of someone in the government . . ." He left the sentence dangling.

"Grandfather has been in an accident," Shelby said, watching his face closely.

He was surprised. Shelby could wager that it was genuine. Surprise was replaced by shock when Shelby told him what had happened. "And the doctor is still up there?" he asked, looking toward the ceiling.

Shelby nodded. The front door opened again, and they all looked out into the hall. "Hayward, Bentley," Pearce called out. "You'll never guess what's happened."

The two came into the drawing room, and Shelby looked at their clothing. Both were perfectly neat, not a sign of hay, grass, or muck on either of them. She watched their expressions carefully as Pearce told them the story. They both looked shocked. *The only one who didn't appear amazed,* Shelby thought with a sick feeling in the pit of her stomach, *is Crawford.* The thought was terrible, almost like a betrayal. The

Crawford she knew would never do such a thing, never. No matter how much he needed money.

Just thinking about it made her dizzy. Her cup trembled and she set it down, thankful the noise of cup shaking against saucer was drowned out by the noise of her cousins and Rose talking. Crawford, however, noticed her pallor. He stood beside her and put his hand on her arm. "Are you all right, Shelby? Do I need to see you upstairs?"

She looked up at him and closed her eyes. "I think I will go up, Crawford, thank you. Thank you very much, but I don't think I need assistance." She stood and excused herself, then went slowly up the stairs into the quiet.

Inside her room, she paced and looked out the window, then did it all over again. Finally, there was a soft knock at her door. She ran to respond and threw it open, expecting a footman or maid with a message. Instead, Gill stood there. He looked up and down the hall. "Do you mind if I come in a moment? I don't want to be discussing anything out here in the hall."

She nodded, stood aside as he entered, and shut the door behind him. "Grandfather?" She was almost afraid to ask.

"He's going to be all right."

She let out a deep breath and sank into the small chair in front of the mirror. Her legs suddenly felt as if they wouldn't support her. "The doctor is sure?"

Gill nodded and sat down in the chair that was beside the window. "He was sure when he first examined the wound. It's a deep slice on his side, but no organs were injured. Evidently, only one tine of the pitchfork hit his body. The blow to his head is really worse. I think he hit himself on the feed box. He doesn't remember. At any rate, Dr. Fish says to keep him quiet for a day or two—and keep a close watch on him." Gill grinned. "I asked the good doctor if he knew what kind of task he was assigning to us. He just laughed. As for the colo-

nel, I've sent Biddle in to him, and he was, of course, asking
for Dick Turpin."

"Did you tell him what a hero Dick Turpin was? If Dick
hadn't come to get us, Grandfather could have been there for
hours. That stall isn't used much, and I doubt anyone would
look there for a day or so."

"I told him. He said he knew Dick would stand by him."

There was a pause, and Shelby knew there was a question
she had to ask. "Was it an accident? Did he slip?"

Gill shook his head. "No, he didn't. Unfortunately, he
doesn't remember much about what happened, but I don't want
anyone except Dr. Fish, Biddle, you, and me knowing that. He
does remember that he heard a noise in the far stall and went
to investigate. It was a yelp that sounded rather like it came
from a trapped animal, he said. He thought Dick had gotten
into something and went down to get him out. He was standing
there, looking around in the gloom, when someone pushed
him from behind. He saw the pitchfork, tines up, and twisted
his body. The last thing he remembers is a crashing pain in
his head."

Shelby put her hand over her mouth to keep from crying
out. "Gill, Crawford came in right afterward. He . . . he had
muddy boots and there was grass and hay on his clothing."

"Did anyone else come in?"

"They all did. Pearce came in muddy as well. He had mud
on his boots and clothing. Grass and hay bits here and there.
He said he'd been out in the meadow experimenting with rockets."

"Did Crawford say where he'd been?"

"No, and I didn't think to ask him. Do you want me to try
to find out?"

Gill rubbed his temple with his forefinger, and gingerly
touched the knot on his forehead. "If you can without being
obvious. We need to find out where everyone was."

"For what it's worth, Hayward and Bentley came in, but

they both looked as if they'd just stepped off a pattern card."
She hesitated. "Rose was with us. She mentioned again that
Crawford was short of funds. It seems everyone knows he
can't publish another issue of *The London Eye* until he finds
an angel." She sighed. "Crawford retaliated by pointing out
that Rose wasn't having any luck in landing a rich husband."
Shelby smiled wanly at Gill. "I trust all our dirty linen won't
prejudice you against our family."

"Every family has some." He grinned back at her. "And it
goes without saying that everything I learn here will go no
further. No matter what it is." He glanced around the room.
"A very pleasant room, Miss Falcon. Do you always stay here
when you visit Wychwood?"

"Always. This has been my room for years."

"I'm right next door. If you need me, all you have to do is
knock on the wall. I'll be here immediately." He paused, then
plunged ahead. "I don't want to frighten you, Miss Falcon,
but you might need assistance. After all, as soon as the solicitor
gets here, you're going to be the new owner of the jewels. You
need to take care."

"Or I might be the one having accidents?"

He nodded and rubbed his temple again. "There is one
thing. I've already talked it over with the colonel, and he's
agreed. That is, he's agreed for the time being. Who knows
when he may get a notion in his head and do whatever he
wants?" He grinned ruefully, then looked at Shelby and continued. "I think it would be best if we simply say that the
colonel believes he tripped over something and fell. I don't
want anyone thinking that we suspect foul play."

"I agree thoroughly."

Gill looked at her in the pale light in the room and was
enchanted by her soft smile. He thought he had never seen
anyone more lovely than she was at that moment. She wasn't
thinking of herself, but of her grandfather. Most of the people
he knew were thoroughly selfish individuals, and were con-

cerned primarily with how they appeared to others or what they owned. It was so wonderful to see a woman who wasn't so concerned about herself or her appearance. It made her all the more beautiful to him. Right now, her skin was pale with worry, and her eyes were troubled with concern. He had to make himself concentrate on something else to keep from sweeping her up into his arms and comforting her as he had done in the back garden. That had felt so wonderful and right to him. He knew that Shelby Falcon belonged there, right in his arms.

If only, the little voice in his head said, *she weren't in love with Crawford.* For a brief moment, he hoped sincerely that Crawford would be the guilty one. Shelby would never love a man who had tried to harm her grandfather. *But,* the voice in his head asked, *would she love you?* It was a question he didn't want answered right now. For the first time in his life, he was afraid of an answer.

"Do you think we should go down now and tell the others that grandfather thinks it an accident?" she asked. "They're all in the drawing room. Perhaps you could watch their expressions and discover something."

He nodded and stood, following her out of the room. His hands itched to touch her, to feel the silky softness of her luxuriant hair as he had in the garden when he'd comforted her. No matter what happened to him during the rest of his life, he would never forget that. Never.

The four men and Rose were still in the drawing room. Briefly, Shelby gave them the news about Colonel Falcon. They all seemed delighted. "Does he remember anything at all about what happened?" Bentley asked.

Shelby hesitated, and Gill stepped into the conversation. "He thinks he may have tripped over something at the door. The only thing he's sure of is a crashing pain when he hit his head." He paused and shook his own head slightly. "He's just fortunate that he fell the way he did. If he had fallen straight down, he would have landed squarely on the pitchfork. When I found him, I noted that if he had done that, one of the tines would have gone right through his heart."

"He's certainly fortunate," Rose said. "Do come in, Mr. Gill, and sit with us." She patted a seat beside her on the sofa. "Have I seen you in London before?"

Gill sat down. "I think not, Miss Meadows. I've been away in India and Java for several years. I came back here to recuperate from a fever."

Rose looked at him frankly. "You look quite healthy to me."

"It's the atmosphere at Wychwood. I've found it quite salubrious."

"Don't we all," said Hayward. His tone was sarcastic.

The conversation turned to London society. Shelby had little interest in the doings of the *ton,* but she listened carefully, trying to hear a clue in what each of them said. It seemed that there was nothing new—the talk centered on the antics of the Prince Regent and the Princess Charlotte. Rose reported that the *on-dit* now was that the Prince was very harsh on Princess Charlotte, even going so far as to deny her friendship with young ladies who had been in her confidence. Miss Elphinstone and Lady Barbara Ashley were forbidden correspondence with the Princess. Just to be sure, gossip reported that Princess Charlotte received no mail which had not been opened. Pearce repeated a story of his own about the Prince, and then Crawford passed on some things that he intended to put in *The London Eye* as soon as it was published again.

Shelby finally excused herself to go upstairs. It was early twilight, and she lit a candle and put it beside her bed. She looked out the window at the deepening dusk, trying to sort out her thoughts, but they were all jumbled. Everything kept coming back to Crawford: the need for funds, the muddy boots, the hay on his coat. Still, it went against everything she knew about him. She couldn't believe him capable of murder.

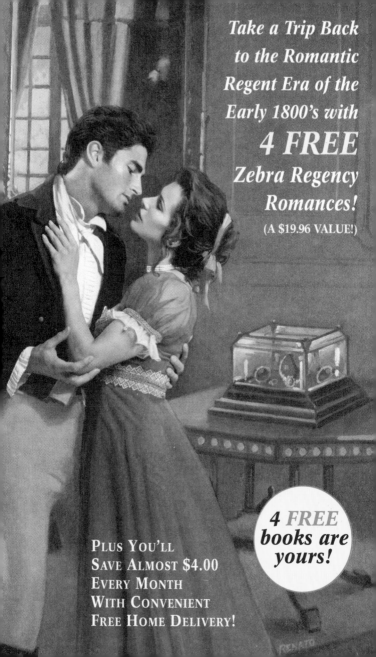

Say Yes to 4 Free Books!

Complete and return the order card to receive this $19.96 value, ABSOLUTELY FREE!

(If the certificate is missing below, write to:)
Zebra Home Subscription Service, Inc.,
120 Brighton Road, P.O. Box 5214, Clifton, New Jersey 07015-5214
or call TOLL-FREE 1-888-345-BOOK

Check out our website at www.kensingtonbooks.com.

FREE BOOK CERTIFICATE

YES! Please rush me 4 Zebra Regency Romances without cost or obligation. I understand that each month thereafter I will be able to preview 4 brand-new Regency Romances FREE for 10 days. Then, if I should decide to keep them, I will pay the money-saving preferred subscriber's price of just $16.00 for all 4...that's a savings of almost $4 off the publisher's price with no additional charge for shipping and handling. I may return any shipment within 10 days and owe nothing, and I may cancel this subscription at any time. My 4 FREE books will be mine to keep in any case.

Name _____

Address _____ Apt. _____

City _____ State _____ Zip _____

Telephone ( ) _____

Signature _____
(If under 18, parent or guardian must sign.)   RG0799

With a sigh, she turned away, massaging her temples. She felt a headache coming on.

She was lying on her bed when there was a knock on her door. Thinking it was Gill, she slipped off the bed and called out, "Come in." To her surprise, it was Crawford.

"I was worried about you," he said gently, leaving the door open so there would be no question. "You were so pale and agitated downstairs."

"I'm fine." Shelby hesitated awkwardly. "I just had the beginnings of a headache."

He came over to her and put his arms around her. She felt herself stiffen and couldn't seem to help herself. "It's all right," he said softly. "I'm sure it was just an accident and that the colonel will be fine." He tilted her chin so he could look into her eyes. He smiled down at her. "No matter that he says he's dying, I don't believe it for a moment. He'll probably outlive the lot of us." He outlined her eyebrows and lips with his fingertips. "I can't understand why I've never before seen what a beautiful woman you've become, Shelby," he said softly. "I know this isn't the time or place, and I should keep myself in check, but I wondered if you have considered what I asked you."

"What you asked me?" Shelby couldn't seem to breathe.

He smiled. "Did my suit mean no more than that? I asked you to be my wife, Shelby. I wonder if you've thought on it at all."

"Crawford, I . . . I . . ." She gulped.

"Isn't this a tender scene?" The words were bitter and caustic. Crawford and Shelby sprang apart as Rose came into the room. "Was I interrupting a lovers' moment?" She looked from Shelby to Crawford.

"Shelby is quite overset, and I was comforting her," Crawford said. "She doesn't need a scene, Rose. She's more than worried about the colonel." He hesitated. "As you should be.

I know you aren't directly related to him as Shelby is, but the colonel has been more than good to you since you were born."

"I don't need a lecture from you, Crawford." Rose paced around the room. Shelby could see another of her famed rages coming on.

"Out!" she said wearily. "Out, both of you! I simply cannot take another thing. Just leave!"

Dovey dashed in the door, bumping into Rose. Rose staggered into the footstool by Shelby's bedside and almost fell. "Did you call, mum?" Dovey asked, white as a sheet. "I was with Countess Rimildi and thought I heard you call."

"You clumsy wench," Rose yelled. "Why don't you watch what you're doing?"

"Rose, get hold of yourself." Crawford tried to be calming. "Shall we leave Shelby to rest? I think she prefers some time alone."

"That's right! Just think about Shelby! Do you ever think about me? Do you . . . ?" She caught herself and took a deep breath, then stood up tall. "A thousand apologies, Shelby. I simply don't know what came over me." With that, she swept out the door.

Crawford looked at the open door, then at Shelby. "Rose doesn't seem quite the thing this evening. I apologize for her. She isn't usually like that." He shrugged and grinned. "I trust you'll feel better," he said. "I'll see you later, I hope." He smiled at her, his smile having a meaning that surpassed his words. As he went out the door, some dried mud fell from his boots. Shelby walked over to it and looked at it. There was straw mixed in with the mud—it was the kind of mud that was in the stable.

Nine

Shelby crawled up onto her bed and leaned back against the pillows, but couldn't rest. After a few futile minutes of tossing and turning, she went to the door and peered out. The hall was empty. She slipped out of her room and went down to her grandfather's room. When she tried the handle, she discovered that the door was locked. She knocked softly, but there was no response. Alarmed, she thought about beating on the door, but then remembered that the colonel had turned her grandmother's room into a sitting room. She went down to the next door, tried it, and it opened quietly.

Biddle was stretched out on a cot, snoring gently while Colonel Falcon was sitting up in one of the big chairs, his feet propped up on a footstool and Dick Turpin on his lap. Dick roused when Shelby came into the room and leaped up to greet her, whining and grinning, dancing on his back legs. She scooped him up and smiled at him. "Did Gill tell you what a hero Dick was in your rescue?" she asked the colonel.

"He did. That dog's worth five of anyone else."

Shelby sat down and looked at him. The bruise on his head was a large, deep purple splotch that spread across most of his forehead. He still looked very pale.

Dick rolled over onto his back on Shelby's lap, and she scratched him absently on his stomach. "How are you feeling, Grandfather?"

"Not worth a demmed farthing." Colonel Falcon shook his head gently. "Could you get me a little whiskey? Not much here to keep a man's spirits up."

"Did the doctor say you could have whiskey?"

There was a long pause. Colonel Falcon could bend the truth, but, like Shelby, he had trouble telling an out-and-out lie. Shelby could see that he was trying to frame his answer. She laughed. "Now, Grandfather, you know whiskey isn't good for you right now. Why don't you let me get you some tea or coffee?"

"You're on to me, aren't you, girl?" He grinned sheepishly at her. "All right, coffee it is if that's the best you can do." He sighed all the way from his toes. "And how about something to eat along with it? I haven't had a thing since breakfast."

Shelby put Dick on the floor and rang for someone to bring coffee and something for the colonel to eat. Then they sat, waiting. Dick tried to jump up onto Shelby's lap, but didn't make it. She had to pick him up again. "I'm glad you're doing better, Grandfather. I was worried."

"Not half as much as I am." He frowned. "Did Gill tell you that someone pushed me?"

She nodded miserably. "I suppose that confirms it's someone on the premises."

"Someone in the family, I'd say, although no one knows how it hurts me to acknowledge that. It makes a man want to disown the lot of 'em." He paused. "I've decided to give it all to you, Shelby. I don't have a thing that's entailed, and it's all yours."

"I'd rather just have you, Grandfather. I don't want to think about inheritances."

"I know you don't, but I'm afraid not to. I need to get my affairs in final order." He looked at her. "I'll leave a small bequest to each of the others, of course, but nothing else. To think they'd try this!"

"Not all of them did. Only one."

He smacked his fist onto the arm of the chair. "Confound it, yes! But which one?"

They were interrupted by Mrs. McKilley coming in with a tray. "Fixed it myself," she said, setting it down on the small table beside the colonel's chair. "I know what you like, and made sure it was here." She moved a napkin to reveal a tray heaped with food and a pot of coffee. When she had gone, the colonel began eating. "Help yourself, Shelby. There's enough here for three or four. I've got a spare cup over there by the bed, so you can have this one." He hesitated for just a beat. "I'd like a little company."

Since she really didn't feel like going down to eat, she pulled her chair closer and began eating with him. It was almost like old times when just the two of them had been at Wychwood and they always ate together. Shelby steered the conversation away from the accident or the inheritance, and talked about those times in the past. She was still sitting there with the colonel, talking, when Gill came. He knocked on the bedroom door, and Shelby got up and let him in.

He was dressed for supper, all in black with a pale blue embroidered waistcoat. His cravat was slightly askew, and he caught Shelby glancing at it. "Ranja hasn't the hang of tying this thing yet," he said, "and I've always been all thumbs. I hate cravats."

She laughed. "This is all you need." She reached up and pulled one side gently, then pulled the bow out on the other side. "There." She glanced up at him and found that he was looking at her with a strange expression in his brown eyes. She looked back, his gaze holding hers. It was the first time she had really looked into his eyes, and she was fascinated. They were a warm brown, flecked with lighter bits of amber. Right now, they were looking at her with an odd expression that she couldn't fathom. Nonetheless, it made her tremble all the way down to her knees. She suddenly felt weak, and there was an odd sensation in the pit of her stomach. To cover her confusion, she turned away quickly. "Have you come to visit Grandfather, Mr. Gill?" she asked.

"Yes." Even that one word had a strange, rich timbre to it. She fought the urge to turn around and look at him again.

She moved farther away and took a deep breath. "Do come in and join us. We were just eating."

"We?" He looked at Biddle on the bed, still snoring.

"Grandfather, Dick Turpin, and I." Shelby walked back to the colonel, and sat down. Gill pulled up another chair and sat so that they formed a triangle. Dick sniffed at Gill's clothes and then hopped up on the colonel's lap. "All I ask, Colonel," Gill said with a smile, "is that you tell me exactly where you found that rat-catching dog. I want one just like him."

"Brussels," the colonel answered promptly. "A friend of mine has a stable there and has several of these Griffons d'Écurie—stable griffons. Best dog in the world." He smiled fondly down at Dick Turpin. In turn, Dick grinned at him. The colonel laughed. "He looks like an ugly Robert Herrick, and God knows, Herrick was ugly enough without any embellishments."

Gill laughed. "Dick's strong point isn't his looks, but his personality." He stopped as Biddle snored loudly and turned over, his snores subsiding. "Your bodyguard isn't doing his job, Colonel," he said. "I think we should bring Ranja in here to stay with you. I'm perfectly capable of fending for myself for a few days."

"Do you think it'll be over in a few days?" The colonel looked at Gill, a deeper meaning to his words.

"I think something will have happened," Gill said slowly. "Whether or not we discover our culprit is another speculation." He paused as the clock chimed. "I've got to go down to supper. Are you going, Miss Falcon?"

"No, I've eaten with Grandfather, and I just don't feel up to talking to everyone tonight. Will you make my excuses?"

He nodded and stood. "I'm glad to see you feeling better, Colonel. I'll send Ranja in to stay with you." He looked back and gave Shelby a fleeting smile. "Lock the door behind me, Miss Falcon."

Shelby read to her grandfather for an hour or so. Then he seemed to be getting restless and wanted to get up and attend to some necessary things, so Shelby left him. Ranja was out in the hall, waiting for her to come out. "I didn't know you were here," she said with a smile, "or I would have opened the door. I didn't hear you knock."

Ranja merely looked at her, nodded his head, and went inside, closing the door softly behind him. Shelby had no idea if the man understood her or not. As she walked away, she heard the turning of the key in the lock. Something nagged at the edge of her thoughts, and it took her all the way to her door to think of it. "Locking Grandfather's door is no barrier," she muttered to herself as she pushed open her own door. "I need to tell Gill that the same key opens all the doors on the floor."

She stayed in her room, writing letters and reading, waiting to hear Gill come up for bed, so she could waylay him in the hall and tell him about the locks, but she heard nothing. Finally, close to midnight, Dovey helped her get ready for bed, and she crawled under the covers. She still couldn't sleep, going over the afternoon's events again and again.

Shelby awoke late the next morning, still groggy. She rang for Dovey and dressed. Dovey had been changing the trim on a pale pink dress that Shelby had never liked. Dovey had embellished it with deep rose and green ribbons, turning part of the ribbons into flowers. The dress had been transformed into a lovely creation that looked perfect when Shelby put it on. Dovey then put Shelby's hair up and twined identical ribbons through it. Then she got busy with the powder and paint pots.

"Just lovely, mum, if I say so myself," Dovey said, moving the mirror so Shelby could see herself.

"Would you consider leaving your family and going to London with me when I go back, Dovey?" Shelby asked. She hardly recognized the woman looking back at her from the mirror.

Dovey fell to her knees and kissed Shelby's hand. "Oh, mum, if you only knew!"

Shelby stood and pulled her upright. "None of that, Dovey. I'm the one who's benefiting. Talk to your mother about it, and let me know." She moved toward the door. "I've got to go check on Grandfather, and I want to see Mr. Gill."

"I don't know about your grandfather as the foreign man has been in there all night, but Martha told me that Mr. Gill wasn't here last night."

Shelby stopped and her heart froze. Her first thought was that something terrible had happened to Gill. She was surprised by the trembling sense of loss that assailed her. Only a short while ago she hadn't even known him, but now she couldn't imagine her life without Gill. "Not at all? Where did he go? I saw him before supper, and he didn't mention going anywhere. Did something happen to him?"

Dovey's head bobbed. "Well, mum, I don't rightly know. Martha was just talking about it belowstairs. She talks to William out in the stables, if you know what I mean. According to Martha, Mr. Gill went out after supper and told William to saddle his horse, saying that he wouldn't be back until today. He didn't tell William where he was going." She frowned. "Or if he did, William didn't tell Martha."

"Mr. Gill said he wasn't coming back until today?"

"That's right, mum. That's what William told Martha, and Martha told the rest of us."

Shelby felt her heart begin to thaw. For a horrible moment, she had imagined Gill in trouble, or worse. If anyone discovered his true involvement with her grandfather, Gill could wind up dead. Shelby shuddered at the thought.

"Are you all right, mum? You appear a little pale." Dovey grabbed a cloth and soused it in the pitcher of water on the washstand. "Do you need this, mum?" She held out the dripping cloth.

Shelby took a step backward. "No, thank you, Dovey. Will you please bring some breakfast up here? I'm going to check on Grandfather, and I think I'll eat here." As Dovey opened a window, she looked at the lovely day. "I may even go riding, Dovey. Get out my habit while I visit with Grandfather."

Shelby knocked gently on her Grandfather's door and was rewarded with a roar from inside. "Just let somebody in, damn your eyes, Biddle!" Dick Turpin barked in chorus.

Biddle opened the door and saw with relief that it was Shelby. "He's a little restless," Biddle whispered as she came inside. "He wants out."

"I don't blame him," Shelby whispered back. She bent to pick up Dick Turpin as he ran to her and jumped up. She held him in front of her and smiled at him. He grinned back.

"I came to see how you were feeling," Shelby said to the colonel.

"I'd feel fine if I could get out of this demmed room. That man of Gill's has been sitting by the door like a wraith. I can't move unless he's right by my side."

"Good. That's what you need."

The colonel sighed. "I know that, but it doesn't make it any easier. Girl, I'm sore all over. I hurt in places I haven't felt since I wrestled with Tippoo Sahib's right-hand man. Have I told you that story?"

"Many times. And you'll win this battle the same way you won that one." She handed Dick Turpin to him and smiled.

"Got to get out of this room first," he grumbled. "Tomorrow, at the latest. I told Ranja that." He chuckled. "He didn't know I could understand the language. I was a little rusty, but we managed a conversation. I discovered that he doesn't like to talk much." He sat down and glowered. "Where's Gill this morning?"

Shelby hesitated, then decided honesty was the best policy. "I have no idea. I heard through the servants' gossip that he left right after supper and won't be back until today."

Colonel Falcon lifted an eyebrow and winced. "That so? He must have discovered something, or else had a good question that needed an answer. Send him up as soon as he gets back, will you?"

Shelby promised to do so and left, going back to her room where she found that Dovey had brought up enough breakfast to feed four people. Shelby had Dovey take the trays to the countess's room, and mother and daughter had breakfast together. Countess Rimildi was still talking about the two of them returning to London immediately. "There's no need for either of us to be here, Shelby," the countess said, enjoying a sugared roll. "I don't think there's a single thing wrong with Colonel Falcon." She shook her head. "He just likes to terrorize everyone. Bates was always in awe of him, poor thing."

"It's easy to be in awe of Grandfather," Shelby answered. "I want to stay a few more days, Mama, just to make sure Grandfather is all right. After that, we'll decide what to do." She smiled at her mother. "I know this is dreadfully dull for you after the social whirl in London."

The countess nodded. "Yesterday was terrible. I was so glad dear Rose was here to talk to me." She lowered her voice. "Do you know that Rose is dodging creditors now? She didn't say so, of course, but I could tell. I talked to her about shopping, and she doesn't dare go into some of the finer shops anymore. It seems she's gone through everything her father left her. That wasn't much, but she could have been comfortable."

"I know." Shelby sighed. "Poor Rose. It must be very difficult for her."

After breakfast, Shelby went outside a few minutes to check on the garden. The day was perfect—warm, but not too warm, a slight breeze fanning the fragrances of the countryside, and the leaves rustling. It was too nice to stay inside. She sent word to William to saddle a horse for her, and went inside to change into her riding habit.

When Shelby came outside to mount, Bentley was there, holding two horses. "William told me you were going riding, and I thought I'd come along. Is that all right?"

There was nothing Shelby could say. "Of course, Bentley. I'd love to have some company."

They rode across the rolling countryside and finally turned onto the road at the fork that led travelers either to Slapton or Wappenham. "Which way?" Bentley asked, slowing his horse to a walk.

"Let's rest the horses a few minutes and then go back to Wychwood by the main road," Shelby suggested.

Bentley helped her dismount, and they walked the horses to cool them. When they came to a bridge over a small stream, they stopped and let the horses drink and graze a few minutes on the grass that grew by the stream's bank. There was a large tree growing there, and Shelby stood under it to enjoy the shade. She was getting quite warm in her habit. She took off her hat, letting the soft breeze blow against the nape of her neck and her cheeks. It felt wonderful.

"You look quite the thing, you know," Bentley said, gazing at her. "I've been surprised at how good you look lately."

Shelby stifled a chuckle. Bentley had never been famous for his tact. "Thank you," she said gravely.

"You still aren't angry with me for what I said the other night, are you? That remark about the rubies?" He looked at her nervously. "I'd had too much to drink and had no idea what I was saying. I'm truly sorry."

"I know you are, Bentley. It's forgotten."

He turned and looked at her. "That's what I like about you,

Shelby. You understand these things and how a man is when he's had too much to drink. You're a right kind of girl; you always have been. Not a bit like Rose. She's always been worried about how she looked and what people thought of her, but you're not like that."

"I daresay on that head I'm more like Rose than you think." Shelby smiled at him. "Society rather demands it of women. Men, of course, can be much more independent."

"I know." There was relief in Bentley's voice. "I'm quite glad I'm a man." He picked up her hand and held it in his. "Since I am a male, everyone expects me to marry, of course."

"I'm sure you'll find the right woman someday, Bentley."

He looked at her. "I already have, Shelby. I think the two of us should marry. I know you've had a *tendre* for Crawford, but with Rose back in the picture, that's over. I just think the two of us would be very happy." He leaned toward her, smiling eagerly. "Would you, Shelby? Would you marry me?"

It took Shelby a moment to get over her shock. She realized that her eyes were wide, and only hoped her jaw wasn't hanging. She had never imagined Bentley had even looked at her twice, particularly with matrimony in mind. "I'm caught by surprise," she managed to say.

"That means you're going to turn me down," he said glumly, looking down at the ground. Then he looked at her again, and seized her other hand. "Think about it, Shelby! Promise me that you'll at least think about it! You owe me that much. After all, it took me a while to get up the nerve to ask you, so the least you can do is consider it."

Shelby stopped the flat *no* that was on her tongue, remembering how sensitive everyone had always said Bentley was. "Very well, Bentley, I'll consider it," she said, hedging. "I'll give you my answer in the morning."

He squeezed her hands tightly. "Good for you! You're always fair, Shelby. I know you'll come up with the right answer." He turned around to check on the horses. "We might as well go back to Wychwood now."

"Definitely," said Shelby faintly.

As they rode leisurely along the main road to Wychwood, Shelby quizzed Bentley about what he knew about the others' finances as well as about his own. He frankly admitted to being without funds. "Although," he said cheerfully, "I'm not anywhere close to Hayward. He's so far down that he's in to the cent-per-centers. If he doesn't come up with some blunt to stave them off, he's going to have to go to the Continent. May even have to head for America."

"Are things that bad for him?"

Bentley nodded. "They're bad enough for him to worry and try to come up with some money. He's exhausted about all his resources, though. I don't know what he'll do this time."

Shelby hesitated. "I understand he's stood good for some of your debts."

"Oh, he has," Bentley said cheerfully. "He's really quite a brother, although he has forbidden me to go about in London unless he chaperones me." He grimaced. "I've had some times getting around that, I can tell you. Crawford always tells Hayward if he sees me out."

"And Crawford? I understand he's strapped as well."

"Strapped ain't the half of it, Shelby. He's used every last farthing he can beg, borrow, or steal." He paused. "That's just an expression. Crawford wouldn't steal anything, I'm sure."

"But he does need money badly." Shelby moved over slightly as she heard the sounds of a horse approaching from behind them.

"He does," Bentley confirmed. "He's dipped in so far that he has to pay up his creditors before he can even borrow enough to publish another paper." He turned and looked behind them at the approaching rider. "Shelby, isn't that Mr. Gill?"

She turned quickly and looked behind them. The rider was wearing a long coat to keep the dust off, but it hadn't been effective. His hat, coat, and boots were covered with a fine film of tan dust. Shelby pulled her horse up and waited. Finally, the rider got close enough to be seen clearly. It was Gill, and from the looks of things, he had been riding hard.

Bentley and Shelby looked at him curiously as he rode up, but he offered no explanation. Instead, after his initial surprised greeting, he fell in beside them and chatted inconsequentially about the weather, the crops, the flora and fauna, and the state of the world in general. Shelby was chafing to get back to Wychwood where she could quiz him.

Bentley insisted on helping her dismount at the front door; then he and Gill took the horses to the stables. Fuming, Shelby went inside to wash the dust off, change back into her pink dress, and have Dovey fix her hair. Over an hour elapsed before Dovey deemed her ready to leave. She started to go searching for Gill, but, after thinking for a moment, sent Dovey down to the servants' quarters to see if Gill was in his room, with the colonel, or somewhere else. Shelby never fathomed how they knew, but the servants always seemed to know the whereabouts of everyone in the house.

Dovey reported that Mr. Gill was in his room and had given instructions not to be disturbed for the rest of the afternoon. For a moment Shelby considered knocking on his door and going in boldly to talk to him, but rejected that idea. There was nothing to do except wait. In the meantime, she thought, she might try to hunt up one of the cousins and see if she could discover anything else.

Rose was in the small music room, practicing on the pianoforte. Aside from all her other charms, Rose had absolutely no gift for music. Her playing was terrible, and her singing was worse. Still, at Aunt Hettie's urging, she was constantly playing and singing in company. Both Rose and Aunt Hettie were unaware of Rose's deficiency in this area.

Shelby tried to keep from wincing as she walked into the music room. Rose had dragooned Pearce to help her with her music, and he rolled his eyes toward the ceiling as Shelby entered. "Perhaps you'd like to stop now and talk to Shelby," Pearce suggested, taking a step back from the pianoforte.

"How was your ride?" Rose asked without preamble. "Did Crawford and Hayward go with you? They said they were going out, and I thought the three of you might be together."

"No." Shelby sat down in a chair and put her feet on a small footstool. "Bentley and I went together. I haven't talked to Hayward or Crawford."

"Just as well," Rose said, taking a chair across from Shelby. "Pearce, why don't you tell Shelby about the visitor who was looking for Hayward?"

Pearce sighed. "It was a rough-and-tumble man who came searching for him. I was glad Hayward was gone. I think the cent-per-centers have run him down." He looked at Shelby and shook his head. "This man was not pleasant."

"Actually," Rose said, "he demanded to see Hayward and threatened Thomas if he didn't fetch Hayward immediately. He created such an uproar that Colonel Falcon came downstairs to see what was happening. He and the gentleman went into the library and talked for a while."

"Do you suppose Grandfather paid anything on Hayward's debts?" Shelby asked. "It would be just like him."

"From what I gather," Rose said, "it would take more than the colonel would have on hand. Hayward is down many thousands of pounds."

"Thousands?" Shelby was aghast.

Pearce nodded. "He's sold everything he owns, borrowed everything he can, and still hasn't enough money. Every time he gets a guinea in his pocket, Bentley gambles it away. Hayward can't keep up with Bentley's debts."

"I heard he stood good for Bentley. Worse, Bentley certainly can't help him," Shelby said. "Bentley has no money."

"Well, I certainly can't help out either Hayward or Bentley, even if they are my half brothers. For that matter, Crawford can't help them either," Rose said. "Crawford needs money as much as the rest of us."

Shelby stood up and started for the door. "Where are you going?" Rose asked.

"I'm going up and find out what the man wanted and what Grandfather told him," Shelby said. "I don't know how this family ever got in such a muddle." She left them and ascended the stairs slowly.

Her grandfather's door was unlocked, and she opened it softly. "Grandfather, are you awake? It's Shelby. I want to talk to you."

"Do come in, Miss Falcon," Gill said, a touch of laughter in his voice. "I've been wondering how long you could hold out before you came up to see what's been happening." He glanced at the clock on the mantel. "Actually, you lasted fifteen minutes longer than I thought you would." He reached in his pocket, drew out some money, and handed it to Colonel Falcon. "You win the wager, sir. You know her better than I do."

Ten

Shelby left after a fruitless hour. Within a few minutes, she had discovered that Gill also knew about the man who had come looking for Hayward. Since there was no point in being discreet about the family linen with Gill, Shelby baldly asked the colonel what had happened.

He shook his head and concentrated on scratching Dick Turpin's throat. "I'm still thinking what to do. I'll let you know when I decide." Then he began talking about an escapade he and Biddle had had during a duel between two army officers outside Seringapatam. The colonel chuckled. "You should have seen old Dunbar. Came to the field that morning full of whiskey and still chewing on ginger nuts. Of course, he fired wide of the mark, and that was the end of it." He paused. "Did I ever tell you about the time Biddle and I intercepted two sergeants making off with a week's supply of arrack?"

"Yes," Gill and Shelby said together. Colonel Falcon looked at them and grinned as Dick Turpin waved his feet in the air and whined to be scratched some more.

Gill called for Ranja to sit with the colonel, and he and Shelby left together. "I think he tells those stories just to distract me," Shelby said.

"I'm certain he does." Gill laughed. "He comes up with one every time he wants to change the subject. He has his maneuvers, doesn't he?"

"Like hearing things selectively?" Shelby looked up at him with an impish smile.

"Exactly. I think we're beginning to know his tricks, Miss Falcon." He stopped at the top of the stairs and glanced down. "Your questions about the man who visited were quite good. I think this is something we need to discover much more about. I'm going to the inn and see if I can find out anything about this man. Why don't you try to quiz the cousins here?"

"Men get to take all the trips," Shelby said with a laugh.

Gill smiled down at her. He was struck by how green her eyes looked today. Dovey had put a touch of something shiny on her lips, and he wanted nothing more at that moment than to see what it was—preferably by tasting. He made his voice light. "Perhaps, but females have more fun."

"We'll have to debate the topic someday." Shelby laughed as she started down the stairs. She paused at the drawing room door as Gill went out. She hoped he hadn't noticed the way her breath had caught in her chest when he'd looked at her. It was altogether a new feeling. "Very strange," she muttered to herself.

"Are you talking to yourself, dear?" Countess Rimildi asked, looking up as Shelby came through the door. The countess was busy working on her embroidery, and, from the pile of silks and linen, she had evidently been there for a while. "Talking to yourself is not a good thing, Shelby. Prospective husbands might think you were touched in the head."

"The last thing I need is a prospective husband," Shelby said with a grin, sitting down across from her mother. "Actually, I'm here hunting Hayward. Have you seen him?"

"Isn't everyone hunting the poor boy? I think he's off at the inn. I suppose he felt the need of fortification." The countess nodded. "I was here working on this shawl—do you like these blue flowers in the corners?—when some perfectly horrid man came in and demanded to see him. The man had no manners at all." She looked around and dropped her voice. "He went so far as to stand in the hall and threaten to do bodily harm to poor Hayward." She knotted off her thread and snipped it. She held the embroidery up and looked at it critically. The one thing at which the countess excelled was fine embroidery, and she enjoyed doing it. Shelby had often thanked her lucky stars that her mother could be occupied by needlework. "I want to put a lovebird with a ribbon in its mouth here," the countess said, "and a heart here." She frowned. "The lovebird can't be white, or it won't show up. What do you think of pale blue, dear?"

"Lovely, Mama. It would match the flowers in the corners." Shelby picked up some pale blue silk from the pile on the table, and pushed it toward the countess. "This will be perfect."

"You have such an eye for color, Shelby," Countess Rimildi said. "You get that from me, of course."

"Of course. Now, Mama, what went on with this man who was looking for Hayward? I heard that Grandfather came down and talked to him."

"Oh, yes, he did." The countess squinted as she threaded the needle. "He was every bit as angry as the man, and you know how intimidating the colonel can be. He was, in fact, very intimidating for a dying man." The countess paused significantly.

Shelby ignored the pause. "What did he say? The other man, I mean. Not Grandfather."

"He merely said that Hayward was a marked man if he didn't pay up. I believe he said that Hayward owed something over twenty thousand pounds."

"*Twenty thousand pounds?* Are you sure, Mother? How in the world can anyone owe twenty thousand pounds?"

Countess Rimildi stabbed her needle into the cloth, the outlines of a lovebird already forming. "I understand it's quite easy, dear. You gamble some, and then you gamble some more, and then you gamble again to try to recoup. But every time you lose." She glanced around again. "Hayward's father was much the same. Every time he went to London, he gambled away everything he could lay his hands on. The colonel usually kept him in line, but still he managed to lose most of what had been left to him." She chuckled. "I suppose that's all right. If he hadn't lost it, Hayward would have. Or Bentley. I understand from Hettie that Bentley is really worse than Hayward."

"So this is something that runs in that family?"

"Oh my, yes. I thought you knew." She dropped her voice. "But you don't need to worry. They inherited that deplorable trait from their mother. The poor thing went quite mad, you know, as did her father. They both had to be—shall we say—put away."

Shelby's eyes widened. "No, I didn't know."

"Well, dear, it really isn't discussed much in the family. Some things are best kept quiet." She peered over Shelby's shoulder out the window. "My goodness. Is that Mr. Gill walking around the garden with Rose? If she's set her cap for him, he must have money." She looked at Shelby, a puzzled expression on her face. "I had thought . . ." She paused and gave Shelby a long look. "Mr. Gill seemed to enjoy your company."

Shelby nodded, remembering that she and Gill were pretending to have a *tendre* for each other. "I find him very appealing, Mama. He's quite charming, and has wonderful manners."

"Ah, I thought as much." Countess Rimildi gave Shelby a beatific smile. "It's good to see you conversing with a handsome gentleman." She frowned slightly. "Still, I haven't heard a thing about that man, and he certainly hasn't said much about his private life. I know I've never heard anyone mention his name in London. Do you know anything about him?"

Shelby caught her breath as she watched Gill and Rose walk about. "No, Mama," she said automatically, her lips wooden. She suddenly felt as if her whole body were numb. Rose. It was going to happen again, just like with Crawford.

"They make a lovely picture, don't they?" Countess Rimildi said cheerfully, turning back to her embroidered lovebird. "Rose is so blond and fragile, while he's so dark. Almost menacing at times, I think." She nodded.

"Lovely." Shelby almost choked on the word. She left and went up to her room, where she could look out over the gardens from her window. They were still walking slowly, Rose pausing for effect now and then and holding a blossom up to her face for contrast. She spent most of the time looking up at Gill, smiling in a coy way. Shelby could almost imagine the conversation. "Rose!" she muttered in disgust as she turned away from the window and fell back into her chair.

Supper began as a dismal affair. Only Rose, Gill, Shelby, Countess Rimildi, and Pearce were there. Crawford arrived about five minutes later, offering his apologies. Hayward and Bentley came in about ten minutes after that, but they offered no apologies. Hayward looked wretched. They had just settled down to eating when there was a curse out in the hall. Colonel Falcon came in, Dick Turpin under his arm. He put Dick on the floor and took his place at the head of the table. "I've eaten off enough demmed trays," he growled. "I thought I'd come down and eat a decent supper, then have a good cigar." He looked around. "You had company today, Hayward."

"I've heard," Hayward said glumly. He said nothing else, and the silence at the table was thick. The tension was so great that Shelby imagined she could hear a hum in the air. The only person who seemed oblivious to it was the colonel. "Thomas," he bellowed, "get Dick a dish and some of this roast beef. He's as tired of pap as I am."

Gill turned to the countess and began asking her questions about Italy. The conversation soon resumed, although there was an element of strain. Bentley was sitting beside Shelby.

"Is Hayward overset?" she asked him.

"Wouldn't you be?" he answered, cutting his roast beef into precise cubes. "I heard that the man threatened to have him transported. Among other things." He turned his plate a quarter of a turn and ate the next thing there, his peas. Those he ate two at a time.

Shelby chuckled. "I'd forgotten how you preferred everything to be orderly, Bentley. When we were children, you always had an idea of exactly how things should be, and if anything went awry, you were all to pieces."

Bentley sighed and turned his plate another quarter of a turn. "I'm still the same. I simply like things to follow a logical, orderly pattern."

"Then how on earth do you manage to gamble?" Shelby asked without thinking.

Bentley dropped his fork with a clatter. Thomas handed him another, and he began eating again.

"How do you?" Shelby asked again. "Gambling has no order, no plan. I don't see how you do it."

Bentley sighed. "No, it's maddening, isn't it? You always think that if you play just one more hand or one more game, then everything will fall into place. You always think you can discover the pattern there." He looked at her. "There has to be one, you know. There's always a pattern."

Shelby frowned. "A pattern? I don't think so, Bentley. From what little I know of gambling, it's fairly random."

He shook his head and turned his plate the last quarter-turn. "No, the pattern is there. Someday I'll find it." He glanced across the table. "Tell me, Shelby, do my eyes deceive me? Is our Rose flirting with the mysterious Mr. Gill?"

Shelby merely glanced across at Rose, but that was enough. She was definitely flirting with Gill, and, worse, he seemed to be flirting with her as well. Shelby hazarded a glance at Crawford. He was carefully studying everything on his plate, pushing it this way and that.

Gill took a deep breath and made himself smile down at Rose again as she made some sort of inane comment. He was most definitely not enjoying supper. He had managed to talk briefly to the countess about Italy, but Rose wasn't going to allow him any conversation except hers. Now she was bent toward him, displaying rather more décolletage than was seemly. Worse, Shelby was looking daggers at him. He knew he wasn't in her good graces. As he and Rose walked in the garden, he had glanced up at Shelby's window and seen her looking at Rose draped all over his arm. Even though he had hastily excused himself and gone on to the inn, he hadn't had the opportunity to explain himself to Shelby. Not only that, he knew she was wondering about his overnight absence. After all, they had promised to share information. He would do that, he vowed—just as soon as he had any.

He glanced at the colonel. Gill was really worried about the old man. With every day, the time drew closer for him to have to go to the Peninsula, and what would happen to the colonel then? Gill had grown quite fond of the old man, seeing in him the father and grandfather he had never known. He let his gaze stray back to Shelby as Rose touched his arm and murmured, then gave out a low, seductive laugh. It was strange, he mused as he only half-listened to her chatter. In any comparison, Shelby would be considered the lesser beauty to Rose, but he thought Shelby had so much more to offer. Whereas Rose was shallow, Shelby was a thinker. Rose seemed to have little sense of family, while Shelby was very involved in her family and had a strong sense of loyalty to them. That was how Gill had always imagined a family would be. He had never known one, and his Uncle Bates had had little time for him. Though his uncle had sent him off to school and, later, had purchased his colors, there had been little real affection, just a sense of duty. Gill felt a sharp jolt of memory, thinking how he used to envy the other boys in school when they complained about their families. How he would have loved to be able to do that! A family was all he had ever wanted.

Later, when he joined the army, he had put those thoughts behind him. The last thing an army man needed was a family.

His first sergeant had told him that. "An army man should be like a penny," the sergeant had said, flipping one into the air. "Not worth much if it's lost, and easily replaceable."

He sighed without thinking.

"A penny for your thoughts, Mr. Gill." Rose's voice held a flirtatious undertone.

"Actually," he said with a smile, "I was thinking of pennies, Miss Meadows." He wanted to look at Shelby again as he heard her conversing with Bentley about their childhoods, but Rose kept talking. Out of politeness, he allowed himself to be monopolized.

It was almost a relief to go into the drawing room after supper. The colonel dispensed with cigars and port in the dining room. He picked Dick Turpin up and headed for the drawing room. "My best brandy is in there," he explained, "and so is a comfortable chair. If I'm going to drink and smoke, I'm going to do it in comfort. The rest of you can stay here if you like."

"Smoke doesn't bother me," Shelby said, following him out. She would have agreed to almost anything to get out of the dining room, where she had to watch Rose make a fool of herself over Gill. Or perhaps it was the other way around.

In the drawing room, Colonel Falcon sat down in his chair, pulled up his footstool, and lit a large cigar. The others declined, and Shelby asked Luke to open the French doors to the garden, so the smoke was hardly noticeable. The countess had a table pulled up near the open doors, and she, Pearce, Bentley, and Crawford played cards for an hour or so. Gill tried to converse with the colonel and Shelby, but Rose kept asking him questions, then offered to sing. Shelby winced, knowing how bad Rose's singing was, but Rose would not be deterred.

Rose's singing was as bad as everyone expected, and, worse, she sang several numbers. Finally, when she launched into a particularly terrible rendition of "Greensleeves," Dick Turpin began howling along with her. Bentley and Hayward broke into gales of laughter.

"That dog's got more sense than some people," Colonel Falcon muttered to Shelby.

Hayward stood finally and made his excuses. "It's been a harrowing day," he said with a rueful grin. "I believe I need some extra sleep. Good night." He smiled at them and left. Shortly afterward, Pearce did the same, saying he had to be up early to do some experiments with his rockets and asking if the colonel had any gunpowder around. "If you don't," Pearce said with a frown, "I'm going to have to go buy some." Unspoken was the comment that he didn't have the funds to buy anything, much less gunpowder.

Colonel Falcon glared at him a moment, then took a puff of his second cigar. "Check with Rankin down at the stables. I think he might have some stored." He frowned at Pearce's back as Pearce walked out. "Be careful!" the colonel roared.

"I always am," Pearce said, his feelings injured. "I never have accidents." Colonel Falcon snorted.

Countess Rimildi and Bentley went up together, leaving Shelby, Rose, Gill, Crawford, and Colonel Falcon in the drawing room. Crawford stood. "I can't credit it, but I seem to be getting accustomed to country hours," he said. "I believe I'll go up as well." He looked around at the others and left.

"Something is troubling that boy," Colonel Falcon said. "He's not been himself since he's been here. I wonder what the problem is?"

"Money," Rose said shortly. "What else?"

Colonel Falcon frowned at her, then shook his head. He started to say something, thought the better of it, and, instead, leaned back in his chair and puffed contentedly on his cigar. "The best time of the day," he said, smiling fondly at Dick Turpin. Dick was lounging on Shelby's lap, on his back, with his paws in the air. Shelby had been absently scratching his stomach. Dick's head lolled back, and he looked at the colonel upside down.

They sat in companionable silence for a short while, Rose trying now and then to begin a conversation. No one seemed to want to talk very much. The cool breeze from the garden smelled of flowers and the dew.

The colonel flipped open the wooden lid of the box that held his cigars and extracted another one that he put into his pocket.

"Grandfather, you shouldn't—" Shelby began.

"My only luxury," he commented, "and I'm saving it for later. I might even give it to Biddle." He grinned at Shelby, and she knew he would be lighting it the moment his chamber door was closed.

"You're incorrigible, Grandfather."

"I know, and I'm delighted you agree." He grinned at her, then took another puff from the cigar in his fingers. He leaned back and stretched as Dick Turpin jumped up on his lap and lazily settled there, looking at the other three. The colonel looked around and smiled contentedly. "Aahhh, there's nothing like a quiet evening, some fine brandy, and a good cigar." He jumped straight up as the sound of a pistol shot rang out upstairs. Rose screeched and grabbed Gill's arm. He shook her off and dashed out the door, Shelby right behind him. Gill took the stairs two at a time, his heart pounding. He fervently hoped nothing had happened to Ranja.

The door to the colonel's room banged open and Biddle came out, a smoking pistol in his hand. "Where is he?" Biddle shouted. "Did you see him?"

"Him? Who?" Gill demanded. "What happened, Biddle?"

"He went out this door into the hall," Biddle said.

"Who, man?" Gill fought back the urge to shake him. "What happened? I saw no one out here."

Biddle sagged against the doorway and looked at the pistol as the hallway filled with the others who had dashed up the stairs. "I don't know who it was," he said dejectedly. "I was taking a short nap—it's been a difficult day, you know—and a noise roused me. I was in the sitting room where he couldn't see me."

"And you didn't see who it was?"

Biddle shook his head. "No. I did see that it was a man, and he was going through the colonel's things. You can see for yourselves—he was just tossing things around, looking for something, I'd say. I heard the noise and slipped over to get the pistol." He looked down at the firearm. "Sad to say, I dropped the thing, and that must have alerted him. I yelled at him to stop as he ran for the door, and when he didn't, I shot at him." He backed up a step and looked at a round hole in the wall. "At least I think I scared him."

The colonel came puffing up the stairs and made his way through the crowd. "Who was it?" he demanded.

Briefly, Gill recounted the story. "Do you have any idea what he could be looking for?" Gill asked. He stepped inside the room and the rest of them followed him. "Any valuables or money?"

Colonel Falcon put Dick Turpin down on the bed and began looking around. "Nothing at all in here except a little money." He opened a drawer in the little table beside his bed. "Well, it wasn't much, but it's gone." He looked again and felt with his hand back into the drawer. Then he turned around and looked at Gill. "So is the new list of things I wanted in my will. And the signed copy of the statement giving the Jewels of Ali to Shelby."

"Why would anyone want that?" Countess Rimildi asked.

"If there's no signed statement, then the old will stands," Crawford explained to her.

The countess still looked confused. "I don't understand."

"That means," Hayward said, "that Shelby wouldn't get the Jewels of Ali if something happened, say, tonight to the colonel. Everything would be divided up the way it was written down in his old will."

There was a sudden silence as everyone thought about this. "But nothing is going to happen to Grandfather," Shelby said slowly. "Not tonight, not ever. Nothing at all. We'll see to that."

"Perhaps we should take turns standing guard," Pearce said, looking around at the others. "There are five men here. We could each take two hours apiece."

"I'll post Luke, Thomas, and Ranja," Gill said. "There's no point in all of you having your sleep ruined." He glanced at the clock. "Why don't we all go back to bed, and tomorrow we can search the house and grounds for the burglar." He glanced out into the dark. "If there are any traces outside, we can't see them until daylight anyway."

"Good idea," Bentley said. "Whoever it was is probably a mile away by now." He turned and went back into his room. "If you need me, just call," he said over his shoulder as he shut the door.

The others dispersed slowly. Shelby wanted to stay with her grandfather, but her mother was ready to weep. "Shelby, we need to stay together tonight. If someone took the list for the new will, then someone might try to harm you." She looked around fearfully. "We could be in mortal danger."

"I don't think that's the case, Mama," Shelby said. "Why don't you let me sit with you awhile until you go to sleep?"

"And then have you wandering around by yourself? No, indeed! I know where my duty to my daughter lies! I don't intend to leave your side until tomorrow." She paused in the hall. "Shall we sleep in my room? We could have a trundle bed brought in."

Shelby knew from past experience that it was futile to argue. She had Dovey bring her night things into the red room. "Such goings-on!" Countess Rimildi said, holding her head. "I can't believe such things are happening at Wychwood. It's enough to make one ill."

"Does your head ache, Mother?" Shelby asked, seeing her chance. "Why don't you let me get you something for it?"

"You're such a good child," the countess said fondly.

It didn't take the countess long to doze off after she had taken the dose of laudanum Shelby gave her. As soon as her mother was sound asleep, Shelby got up from the trundle bed and put on her dressing gown. She went out into the hall, which was lit from one end to the other, candles in every sconce. Shelby wondered briefly who had ordered this to be done.

Undecided, she wondered if Gill was in his room or her grandfather's. She wanted to ask him what he thought of this occurrence, and perhaps discover why he had left so suddenly and stayed away all night. She tried the handle on her grandfather's door quietly, but it was firmly locked. Remembering that every key fit every door on the floor, she slipped back to her room and found her key. She inserted it quietly in the lock on the colonel's door and it turned, making a faint scratching noise. She opened the door and went inside.

Suddenly she was attacked from behind. She was pulled backward and a hand went over her mouth so she couldn't make a sound. She kicked ineffectually with her feet, which were off the floor, but made no impact. She tried biting, but the hand over her mouth was too strong. Finally, making noises in her throat, she went limp. Her captor bumped the door closed and half-dragged, half-carried her into the sitting room where a single, shuttered candle burned. The door to the sitting room was closed behind her and her assailant as well, and she was unceremoniously plopped onto a chair. Gill was standing over her.

"You," he said with a sigh. "I should have known."

"I had to see if Grandfather was all right. Luke or Thomas could go to sleep or anything could happen. I wanted to come sit with him myself." She looked up at him poised over her.

He looked huge in the weak light from the shuttered candle. The word her mother had used to describe him popped into her mind: "menacing." At this moment, it was an apt description. "Must you loom over me like that?" she asked. "Why don't you sit down?"

He seated himself across from her and turned the candle so it illuminated them. "How did you get a key to that door?" he asked. "I have it in my pocket."

Shelby sighed. "I was going to tell you last night, but you left. Every door on this floor opens with the same key."

"Hell and damnation! That's how it was done!" He hit his knee with his fist. "Anyone could get in here at any time."

"Exactly." Shelby cast an uneasy glance in the direction of the colonel's bedroom. "Shouldn't we have that door open? Someone may try to get in and harm him."

"He isn't in there. I put him in my bedroom with Luke and Ranja to guard him. And"—he grinned, his smile very white in the gloom—"Dick Turpin, of course. I think Dick will be a better guard than anyone."

Shelby smiled back and settled into the chair, her tension ebbing. "You're probably right." She looked around. "Since we're here and it's private, perhaps you might want to tell me why you left last night. Did you find out anything new?"

Gill shook his head. "I left for two reasons. I wanted to check with a friend in Oxford who has London connections. I thought he might know something about Hayward's gambling debts."

"They're becoming legendary," Shelby said with a smile.

"True. My friend didn't even have to ask around in London. He told me that both Hayward and Bentley are badly dipped."

"And you've heard about Hayward's visitor?"

He nodded, looking at her. He was trying hard not to look at her, but it was impossible. She was sitting there, all that glorious auburn hair tumbling down, spilling around her shoulders. All she had on were her night things, a thin dressing gown that was a cream color and was beautifully embroidered all around the collar. Gill kept wondering exactly what was underneath it. He made himself take a deep breath.

"And the other thing?" Shelby asked. "What was that?"

"It was a personal thing," he said slowly.

Shelby hesitated. "Is it anything I can help you with? Or is it one of those personal things that can't be shared?" She smiled at him, thinking again how handsome he was. A curl of dark hair had fallen onto his forehead in their tussle, and she clenched her hands into fists to keep them still. If she didn't, she feared she would reach over and smooth his hair back. Her fingers tingled as she wondered how that would feel.

"A messenger came from my uncle Bates just before nightfall." He paused. "I don't believe you know the family, but he has one son, Charles, my cousin. Charles was in Ireland, and was in a boating accident. He was pulled from the water, but he seems to have developed lung complications." He stopped and there was a catch in his voice when he continued. "He isn't expected to live."

A dozen thoughts ran through Shelby's mind, but the most pressing she had to deny. She wanted to put her arms around him and comfort him. Instead, she made herself sit still. "I'm so sorry. Will you need to leave and go to him?"

Gill shook his head. "No, Uncle Bates felt I should stay here." He ran his fingers through his hair. "Charles and I were never particularly close."

Shelby leaned toward him. "No matter. It's always a shock when something happens to one of your family."

Gill almost choked. He said nothing, and she reached over and put her hand on his. "Is there anything I can do for you?"

He closed his eyes. The thing she could do for him didn't bear repeating. He fought against the image of all that auburn hair spread out on a white embroidered pillowcase. He swallowed hard and made himself speak. "No," he said hoarsely. "Nothing."

She leaned back and looked at him with sympathy. "I was

going to sit with Grandfather tonight, but I suppose that's not necessary. Are you going to stay here all night?"

"Yes. I thought the person Biddle frightened off might return to see what else was here. Now that I know about the keys, though, I may just go to bed. The intruder could come any time, and it will be impossible to keep someone on watch around the clock."

Shelby looked at him with sympathy again. "I know you're exhausted if you didn't sleep last night. When Bentley and I saw you on the road, you looked as if you'd ridden for hours. Why don't you go to sleep, and I'll sit beside you. I could wake you if I heard anything." She patted his hand. "I insist."

"Miss Falcon," he said slowly. "You cannot. You know enough about London gossip to realize that you can't spend the night in this room with me, no matter how innocent it may be. You shouldn't be here now." He stood up and extended his hand to her. "I suggest you leave now before anyone barges in here." He glanced around. "I'll barricade the door and get some sleep."

It took him a few minutes to convince her, but he finally got her to the door. She stopped and looked up at him, her eyes dark green in the half-light. "Take care, Gill," she whispered.

He nodded and quickly shut the door, leaning back against it as he gulped in air. His hands were almost shaking with the desire he had felt. He had come close to simply grabbing her and kissing her until she . . . "Dear God," he muttered, hitting his forehead with his palm. "What am I thinking?"

He threw himself down on the bed, thanking God it had been too dark for her to see what she had been doing to his body. That thought didn't help him at all, and he groaned and sat up, his body aching all over.

It was going to be a long, long night.

Eleven

Gill looked haggard when he came downstairs the next morning. His luck held, and he saw no one until he reached the stables. Rankin looked at him curiously as he saddled a horse, but Gill offered no explanation for his swollen, red-rimmed eyes. Once out in the fields, he rode hard, trying to get last night's images of Shelby out of his mind. It didn't work at all.

When he came back inside, she was in the breakfast room, along with Hayward and Bentley. Gill nodded good morning to them.

"Do come join us, Gill," Shelby called out.

Gill glanced down at his boots. "Let me go change out of these, and I'll be right back down."

She smiled at him. "Don't stand on ceremony. I'm sure riding boots at the table won't bother any of us. We've all done that." She motioned to a seat across from her, and Gill entered the room and sat down. Shelby rang for Mrs. McKilley, and the conversation was about the weather until Gill had been served his breakfast.

"Did anything occur last night?" Shelby asked.

He shook his head. "Nothing. Have you heard any word from the colonel? I got out early and haven't checked on him."

"Biddle came down to make sure Grandfather's favorite

breakfast was here. He said Grandfather would be down in a few minutes."

"We're just waiting," Bentley said.

They didn't have long to wait. They could hear Dick Turpin yipping before the colonel appeared in the doorway. "How is everybody?" he asked, putting Dick Turpin on the floor. "You look like the very devil, Gill. Didn't you sleep?"

"Very little." Gill looked down as Dick Turpin sat on his hind legs and tried to beg for some sausages. Dick grinned at him.

"What did I tell you?" Colonel Falcon said. "He's Robert Herrick's very image."

"That's something of an insult to Herrick." Hayward gave Dick an evil look and sneezed as Dick stood on his back paws beside him.

"Just feed him and he'll go away," the colonel said.

"Let me fix Dick something to eat," Shelby said, trying to contain her laughter at Dick's antics. He heard the word "eat" and came dashing over to her. She got a saucer and put some sausages on it. Dick was ecstatic.

"Got a letter from Wharton, the solicitor," Colonel Falcon announced as Mrs. McKilley brought him a heaping plate of food. "He'll be back from London tomorrow, and over here the next day." He looked at Shelby. "Now don't you worry, Shelby. I'll take care of things. I want to see you a rich woman before I die."

"I wish you wouldn't talk about dying, Grandfather." Shelby put her napkin beside her plate. "I don't like to think on it."

"It's going to happen, girl," he said. "If not now, later. I want everything all fixed up legally so there's no question about your inheritance."

"Ah, Shelby," Hayward said with a grin, "you'll be the toast of London when you get out and about wearing those jewels. There'll be eligibles falling at your feet." His dark good looks set off his smile. Shelby hadn't noticed before how handsome he was when he was smiling. But then, Hayward didn't smile very often.

"All the eligibles, including you, I suppose," Bentley said, folding his napkin precisely and putting it in line with his fork.

"Thank you, no. I've already had my comeuppance." Hayward rose and made his excuses. "Colonel, you'll be pleased to know that I'm off to talk with your steward about farm management, as you suggested."

"If you don't, you'll be begging in the streets," Colonel Falcon said with a snort. "Next, you'd better work out something with your creditors. I don't want to hear of you being in London again except for a business visit."

Hayward turned and looked at him. He started to say something, then thought the better of it. "I'll see the rest of you later," he said, going out.

"I'll be leaving as well," Bentley said, rising. "I promised Pearce that I'd help him this morning. He has a design for a new rocket that he wants to try." He made a face. "This is certainly not what I'd make a choice to do today, but I did promise."

"See if you can convince the boy to turn to fireworks instead," the colonel said. "At least he could sell those to the Prince Regent." He glanced after Bentley as he left. "Rockets," he said with scorn. "They'll never amount to anything." He paused. "Now the Chinese know what to do with gunpowder. They have wonderful fireworks. Did I ever tell you about the time I was in Madras and the fireworks frightened our horses?"

"Yes," Shelby and Gill answered together.

"I thought I had." He looked around. "Gill, since nothing untoward happened last night, don't you think I could sleep in my own room tonight? Perhaps this foolishness will stop as soon as Wharton gets here and I make my will."

"I doubt it," Gill said with a sigh. "And, no, I think you'd better sleep in my room again. There's only one door, so it's more easily defended. If we keep two men in there, you should be safe."

Rose came tripping into the room. "Oh, there you are, Mr. Gill. I've been looking all over for you! I thought you might like to take a carriage ride with me around the area. We could stop in the village if you like. There are some very fine ruins near there." She sat down and waited for Thomas to pour her a cup of tea. "How do you manage to eat so early in the morning, Shelby?" Without waiting for an answer, she turned back to Gill. "Shall I have the carriage brought around?"

"As much as I would like to go, Miss Meadows, I must decline. I have some rather pressing things to do here."

Rose forced her expression into a mock pout. "Now, Mr. Gill, what could be more important than accommodating a lady's request? Surely you could defer your business until later. I so wanted to go to the village."

"Perhaps Shelby could go with you," he suggested.

Rose's face fell. "Why don't the four of us go? Shelby, would you like that? Mr. Gill and I, and you and Crawford. It's perfect!"

"Gill, if you're staying around because of me, don't," Colonel Falcon said. "I'm going to ride around the estate today with the steward as soon as he's finished with Hayward. On second thought, Hayward could go with us. If he's going to try to salvage his finances, he might as well see how a profitable estate is run."

"Grandfather, are you sure that's wise? Perhaps you should stay indoors for a few days." Shelby looked at him with concern.

"I'm not going to stay here wrapped in cotton wool. If something happens, then it happens." Colonel Falcon stood up. "I'll be all right, girl. Haven't I made it through too many wars to count? I've always come through." He whistled for Dick Turpin and left, the dog right at his heels.

"I hope he's right," Shelby said. She had a bad feeling.

"You worry too much," Rose said. "Are you going with us, or are you going to stay here? If you're going along, I'll go convince Crawford to accompany us. When I looked out the window, I saw him prowling around in the back garden." She jumped up and went out. "Perhaps we should plan a picnic," she said over her shoulder as she left. "What do you think about that?"

Shelby made a face. "I hate picnics," she said to Gill.

"So do I." He gave her a wry smile. "Perhaps I've eaten one too many meals while I was on patrol. I much prefer my meals indoors in comfort."

Shelby smiled at him. "I believe we've been dragooned into this trip, but at least we can insist on lunch at the inn in the village. Are we in agreement?"

"We are always in perfect agreement, Miss Falcon," he said. There was a strange expression on his face that Shelby couldn't read. She wondered what he meant.

The outing was exactly what Shelby had thought it would be. They had been obliged to ask the countess to come along, and she did. "I know my duty is to chaperone my daughter," she had said. "I would certainly never shirk that responsibility."

Because the countess went along, Gill and Crawford rode along beside the carriage, much to Rose's dismay. "Did you plan things this way?" she whispered to Shelby as they got out at the ruins of an old church on the edge of the village. A castle had been right beside it, and the tall keep was still standing, dominating the village.

"Certainly not." Shelby couldn't say more as the countess called to her.

"Shelby dear, I do believe I'll just sit here in the shade and wait for you," she said. "I brought along a little embroidery to pass the time." She looked at Shelby and frowned slightly. "Do remember to pull your bonnet forward, and don't let the sun get on your skin."

"I'll remember, Mama." With a sigh, Shelby went back to the others. Crawford was waiting for her. "Rose has captured Mr. Gill and taken him off to view the ruins," he said with a small smile. "I rather sympathize with the gentleman."

"Why is that?" Shelby looked up at him quizzically.

Crawford shrugged. "Because Rose usually gets what she wants, and right now she seems to want Mr. Gill. I suppose it's because he's really the only eligible man at Wychwood." He paused. "Rose must know something about his finances that the rest of us don't."

"He's in the army, and I've never heard him mention any prospects. I imagine he's comfortable, but not particularly wealthy."

Crawford took another look at Rose and Gill as they strolled across the grass, then shook his head. "They're certainly not my worry since I'm here with the most lovely woman at Wychwood." Shelby had put her hand on his arm, and he now covered it with his. They walked on in companionable silence for a few minutes until Crawford suggested that they sit on a rock in the shade. "It's hot today." He took off his hat and fanned himself with it briefly. "Too hot for this kind of outing." He paused, then put his hat down on the rock beside him. "Shelby, have you thought about what I asked you?"

"What you asked me?"

He looked at her, his blue eyes looking right into hers. "About marrying me. You do recall that I asked you?"

Shelby felt herself blush. "Of course, I recall that, Crawford. With all the excitement of things happening to Grandfather, I simply haven't had much time to think about it."

"So the answer is no," he said, looking off into the distance. "I thought it might be."

"I didn't give you an answer, Crawford."

He looked at her and smiled sadly. "No, you didn't in so many words, but your actions did. You favored me once, didn't you?" He took off his glove and touched her cheek with his fingertip.

"No, I . . ." Shelby stopped. There was no use to deny it. Everyone in the family knew. "Yes, Crawford, I did."

"It was the thing with Rose that changed your mind, wasn't it?"

Shelby hesitated. "I believe you still care for Rose. Do you think I would want to marry a man who loved someone else?"

He looked away from her. "I'm sorry. I truly am. I thought I was over Rose. Then she came to Wychwood." A touch of bitterness tinged his voice. "Before, she told me she cared for me, then broke the engagement because of my finances. At the time, I believe she thought she could get Armstead to come up to scratch. He's got more money than the Bank of England."

"I've heard about his funds, and I think that's an exaggeration, Crawford," Shelby said lightly. She reached up and turned his face to look into hers, and smiled at him. "Have you ever thought of talking to Rose about how you feel? She may have changed her mind and not know how to approach you. Women are sometimes limited in their actions." Shelby hesitated. "Do you think you could forgive her for breaking your engagement?"

"I don't know." He took her hands in his. "It was a betrayal of the worst sort."

"Perhaps Rose felt desperate. You and I know that she's often done rash things in a desperate moment. Things that she regretted bitterly later." She gave him a rueful smile. "I do care for you, Crawford, but more as a brother. I admit that once I thought I had other feelings, but I know better now."

"Sweet Shelby," he said, giving her a chaste kiss on the forehead.

From the top of the keep, Rose and Gill watched them. "Heavens! What a breach of propriety. My mother would never allow such." Rose's voice had an odd tone. "Do you think . . . ?" She didn't finish the sentence. "What do you think they're discussing, Mr. Gill?"

Since Shelby had told him of Crawford's offer, Gill had a very good idea of the topic under discussion. His heart almost stopped as Shelby touched Crawford's face with her fingers and turned him to look at her. He gripped the edge of the crenellated wall until his fingers went white, wishing with all his heart that it was Crawford's throat.

Beside him, he could feel Rose tense as the pair below seemed to move closer. "They seem almost. . . . almost *intimate*," Rose muttered in disbelief. She made fists of her hands and rested them on the parapet. "She's always been in love with Crawford, always." Her voice sounded harsh.

"Is that why you suggested the two of them come along?"

"I don't know," Rose said miserably. She put both hands over her mouth and turned away as Crawford kissed Shelby on the forehead. Gill knew he should comfort her, but he had his own problems. What if Shelby was really in love with Crawford and had accepted him? She had indicated that she no longer cared for Crawford that way, but she could have changed her mind. If Shelby married Crawford, Gill knew there would be a hole in his heart that would never heal. Why had he allowed himself to feel this way? He turned away, cursing himself a thousand times, and took Rose's arm. "Perhaps we should go down. It's almost noon, and I think the inn is expecting us for lunch."

Nothing was said over lunch to make Gill think that Shelby had accepted Crawford. The talk ranged from topic to topic in government and finally settled on Crawford's paper. *"The London Eye* made a favorable impression on many," Gill told Crawford. "I know my uncle said it was the finest comment on politics available, and he doesn't give compliments lightly."

"I'm flattered," Crawford said with a smile. "I can only hope there will be more issues."

"Why don't you try to get a consortium together?" Gill

suggested. "I'm sure there are many like my uncle who would like to see the paper succeed. You could get, oh, say, twenty investors together, and that should give you enough capital."

Crawford looked at him with respect. "I really hadn't considered that a possibility, Mr. Gill. Do you think you could help me with some suggestions or some names?"

Gill looked surprised. "Of course. My uncle has gone to Ireland right now, but when he returns, I'll ask him if he knows any like-minded people who would be willing to invest."

"I may go to London and talk to some people. I've been trying to find just one patron, but I might be able to find many people who would invest a small amount."

"Small amounts add up to large amounts," Shelby said with a smile.

"Exactly." Crawford smiled back at her.

Rose dropped her reticule. "Crawford, would you mind getting that for me?" She put her hand to her head. "I'm afraid I'm coming down with a terrible headache. Do you think we could return to Wychwood now?"

"It's the heat," Countess Rimildi said. "I kept a headache during those Italian summers. Dear Count Rimildi always suggested that I go to the countryside and stay." She peered out the window. "I do think it may storm this afternoon; that's probably why it's so hot and sultry now. A nice thunderstorm will break the heat."

"It will be just as well that we go back then," Gill said, looking through the small panes of glass. "I agree with you, Countess. It does look like rain."

They were almost back at Wychwood when they saw the smoke.

Crawford and Gill stood in their stirrups and looked. "I think it's the back field," Crawford said.

"It looks like quite a blaze." Gill took another look and turned to the countess. "Would you see everyone home, Countess?" he asked. "They may need help in the field." At the countess's nod, he and Crawford took off at a gallop.

"I hope he doesn't ruin another coat," Shelby said before she thought.

Back at Wychwood, everything was in chaos. Shelby went hunting for her grandfather, but couldn't find him. There didn't seem to be a male on the place. She went out the back and looked into the distance, watching the smoke billow up. The past two days had been hot and the past week had been dry, so the grass blazed quickly. Shelby looked up at the sky. The rain predicted by Gill and her mother was nowhere in sight, although heavy clouds were building quickly.

Luke came running up to the house. "What's going on?" Shelby asked him. He was dirty, sweaty, and covered in soot.

"The back field is burning fast. I came to ask the colonel to send to the village for men to help us."

"He's not here, and I don't know where he is." Shelby felt a sudden drop of her heart. "None of the men are here."

She and Luke looked at each other in fear. "What shall I do?" Luke glanced back at the blaze.

"Go to the village and get some men," Shelby said quickly. "I'll look for Grandfather. If I don't find him anywhere, I'll go get Gill."

Luke nodded and left. Shelby put her head against the warm wood trim of the back door and took a deep breath. She had to find her grandfather, and she had to do it quickly. She consoled herself that he was out riding with Hayward and the steward, and ran to ask Mrs. McKilley.

"No, they came in around noon," Mrs. McKilley reported. "Then Mr. Hayward rode back out toward the back field. I don't know where Colonel Falcon went."

Shelby closed her eyes and hoped. Would Hayward do anything to the colonel? The thought sprang into her mind unbidden. Hayward would certainly benefit, as would the others. Shelby had a sense that the colonel was in trouble. Quickly she ran into the house and changed into the sturdy brogans she used for walking. She dashed through every room in the house, calling for the colonel as she went. He was nowhere to be found.

She ran to the stables and searched there, pressing Mrs. McKilley and Dovey into searching with her. "He's nowhere, mum," Dovey said, wringing her hands. "Mayhap he went to help fight the fire."

Shelby looked again at the blaze. From where she stood, she could see the silhouettes of the men working against the flames. If her grandfather was there, anything could happen to him. In the chaos, anyone could harm him, or he could just quietly disappear into the flames. She began to run across the field, paying no attention to Dovey's call for her to stop.

The smoke was thick as she drew near to the field. She clambered over the gate that blocked the road and ran on, gasping for air. The first person she saw was Biddle. "Have you seen Grandfather?" she asked, almost choking on the smoke.

"He's out there somewhere," Biddle said with a worried look. "He came out here—nothing could stop him—and then Dick Turpin got loose and ran behind the fire line. The colonel went after him. That was just before the fire shifted, and now I don't think he can get out." Biddle shook his head and looked near tears.

"Gill! Where is Gill?" Shelby grabbed Biddle's sleeve. "Where is he, Biddle? Where is Gill?"

"Right down there." Biddle pointed to a blackened figure flailing the fire with his coat.

Shelby ran down to Gill. "What are you doing here?" he shouted. "Get back to the house before you get hurt!"

"Gill, Grandfather's in there somewhere!" she cried, grabbing at his arm. "Biddle said Grandfather went in there after Dick Turpin! Right before the fire shifted."

Gill stood still and looked at the consuming flames.

"Shelby," he said quietly, "you know he can't survive in there."
He put his arms around her. "Let me take you back to the
house."

She shook her head. "No, I won't go until Grandfather is
found."

Gill sighed. "Shelby, it may be tomorrow or next day before
they find him. It may take a while to identify. . . ." He stopped
and released her, turning to look at the line of flames across
the field. "Isn't there a pond back there? I thought I saw it
when I was out riding."

She nodded. "The bream pond. Grandfather keeps it
stocked, and Dick likes to swim there." She looked up at Gill,
hope in her eyes. "Gill, do you think there's a chance . . . ?"

He moved away and ran back toward the house where his
horse was standing in the back garden, nervously tossing his
head. Gill grabbed the reins and mounted. "I'm going to try
to ride around the fire and come in from the side. I think I
may be able to get to the pond. If I know the colonel, he'll
try. It'll be his only chance, and I think he'll take it." He looked
down at her. "Promise me that you'll stay here by the house
and wait." She nodded, and he galloped across the field to the
fire, down the line of the flames, then turned left. Shelby
couldn't see him anymore because of the smoke and fire. She
leaned up against a tree and tried to see him in her mind, but
couldn't. All she could do was imagine the worst, both for her
grandfather and for Gill.

Luke came tearing through the field, driving a cart that
bounced at each rut and rock. Most of the village men were
in it, and they all tumbled out to help. They brought shovels
and pitchforks, and went to work digging a ditch so the fire
couldn't cross. Shelby stayed next to the tree, hoping despite
the odds, looking up at the sky and praying for rain. The clouds
were building higher, but there was no sign yet of rain.

After almost half an hour, it started to rain. The men raised
a cheer as the first huge drops began to fall. Overhead, the

storm broke as lightning and thunder rolled across the sky. "Get away from that tree, Shelby," Crawford called out, running up to grab a bucket. "Go back into the house."

Shelby shook her head. "I can't, Crawford. I have to know about Gill and Grandfather." He came over to her, and she told him the story.

Hayward came up as well and heard her. "We spent the morning riding, talking to the steward; and the colonel was showing me how things should be run," he said. "I can't believe anything could happen to him. Not now." On his face was a look of anguish. Pearce came up to them, wiping soot and smoke from his face with his sleeve.

"How did the fire start?" Crawford asked.

Pearce looked guilty. "Bentley and I thought we were careful. We saw the colonel and Hayward out riding, and I suppose that distracted us. At any rate, we must have done something wrong. Right after lunch, we went out to set off the rockets. One of them must have set the blaze."

"You damn fool, setting rockets in this dry grass," Hayward said. "Make that fools—I should have stopped you." He looked up at the streaming rain and lightning. "This will stop the blaze, I think." He looked anxiously at the fire.

Bentley wandered up to them. "Quite a blaze," he said with a grin. "It's better than Prinny's last fireworks show. Pearce and I certainly know how to get everyone out."

"Grandfather is still in there." Shelby's voice broke. "He may be. . . ." She faltered and couldn't say the word.

"Perhaps Gill can find him in time." Pearce sounded as if he were going to cry.

"I'm sure the colonel will be all right. Think of all the things he's been through," Crawford said.

"Well," Bentley said, glancing out at the rain falling on the last of the fire, "everybody's luck runs out at one time or the other." Hayward cuffed him on the arm, and Bentley looked in surprise at his brother. "Well, it does, you know."

"Shelby, you're going to have to go inside," Crawford said gently. "You'll catch your death of cold out here in this. You're soaked already."

Shelby looked down at her clothes. They were drenched and clinging to her. She could feel her hair sticking in little bunches around her face and dripping down her back.

"Crawford's right," Pearce said, as the others nodded in agreement. A fierce crack of lightning struck, and the village men clambered into the wagon and drove toward shelter.

"I can't leave." Shelby started to cry. "I can't."

"Well, I'm leaving," Bentley said. "I'll come back when the storm is over." He looked at the others. "Are you coming?"

Pearce went with him, while Hayward and Crawford stayed to persuade Shelby to go. Finally she gave in. She stood up, swaying slightly, clinging onto their arms. She took one last look at the fire, and saw something on the ground. It was Gill's coat. Quickly she ran and picked it up, holding it next to her. Just having something of his gave her hope. He would come back, she knew.

They had been back inside Wychwood for almost an hour. Outside it rained heavily. Shelby agreed to stay inside while the storm was raging, but she refused to leave the back door and go change her clothes. She just stood there, holding yet another of Gill's ruined coats, waiting. Finally the storm broke, and the heavy deluge changed to a soft, gentle rain. Ranja came in, silent as a wraith, and joined her at the door. He looked at her and nodded his head, then touched the coat with his fingertips. "He will come," he said. He sat down beside the door to wait.

"I didn't know you spoke English, Ranja," Shelby said, surprised.

He looked at her, but didn't answer. Instead, he turned back to the door and began looking outside. After a few minutes, he cried out a strange word, leaped to his feet, and ran out the door. Shelby followed his gaze across the field, and then she began to run. Gill was walking wearily toward them, leading his horse. There was someone sitting on the horse. Shelby ran to meet them, heedless of the mud in the garden or the rain that was still falling. Ranja ran right beside her.

Gill was covered in smoke and soot, and his clothes were plastered to him. His shirt was torn, and his hair was singed. His chin and nose were black from smoke. "I followed the stream up to the pond," he said, "and there he was. Getting out was worse than getting in because of the smoke." He turned and looked at Colonel Falcon, then glanced back at Shelby and spoke in a low tone. "Thank God the rain came when it did. I don't think we would have made it if it hadn't rained."

Colonel Falcon said nothing at all. He sat on the horse, his face a stiff black mask until they reached the back of the house. There he allowed Gill to help him off the horse, and then he turned to look at Shelby. Ugly red burns splotched his face, mixed with cuts and scratches. It was difficult to see how badly he was hurt as his skin, like Gill's, was blackened with soot and smoke. His eyebrows and hair were singed and burned, and his clothing was torn, blackened, and drenched. As far as Shelby could see, he didn't appear to have any serious wounds or broken bones. "Oh, Grandfather!" she cried, throwing her arms around him. He stepped back, patted Shelby on the arm, and went into the house without speaking.

"I don't understand," she said in confusion to Gill. "I thought he would be delighted that the fire is out and he's home safely. I know I am."

Gill took a deep breath. "His heart is broken, Shelby." He paused an instant. "He can't find Dick Turpin."

Twelve

The house was quiet that night. Colonel Falcon was in seclusion and refused to see anyone, even Shelby. Everyone else either ate supper from a tray upstairs, or went down for a cold supper. It was a house in shock. Everything was hushed; the only sounds were the calls the village men made to each other as they patrolled the boundaries of the fire, making sure that it didn't break out again.

Shelby went down to the drawing room when she could stand the misery no longer. Everywhere she walked, she remembered Dick Turpin being there. She found her mother sitting in the drawing room, busy with her embroidery. Her silks were piled up on the case that held the Jewels of Ali. Shelby sat and looked around, remembering Dick Turpin slurping her grandfather's whiskey, jumping up on her lap, or just grinning at everyone.

"I'm afraid Dick's loss may break Grandfather's heart," Shelby said to her mother.

Countess Rimildi snipped off a thread. "What he needs is another dog," she said practically.

"Another dog couldn't take Dick's place."

"No, but it would distract him. I'm sure that for him no animal or person could take Dick's place."

Rose wandered in to hear the last of the conversation. "I, for one, am glad that horrid animal is gone. The dog had no manners whatsoever." She sat down in the chair opposite Shelby and glanced at the silks on top of the case. "I understand the solicitor is coming tomorrow, Shelby," she said. "The jewels should be yours by tomorrow night."

"I don't care." Shelby glanced at the case. "I'd rather have Grandfather happy and contented and well." She looked up as the front door opened and Crawford and Hayward came inside. "We're in here," she called to them.

The two entered the room, damp from the heavy mist outside. "What happened to you?" Shelby gasped. "Did you go back and get hurt in the fire? You were fine when I last saw you." She gave Hayward a horrified look. He had been battered around the face. One eye was almost swollen shut and was rapidly turning black. There was a nasty cut on his chin, while one side of his face was red and skinned.

"No, not the fire," he said, looking uneasily at Crawford. Shelby looked at Crawford then. He didn't look a great deal better, but at least he wasn't bleeding. "I may as well tell you, I suppose," Hayward said with a sigh. "After we all got the news about Dick Turpin, I went to the inn to get away from the house for a while, and ran into Mr. Biggs there. He had a friend with him." He grimaced. "I believe you've heard of Mr. Biggs—he was here talking to the colonel yesterday."

"And he—they—did that to you?" Shelby was appalled.

Hayward managed a grin. "Well, yes, they did. Although I think Mr. Biggs got the worst of it. Crawford and Gill came in at a critical time, and, with their assistance, I think Mr. Biggs will be in bed most of the day tomorrow."

"Gill?" Shelby looked around wildly. "Where is he? Did he get hurt?"

Hayward shook his head. "No, he really didn't do much except keep Biggs's confederate out of the way while Mr. Biggs and I had our, um, conference." He looked at Crawford. "Fancy Gill carrying a small pistol on him. I would never have known."

"Mr. Gill is full of surprises," Countess Rimildi said, selecting an emerald green silk for a leaf.

"Yes, but how is he?" Shelby asked. "Are you certain that he didn't get hurt?"

"No, that is, he didn't get hurt there," Hayward said. "He's on the edge of exhaustion of course, after that bout this afternoon. It wasn't easy fishing the colonel out of the bream pond."

"Where is he?" Shelby couldn't keep a touch of anxiety out of her voice.

"Oh, he stayed to shepherd Pearce and Bentley home. They're both trying to drown their guilt over setting the field on fire."

"So they were the ones?" Rose asked.

Crawford went over and sat down beside her. "Yes, although it was accidental, I think. They were playing with Pearce's rockets and managed to set some dry grass alight."

Rose looked up at Crawford's face and touched a bruise with her fingertips. "You should have that sponged," she said. "It's going to be purple in the morning."

Crawford looked down at her and caught her hand in his. A look passed between them that Shelby knew. They quickly glanced away from each other, and Crawford released her hand.

Countess Rimildi snipped a thread off the end of her leaf and frowned. She put her embroidery down and covered a yawn. "I do think I'm going to retire," she said. "I can't believe I've become accustomed to these country hours so quickly." She glanced at Shelby. "Are you coming up, dear?"

"I think all of us should retire. We've had too much excitement lately." Hayward stood and made his excuses; then Crawford joined in. Shelby and Rose hesitated a moment before following the countess up the stairs. Shelby sat down in her room to wait for Dovey to come help her get ready for bed, but then decided to act on the look she had seen pass between Crawford and Rose. She walked down to the gold room and knocked on the door. Rose opened it, a happy smile on her lips. "I thought . . ." She stopped and her expression changed, becoming closed and shuttered. "What do you want, Shelby?"

Shelby gave the door a little shove and walked inside the room. The gold room was a beautiful topaz color, but the hue really did nothing for Rose at all. "I want to talk to you." Shelby sat down and glanced around at the clothing and cosmetics strewn everywhere. "About Crawford."

Rose sat, facing her, her expression angry. "Are you going to marry him?" she asked bluntly. "I know you've always been in love with him, and I know he's asked you."

"No. No, I'm not," Shelby said slowly. "And the reason I'm not going to marry him is because he doesn't care for me." She leaned forward. "I own that for years I thought I was in love with Crawford, but now I know better. What I felt for him before was just a young girl's fantasy." She shrugged. "Crawford was older than I, and when he came here, he brought his town bronze and stories of London. I was enchanted"—she paused—"but not, I think, in love. So that's one of the reasons I don't intend to marry Crawford."

"And the other?" Rose asked. She was pale.

"The other is that he's in love with you, Rose. If you had any sense at all, you'd go see him, own up to your feelings, and marry the man."

Rose looked around at all the things strewn around the room. "I can't go to him like this, Shelby. I have nothing at all." She turned back to look at her. "I can't live in poverty. I simply can't."

Shelby sighed. "That's a choice you're going to have to make for yourself, Rose. I can't tell you what to do. I know what I would do if I loved someone truly."

"Yes, but you have money. You'll have the Jewels of Ali. What man wouldn't want to marry someone with that?"

"Is money really that important to you? Besides, Crawford will probably be quite successful if he can find backers for his newspaper. I doubt he'll be hounded by creditors all his life. He has the estates, and they're in good shape, Grandfather says. You could be comfortable." She stood up and went to the door. "As I said, it's something you need to decide, Rose. Crawford loves you very much, and you love him. It would be a shame to throw all that away." She went outside and closed the door behind her. Out in the hall, she leaned back against the door and took a deep breath. She should feel terrible, tossing away all the dreams of her adolescence, but instead she felt relieved. From this vantage point in her life, she knew she had never been in love with Crawford. She had been more in love with the idea of being in love.

She smiled as she was flooded with a new sense of exhilaration. She stretched, grinned, and went downstairs. Luke was there by the door, extinguishing the candles in the lower hall. "I'm going out for a few moments, Luke," she called. "I thought I'd get some fresh air in the garden."

"Do I need to accompany you?" He looked alarmed.

She shook her head. "No, I'm not going far. I just felt the need to get out and breathe some fresh air."

"The night air isn't good for you. Mrs. McKilley insists it will bring on the ague and all sorts of other complaints."

"Perhaps." Shelby smiled at him. "I won't be out long. I just wanted to walk in the garden a moment."

Luke looked at her as if she'd lost her mind, then shrugged. The ways of the gentry were always beyond him. "The mist has cleared," he told her, "and the moon is coming out. But you'd best stick to walking on the gravel—the grass is still wet."

Shelby went outside and paused at the top of the steps. It was a soft night, and the moon was just coming out behind the clouds. The smell of smoke was still in the background, although the rain had washed most of it away. She went down the gravel path, breathing in the fresh air. She wandered a moment, reveling in the sensation of at last being free of her foolish ideas about Crawford. She had known it for a while, but there was something about just saying the words. She laughed to herself and started back inside, pausing before the door to take one last look around.

In the distance, she saw a dark figure prowling around the stables. She thought of investigating herself, but knew she'd be no match for someone like Mr. Biggs or one of his ilk. She went back inside and sent Luke out while she waited for him on the gravel path. "I knew it wasn't a fit night out," he grumbled as he left. Shelby noted that he picked up the poker from the drawing room and took it with him.

He returned in just a few minutes. "It's Mr. Gill," he told her. "He brought Mr. Pearce and Mr. Bentley in the back way, then went down to the stables. He wanted to check some things before he went to bed." He replaced the poker.

"Thank you, Luke," she said, pretending to sit and start winding her mother's embroidery silks. "I'll just stay here for a while. You can go on to bed."

As soon as Luke had disappeared, Shelby peered out of the drawing room. No one was about, so she slipped out the door and ran down the gravel path to the stables.

Gill was sitting on a rough wooden bench at the back of the stables, looking out over the field. In the distance, lantern lights gleamed and disappeared, gleamed and disappeared as the village men checked to make sure the fire was truly out. Gill ran his fingers through his hair, feeling the singed ends that would have to be cut. *I need to go to the barber, anyway,* he thought. He had planned to go before he left for the Peninsula.

He grimaced. He didn't seem any closer to discovering the identity of the person trying to harm the colonel than he had been a week ago. He was convinced that the fire, unlike the other things that had happened to the colonel, had been a true accident.

Gill had brought Bentley and Pearce home, and turned them over to Thomas. They were sober enough now, but still feeling guilty. Or at least Pearce was. "After all," he had said earnestly to Gill over his fifth or sixth ale, "it was my fault. I knew those rockets shot sparks, and I knew the grass was dry, although I thought I had every one of them aimed to go into the pond."

"It could happen to anyone," Gill had told him.

"Yes, but I should have been more careful." Pearce had sighed. "When we saw Colonel Falcon and Hayward riding through the hay toward the house, I even remarked to Bentley that the grass would blaze up in an instant if a spark hit it. I told Bentley to be sure everything was aimed toward the pond." He had hesitated and then had downed the rest of his ale. "I thought that last rocket had landed in grass, and I sent Bentley over to check and see if anything had caught. He said everything was fine, or I would have looked myself." He had looked miserable. "Poor Dick." He'd signaled for another ale, but Gill had stopped him.

"These things happen," Bentley had said. "Dick was a pest anyway. No one was hurt."

"No one except the colonel and Mr. Gill," Pearce had said morosely. "And Dick."

Gill had glanced at the clock. He'd been bone-weary and wanted nothing except to go somewhere quiet and close his eyes. He'd almost had to insist that the two go home with him. He had escorted them to the back door and sent them inside, then had gone down to the stables where he could sit in the cool night air and think.

He heard someone on the gravel before he saw anyone. Luke came around the corner of the stable, carrying, of all things, a poker. "Who's there?" Luke asked, his voice betraying him with its quiver.

"Just me, Luke." Gill stretched his legs out and leaned back against the stable. His head was feeling better. "I just wanted to come here and check on a few things before I went to bed. I'll let myself in."

Luke lowered the poker. "Very well, Mr. Gill. I'll leave the door unlatched for you. Call me if you need anything." He peered at Gill in the wispy moonlight. "Are you all right, Mr. Gill? Do you want me to send Ranja down to you?"

"No, Ranja is with the colonel." Gill took a deep breath. "Considering the circumstances, Luke, I'm just fine. I'll be along in a few minutes. Don't wait up. I'll be glad to latch the door behind me."

As Luke went back toward the house, his feet crunching on the gravel path, Gill looked out at the fields. He hadn't come here to check on anything—he had come here to sit and think. He was worried about Colonel Falcon. The fire today could easily have been fatal if the colonel hadn't been able to get into the pond. As it was, inhaling all the smoke certainly wasn't good for him. Gill felt as though he had been remiss in his duty.

Then, too, he wasn't any closer to discovering the identity of the person trying to harm the colonel than he had been when he'd first arrived. Every time he'd thought he had a likely candidate, he had changed his mind. He had been almost certain that Crawford might be the one, but he had now ruled that out. Hayward was an excellent possibility, but Gill found he was coming to like the man and didn't want to find him guilty. That left Bentley and Pearce, and neither of them seemed capable of doing such heinous things.

Worse, and perhaps the thing that had preoccupied him more than it should, was something he didn't want to admit. Miss Shelby Falcon. Gill thought about her constantly. *Hell,* he thought to himself, *I even dream about her.* And those dreams, he reflected, had nothing to do with how charming and sweet Miss Falcon was. Rather they had to do with seeing all that glorious auburn hair in his bed, spilled on a pillow. Seeing those eyes looking at him with an expression of desire, or. . . ." He shook his head, trying to control his breathing. Granted, their acquaintance had been short, but how long did it take to fall in love with someone?

Love. The word brought him up short, and he sat up straight. He tensed as he heard a noise, then made himself put thoughts of Shelby out of his mind as he heard someone walking toward him on the gravel path.

"Luke said you were here," Shelby said, rounding the corner of the stable and sitting down beside him. "I thought I should come see if you were truly all right."

"I am." He thought he sounded brusque, and changed his tone. "I'm fine, really."

She put her hand on his arm and her touch seemed to burn right through his coat. "Thank you for saving Grandfather. I know he would be dead now if you hadn't gone into the fire and rescued him. I'll never forget it."

"I didn't do it for thanks."

"I know that, but I wanted to thank you anyway." She sounded hurt, and he realized that he had been churlish. She couldn't possibly know what her nearness was doing to him.

"I understand," he said softly, trying not to look at her profile in the thready moonlight. "You're welcome. You know I would do anything I could for the colonel. I almost think of him as family."

She smiled and turned to him. "He has that effect on people. They shy away from him because he seems so irascible, but as soon as they get to know him, they love him. Once he considers you a friend or part of his family, he'll do anything in his power to help you."

"Even paying gaming debts?"

Shelby drew back, alarmed. "You? I really didn't. . . ." She checked herself.

Gill chuckled. "No, not me. I may be many things, but I'm no gamester. I was thinking of Hayward and Bentley."

Shelby sighed. "All right, I take back some of what I said. Grandfather paid off their debts for a long time, but then he finally saw that they weren't going to change as long as he helped them. He told them last year that, as of that moment, they would have to meet their own obligations." She paused. "Of course, I don't think the sums were ever as large as I understand them to be now." There was a long silence. "You're probably also wondering why he isn't financing Crawford, aren't you?"

"It had crossed my mind."

"Grandfather financed the first issue, which was expensive. Then he came to much the same conclusion as he did with Bentley and Hayward. He will help, but he is also always saying that 'God helps those who help themselves.' Besides, he needs to look after himself and Wychwood. He usually plows any profits back into the place."

"And that's the way it should be." Gill breathed in the night air that was still touched with the scent of smoke. "I know he hates to lose a fine field of hay."

Shelby leaned back against the stable wall, content to just be beside Gill. There was something special about being around him. He interrupted her reverie.

"Have you had any more proposals?" he asked. "Crawford, Hayward, and Pearce to date, isn't it?"

"Bentley. He offered for me when we were out riding, right before you came up to us."

"Are you giving any of your offers serious consideration?" There was a strange note in his voice.

Shelby glanced at him. He was looking straight ahead to the field, and the moonlight fell on his profile. A curl of dark hair fell down on his forehead, but it didn't soften the strength in his face. Just looking at him did strange things to her body—she felt strong and giddy at the same time. "No, I think not," she said to him.

"Not even Crawford," he said quietly, turning to look at her.

"No, especially not Crawford." She smiled briefly. "Crawford is in love with Rose. I went to see her tonight and told her she was a fool if she didn't patch things up with him. As for the others, Pearce is much too young to know what he wants, Bentley is much too odd for anyone to marry, and Hayward . . . well, Hayward doesn't really care for me at all either." She laughed in the moonlight. "Quite unloved is Shelby." She had meant to strike a light note, but it didn't turn out that way.

"Not quite, I would say."

She turned away to look back out at the field. "No, there's Mother and Grandfather. I'm quite content with my life as it is."

"Are you?" His voice was husky in the dark.

Shelby looked at him again. He had turned toward her and his face was partially in the moonlight, partially in shadow. She didn't know how to answer him. "I . . . I . . . ," she began, but stopped as he touched the side of her face with his fingers. He pushed a stray wisp of hair behind her ear, then ran his fingertips down the edge of her jaw. When he reached her chin, he put his finger under her chin and tipped her face up slightly.

"Gill," she whispered.

Her whisper of his name was his undoing. Gill had thought he could simply look at her and then suggest they go back inside. Her reputation would be ruined if anyone knew they were there, alone, at that time of night. Instead, she had whispered his name, and everything fled out of his mind except an overwhelming desire to know her, to touch her. He bent to kiss her, and found her lips as soft and willing as he had dreamed they would be. *Just kiss her lightly,* he said to himself, *and that's all.* He did—he made his touch featherlight and just teased her lips, but she pressed into him, and put her arms around his neck, drawing him closer. He felt a surge of desire like none he had ever known. He crushed her to him and kissed her hungrily, then pulled back a fraction so he could tease open her lips. She was as eager as he was. She brushed her fingers over his forehead, running her hands through his hair, then whispering his name again against his lips. From somewhere deep inside him, there came a warning. If he didn't stop now, he would have her down on the grass in a moment. He couldn't, wouldn't, do that to her—he cared too much.

With a groan, he pulled away from her and got unsteadily to his feet, propping himself against the stable wall with one hand. He was breathing heavily.

"Gill?" Shelby's voice was perplexed. "Did I do something wrong?"

"Wrong? Good God, no." He turned away from her and managed to walk a few steps. His body was screaming for her, for release, and he didn't dare look at her sitting there in the moonlight.

"I didn't know. . . ." She hesitated. "I don't usually. . . ."

"I know that." His breathing was still ragged, but he was beginning to get it under control. Now if only he could get his body back to normal, he could turn around and comfort her. "You don't know what you're doing to me, Shelby. I can't sit back down with you. Perhaps you'd better go back to the house."

To his dismay, instead of going back, she got up and came over to him. "Gill," she whispered, touching his back. "I'm sorry."

"Sorry?" He wheeled and looked at her. "I'm the one who should be sorry. I came within an inch of ruining your reputation right there on the grass by the stable. What kind of man would even think of doing that?" He took another deep breath. "Go back to the house. Please." He was hanging on by a thread. He closed his eyes so he wouldn't look at her. He knew that if he turned and looked into those green eyes, he would be lost, and her reputation probably would be as well.

"All right," she said in a small voice. "If that's what you want."

"It's not what I want, dammit. What I want is. . . ." He stopped himself. "You'd better go, Shelby." His breathing was more regular now. "Would you like me to walk you back to the house?"

"I'd like that very much." She looked at him in confusion, then turned away, obviously hurt. He fell into step beside her, and the only sound in the night was their footsteps on the gravel.

Suddenly Shelby stopped. "Wait!" She grabbed his arm.

"What?" He stepped warily to the side. He was holding himself together by a fragile tether.

"Listen. Do you hear that?"

Gill stood still, scarcely daring to breathe, waiting for a sound. At last it came, a soft whimpering that spoke of pain.

"What could that be?" Shelby asked. "It sounds as if something's been hurt."

"Wait here, and I'll search." Gill looked up at the moonlight making its way through the clouds. "I'd do better with a lantern."

"I'll run get one." Shelby dashed away toward the house. When she returned with Thomas and a lantern, Gill was busy walking along the edge of some bushes that edged the back garden.

"Bring the lantern over here. I can't find anything, and the sounds aren't regular," he said. "It might be a rabbit or something that's frightened. I think it's under this hedge."

Thomas held the lantern, and Gill crawled on hands and knees along the hedge. Shelby heard the sound again, and dashed to where she thought it was, falling down to her hands and knees. "Not over there, Gill. Here, I think. Try here."

She knelt as Gill crawled up to her, and their noses almost

met as they looked at each other. "Give me the lantern, Thomas," Gill said. Thomas handed it over, and Gill put it on the ground, then slowly parted the brushy hedge. "There it is," he said, "but I can't see what it could be. Here, hold back this limb."

Shelby pulled the limb back and peered under the hedge. Something was cowering against the back of the hedge, pulling away from Gill's outstretched hand. Shelby moved the lantern closer, then cried out in joy. She held the limb back with her body and plunged into the middle of the hedge. "Gill, it's Dick Turpin. He's alive!" She held out her hand to the little dog, and he managed to move his head and lick her outstretched fingers.

"Easy with him," Gill said. "He seems to be frightened as much as hurt." He thought a moment, then rose to his knees and took off his coat. "I'm going to run out of coats if I stay here much longer," he said with a grin. "Here, let's see if we can get Dick onto my coat, and then we can carry him into the house. I'm afraid to pick him up until we see how badly he's hurt."

Shelby flashed him a smile of gratitude and put the coat down beside Dick. Carefully, she and Gill moved Dick onto the coat; then they slowly pulled it and the dog from under the hedge. Gill tried not to wince as his coat caught on a broken limb and ripped. After all, he thought with resignation, it was being ruined for a good cause.

In the harsh yellow lantern light, Dick looked terrible. The little dog had lost a great deal of his fur, and was soaking wet as well. It looked to Gill as though part of his fur had been burned, and part had been torn off some other way. He couldn't see well enough in the lantern light to discover exactly what had happened. One thing was painfully obvious, though; one of the little dog's legs was hurt. There was a gash along his hip and leg, and, unless Gill missed his guess, Dick Turpin had lost a great deal of blood. Gill couldn't bring himself to tell Shelby, but it could be touch and go with Dick for a day or so. Still, the little dog had courage and heart. Somehow he had made it out of the flames and to safety under the hedge at Wychwood.

Shelby touched Dick's head, wishing he would grin at her once more. "Oh, Dick, you don't know how glad we all are to see you." Impulsively, she bent down and kissed him on his singed head.

She looked up at Gill through her tears. "Let's go tell Grandfather."

Thirteen

Gill gingerly held Dick Turpin, curled up on his coat, as he and Shelby reached the top of the stairs and turned toward his chamber. They had walked slowly from the hedge so they wouldn't jar the little dog, but Dick still trembled and whimpered as Gill carried him gently. Shelby knocked softly, and they heard something sliding away from the door. It sounded as if someone was moving a chair or dresser from in front of it. "I told Ranja to bar the door with something since the locks are useless," Gill said with a small smile.

She turned and looked at him, her eyes luminous. "I can't tell you how much it means to me that you're so concerned about Grandfather."

Before Gill could answer, Ranja opened the door silently about a foot or so, looked at Shelby and Gill, then spoke to Gill in his native language. Gill answered him, and in just a moment, there was another scraping sound, and the door opened.

Colonel Falcon was sitting in front of the small table by the bed. His elbows were on the table, and his head was propped in his hands. He looked old, beaten, and hopeless. Shelby ran to him. "Grandfather," she said, putting her hand on his arm.

"Go away, girl," he said gruffly. "Now isn't the time. Just leave me be."

She stepped back, surprised. No matter what had happened

in the family, she had never seen her grandfather like this. He looked away from her, but at her exclamation of dismay, turned his face so she could see it. He had been crying. With a surge of affection, she threw her arms around the colonel. "It's all right, Grandfather. We found him. Gill and I found Dick Turpin."

Colonel Falcon twisted around to see Gill and wiped at his cheeks. "Is he dead?" he asked gruffly. "Did he suffer?"

Gill shook his head, and placed the coat with Dick Turpin on it on the bed. The little dog reached forward to try to lick Colonel Falcon's fingers. The colonel's hand trembled as he gently touched Dick's tiny body. "That leg needs sewing up," Gill said, "and I think some salve is in order for the rest of him. We might get some scissors and do what we can to cut off the charred fur." He slipped a finger under a burned ear. "He may lose the bottom of this ear, but we can try to save it."

Colonel Falcon turned away, leaving one hand resting on Dick's front paw. His shoulders began to shake, and he tried to speak, but no words would come as he sobbed. Dick reached out again and began to lick his hand. "Dick," the colonel said in a strangled voice. Dick whimpered, and the colonel straightened up. "What are we waiting for? Shelby, go get some salve and bandages. Get a needle and thread while you're at it. Gill, are you any good at sewing up a wound? My fingers have gotten so feeble that I hesitate to do it." He pulled up his chair and sat down so that he was eye to eye with Dick Turpin. "We'll have you fixed up in just a few minutes, boy. And then I want you to get well and go bite the hell out of whoever did this."

Gill laughed aloud as he went to help Shelby gather the things they would need. They even remembered to bring a bottle of brandy for the colonel to use while Gill sewed up Dick's leg.

Very carefully Gill sponged Dick off while Shelby held him gently. Colonel Falcon was making good use of the brandy, and offering many suggestions, all of which Gill ignored. He snipped off the charred fur with scissors, being gentle beyond belief with the little dog. With a great deal of his fur gone, Dick resembled one of the rats he was famed for catching.

"I didn't realize he was so small," Shelby said, as Gill toweled Dick dry. He had washed the wound carefully, and now bent to examine it closely. "What do you think, Colonel?" he asked.

"Looks like a knife wound to me," the colonel said. "The edges are too clean for much of anything else."

"That's what I thought." Gill threaded his needle and ran the thread through a piece of wax so it would sew better.

"A knife wound? But who would do that to Dick?" Shelby was incredulous.

"The same sort of person who would try to cause other accidents or set a fire," Gill said.

Shelby frowned. "Yes, but this fire was accidental. Pearce and Bentley have already apologized for being careless with their rockets." She had to stop and hold Dick as Gill began to sew, taking his time and being as gentle as possible. When Gill was finished, he looked at the colonel. "Where do you want us to put him?"

"Just you leave him right there. I'll sit in this chair and watch him. He's comfortable, and he can just stay there."

Gill took a last look at his ruined coat, then turned to Shelby. "Thank you for your assistance, Miss Falcon. I believe I'll go to bed now. Colonel, if you need anything, or if Dick Turpin gets worse, send Ranja for me." With a faint smile, he went out the door.

"Fine boy, that," Colonel Falcon said. He looked up at Shelby. "It's past midnight and you need to get to bed yourself, girl. I'll see you in the morning." He pulled the small table and candle over next to him, propped up his feet, and settled back to watch Dick Turpin.

Shelby went on to her room, pausing at the door to look

down the hall to her grandfather's room where Gill was sleeping. Without thinking, she touched her lips where Gill had kissed her. It seemed both an instant ago and forever ago. He had feelings for her—she had sensed that. For a moment, she thought about going in to see him, but realized she couldn't do that. As tired and sore as he probably was, most likely he was already in bed. She went on into her room.

Dovey was there, sound asleep in the chair. Shelby woke her gently and, with the minimum of preparation, went to bed. As soon as the room was quiet, she tried to rest, but found she was too overwrought to go to sleep. All she could think of was the way she had felt when Gill was kissing her. This, she decided, was what love was really like. Never in her wildest dreams could she imagine Crawford making her feel that way, making her want to be a part of him. Just reliving the moment in her mind made her quiver. Her lips almost ached for Gill to kiss them again. She could even recall the exact smell of him—the touch of smoke that still clung to him, the sweat, and the indefinable scent that was his alone.

She wondered if he cared for her in the same way that she cared for him. She could imagine spending every day of her life with him, every day a delight. Was that what he felt, or did he simply feel lust? She had listened to enough women's talk to know that most women felt men were motivated by lust rather than love. She couldn't believe it of Gill. He had to care about her. She couldn't imagine anyone sharing a kiss like theirs without love.

Shelby tossed and turned, but couldn't sleep. One minute she believed Gill loved her, the next she didn't. She went over every conversation they had had, mentally relived every look, but she still couldn't fathom his feelings. She heard the big clock in the hall chime four before she slept.

It was late the next morning before she rose, and when she came out of her room, Bentley was waiting at the top of the landing. "I thought you might like to go for a ride this morning," he said, glancing at the clock. "Even if it is almost noon. A ride would be just the thing."

Shelby shook her head. "I don't believe I'm quite up to it today, Bentley. I couldn't get to sleep, and woke up with a headache. Right now, I'm just going out for a breath of fresh air before I get something to eat."

"I'll go with you," Bentley said, leaping to his feet. "I understand that Colonel Falcon's solicitor is coming today," he said, stopping on the bottom step to look at Shelby. "Is that true?"

"I really don't know. I've given it no thought at all." She smiled at Luke as he opened the door. Outside, the day was overcast, but warm. Shelby took a deep breath and rubbed her temples to ease the ache before going down the stairs and into the side garden, Bentley right behind her.

They strolled in silence for a few minutes. Then Bentley pulled a flower from its stem and began shredding the petals. "Have you had time to consider my offer?" he asked, not looking at her, but concentrating on the ruined petals.

Shelby walked to the small garden bench that faced the French doors to the drawing room. "Let's sit a moment, Bentley." As soon as they were seated, she turned to him. "I'm honored that you thought of me, but I simply don't feel that I can accept."

"Why not?" Bentley's mouth set in a straight line.

"For several reasons, Bentley. Chief among them is the fact that, while we hold each other in esteem, there is no real regard. It simply wouldn't be fair to either of us if we married."

Bentley looked at her and tossed down the ruined flower. "We could learn. I understand that most of the married folk in the *ton* don't even like each other, much less hold each other in real regard. I think we would rub along most excellently."

Shelby shook her head. "No, Bentley. It just isn't possible."

He frowned and stared down at his dusty shoes. "It's Crawford, isn't it? You're planning to marry him."

"No, I'm not. I'm not planning to marry anyone." Shelby stood up and touched her head. "Bentley, I have the most terrible headache. I need to go back inside and get some coffee. I do hope you excuse me."

Instead, Bentley stood and walked back to the house with her. "I think it must be Crawford," he said. "The reason you say you're not planning to marry anyone is that you're waiting to see what Crawford and Rose do now that they're thrown together." He looked at Shelby. "You'd be better off with me rather than Crawford, Shelby. That's a fact."

Shelby paused at the door. "No, Bentley. There's no point in asking me further. The answer is no. I simply cannot marry you." She went inside. Bentley stuck his head into the hall and shouted at her as she went up the stairs.

"You're making a mistake, Shelby. Don't say I didn't tell you. Tell me when you reconsider."

Gill was just coming out of Colonel Falcon's room. He looked at her quizzically, but said nothing. Shelby started to tell him about the episode, but dismissed the thought. Instead, she looked at him. He looked no better than she felt. "Are you all right today?" she asked.

His laugh was short. "If you knew how I really felt, you wouldn't ask that question." He stepped out onto the landing where he could see her better. "Perhaps I should ask you the same thing." He grinned.

"I had a wretched night, and a worse headache today. I thought I'd go check on Dick Turpin and then lie down and try to overcome this dreadful ache."

He looked at her slowly, as though savoring her features. "I'm sorry you're not well. Let's go see Dick Turpin together, shall we? Then I'll make sure Dovey comes to you and brings something to help your pain." He held his arm out for her, and within moments they knocked on the door to the blue room.

Colonel Falcon was still sitting by the bed, and Dick Turpin was still resting on Gill's coat. The colonel turned when Gill and Shelby entered. "He's holding on and seems to be improving," the colonel said. "If it can be done, Dick Turpin will do it."

"I know he will, Grandfather." Shelby came closer to Dick. The little dog lifted his head and tried to grin at her, but managed only a sickly grimace. "The spark is still there, Grandfather," she said.

Gill moved to the side of the bed and looked at Dick's burns. Then he examined the wound on the dog's leg. "He's not bleeding. Has he been drinking any water?" He frowned at the colonel. "I don't think he should have brandy or whiskey. Just water."

"I know, and he hasn't had any. Whiskey isn't good for him, even though he loves it." The colonel sighed. "I did offer him a little nip of brandy, but he didn't want it. I've always heard that dogs know what's best for them when they're sick." He looked up at Shelby and winked. "Now don't you tell me you wish humans were that way. I know that's what you're thinking."

"I'd never say it." Shelby smiled back at him and gave him a quick kiss on the forehead. Then she and Gill left. Out in the hall, Shelby turned to Gill before she went into her room. "Do you think Dick will make it?" she asked.

"Dick Turpin? I certainly do. He's a tough little dog." He smiled down at her, a strange expression on his face. "Now as for you . . . I believe you're going in to your room, and I'm going to send Dovey up with something to ease your headache." He opened the door and stood back until she went inside. "Perhaps we can talk later," he said seriously. "I think we may need to discuss some things."

"What things?" Shelby whispered, but Gill had already shut the door.

Gill went outside into the day, feeling about as bad as he had ever felt. Every muscle in his body ached from the strain of yesterday. Worse, his mind and emotions were so overwrought from his encounter with Shelby that he couldn't seem to think straight. He decided to go for a ride; that always cleared his mind, even if his body protested that he couldn't do anything except sit quietly in a chair.

He was almost ready to mount when Crawford came into the stables. "I thought you might be here, Gill," he said. "I wanted to talk to you about yesterday."

"What about it?" Gill kept his voice carefully even.

Crawford hesitated a moment. "I may as well be blunt. I was just wondering if you thought the fire was an accident or if it was set."

Gill turned and looked at him. "You don't mince words, do you?"

"No. That's an asset in the newspaper business, but I'm not so sure how it flies with people." He paused. "What do you think? I respect your opinion, so I'm asking you. Also, you were in the thick of it."

"Pearce said it was an accident. He said a rocket set the hay on fire." He paused. "It was dry. Just a spark could have ignited it."

"Yes, but did it?" Crawford grimaced and hit the wall with his fist.

"I don't know." Gill shook his head. "At first I thought the fire was deliberate, but Pearce was so convincing that I began to doubt myself." He glanced at his horse and moved him back into a stall. "Miss Falcon and I found Dick Turpin last night. It appears that someone tried to slash at him with a knife. His upper leg and hip were cut."

"Pearce wouldn't do that."

Gill regarded Crawford. "I don't think he would either. Also, I don't think Pearce would deliberately set a fire."

Crawford ran his fingers through his blond hair, rumpling it. "Pearce showed me where he fired the rocket. I followed the arc and the rocket should have landed in the pond. I know rockets are erratic, but the fire seems to have started well to the right."

Gill tried to keep his expression blank. "I hadn't checked that, Crawford. I was taking Pearce's word for it that the fire was accidental. He was really down in his cups about it last night." He paused. "So you think Pearce could have set the blaze?" His tone was perfectly bland.

"No, I agree with you." Crawford leaned against the wall. "I don't want you to think I'm defending my brother, but setting fires just isn't like Pearce."

"I agree completely."

Crawford looked at him briefly. "Thank you for that, Gill. You've eased my mind considerably." He paused.

"But that leaves Bentley." Gill's tone was flat. "If the fire was set, why would he do such a thing?"

Crawford looked at him. "That's what I can't figure out. There's no reason for him to try to set the field on fire. Do you know of anything? I know he's dipped at the tables, but from everything I've heard, Hayward is standing good for his debts. That's why Hayward is up the River Tick. He could handle his own debts, but Bentley's are just too much." He sighed. "Besides, what would it signify for Bentley to burn the field? That certainly wouldn't do him any good unless he hoped to burn Wychwood.

"And that's no gain for anyone." Gill frowned. "I don't know the answer. I'm trying to think through things." Gill led his horse back out of the stall, turned to mount, and swung himself up into the saddle. Every muscle protested. "I'd appreciate it if you would try to think about these questions and share your answers with me."

Crawford smiled up at him. "All right, but don't count on me for answers. I'm still trying to discover the questions."

"Aren't we all?"

When Gill returned to Wychwood, he still had no answers, but he still ached in places he didn't even know could ache. He'd started across the entry when Colonel Falcon called out to him from the drawing room. "Gill, come in here." The colonel sounded just as though he were still in the army and Gill was a lowly private.

Gill felt like saluting when he entered the drawing room, but there was a strange man sitting there. "This is Mr. Wharton, my solicitor," Colonel Falcon explained. "I'd like you to witness what I'm telling him."

"I don't think that's necessary," Mr. Wharton said hastily. "I've written down all your instructions, and it won't be necessary to witness anything until you sign your will. That will have to be witnessed, of course."

"I know." Colonel Falcon leaned back in his chair and drained a glass of whiskey. "The way accidents have been happening around here, I want everyone to know exactly what my intentions are." He set down his glass. "First, Shelby gets the Jewels of Ali and Wychwood, along with any moneys over and above the bequests I've listed. Also, Shelby has to provide a good home for Dick Turpin as long as he lives. Third, I want her married within four years."

At the last statement, Gill stared at the colonel. "Colonel Falcon," he began, but the colonel held up a hand to stop him. "I want this place to be full of children. That's the way it should be. Shelby needs to get married, and the sooner the better." He paused. "Maybe this will light a fire under someone."

"What will happen if she doesn't marry?" Mr. Wharton asked.

"Then it all goes to Dick Turpin if he's still alive. Dick is to leave it to Shelby." Colonel Falcon drew his singed eyebrows together. "If Dick isn't still alive, then I'll think of something." He glared at Mr. Wharton. "Just make out the will and leave a blank space there for me to write something in when you bring the dratted thing back. I'll have all the provisions clear in my mind by then." He hesitated. "No matter what, Shelby gets everything."

Gill let out his breath. "So, you want her to marry, but there's no penalty if she doesn't?"

Colonel Falcon nodded. "I can't really force her, can I? Still, I don't want her to know that. Let her think she's got to marry within four years."

Mr. Wharton shook his head as he prepared to leave. "Odd," he murmured so Gill could hear. "Very, very odd." He looked at Colonel Falcon. "I'll have the will prepared and return with it in three days. Will you be here to sign it?"

"I sincerely hope so," said the colonel, forcing himself out of the chair. He made himself stand ramrod straight. "I sincerely hope so."

Gill watched Mr. Wharton leave, fervently hoping so as well.

Upstairs in her chamber, Shelby awoke as the front door shut. Dovey was sitting beside her bed, waiting. "Who came in?" Shelby murmured, still half-asleep.

"That's just some man who came to see the colonel," Dovey said, dipping a fresh cloth in lavender water, wringing it out, and putting it on Shelby's forehead. "He's been here a while, but he's leaving." She patted the cloth gently. "Now, mum, this should make you feel much better."

"Thank you, Dovey." Shelby smiled at the maid and closed her eyes again for a moment while she assessed her body. The pain in her head was gone, and she felt reasonably rested. She glanced out the window. It appeared to be late afternoon. She sat up slowly. "I think I feel well enough to go down for supper, Dovey. Send for a bath, and lay out a dress for me."

"Oh, I was so hoping you'd say that! I've been working on this one." Dovey picked up a green dress from the foot of the bed.

"Not that," Shelby said. "I've always hated that dress, and don't even know why I brought it with me. I was just throwing things in my trunk."

Dovey's face fell. "But I've been working on it. You might like it now." She held the dress up for Shelby to see. Shelby couldn't see much difference, but acquiesced. "All right, Dovey, you know best. I'll wear it tonight if you think it's right."

When she put on the dress, it did look wonderful. Dovey had just taken a tuck here and a nip there, added some lace at the neckline, and put a green velvet ribbon just under the lace. The dress fit her body like a silk glove, and the trim set off Shelby's skin. The cloth was a vivid emerald, and it brought out the green in Shelby's eyes.

"You've worked magic again, Dovey," Shelby said as she started down for supper. Dovey's expression was all the thanks she needed.

Pearce was alone in the drawing room when Shelby walked in. He was looking out the window pensively. "Crawford and Rose are taking a turn around the garden," he said, turning when Shelby came into the room. "What do you suppose they're discussing?"

"The weather probably." Shelby sat down on the sofa. "How are you today, Pearce?"

"I'm still feeling guilty, but you don't know how glad I am that you found Dick Turpin," he said, sitting down next to her. He gave her an admiring look. "That's a beautiful dress, Shelby. You look quite fetching in it."

She smiled back and thanked him. "I think Dick is going to be fine, and, as for the fire, you don't need to feel guilty, Pearce. Everyone understands that rockets are dangerous."

"I just don't see how it could have happened. I could have sworn the thing landed right at the pond." He sighed and ran his fingers through his hair. "Uh, Shelby, there was something I wanted to discuss with you." He squirmed. "If you recall, the other night, I . . . I . . ." He stopped, his face red.

"You offered for me on the spur of the moment," she said gently. "I certainly don't hold you to that, Pearce."

She could almost hear his sigh of relief. "Still, if you want to, I'd be glad to marry you," he said. "Crawford says that a man should always honor what he says."

"I'm glad you feel that way, but I do feel we shouldn't suit. We aren't at all alike."

"Even for cousins," he said, musing. "I've noticed that. You don't like rockets at all." He smiled broadly at her. "We can still be good friends though, can't we, Shelby?"

"Of course, Pearce."

"Then, since we are cousins and good friends, do you think when you get the jewels and whatever, you could loan me some money to build a rocket factory? I could pay you back every cent, I'm sure."

Shelby was mercifully prevented from answering him by the entrance of Hayward and Bentley. Hayward walked in and took a deep breath. "No sneezing since Dick Turpin hasn't been running around. It's wonderful."

"The best of all possible worlds," Pearce said with a grin.

After supper that evening, Colonel Falcon left them and went upstairs to sit with Dick Turpin. Hayward, Bentley, Pearce, and Countess Rimildi played cards for a penny a point. Shelby noticed that, as terrible a card player as her mother was, she had already accumulated a tidy pile of pennies. Crawford and Rose sat and talked, while Gill and Shelby went off to the other side of the drawing room to sit. "I think Crawford and Rose may be sorting things out," Shelby said.

"Does that bother you?"

She looked at him, surprised. "No. I don't care for Crawford in that sense. He's more like a brother to me." She turned and smiled at the two across the room. "I wish him well. If Rose is the one he wants, then I hope it works for him." She lowered her voice. "I truly don't think she is the right sort of wife for him, but that, of course, signifies nothing to Crawford."

"Men seldom think along those lines—whether a woman is right or wrong, I mean. Most men are influenced by, shall we say, other considerations." He chuckled. "I'm glad we're sitting here talking, Miss Falcon. I do recall that we agreed to appear to have a *tendre* for one another. We've been somewhat remiss in displaying that. In public, at any rate." There was laughter in his voice.

"We've hardly had time." Shelby didn't look at him. If last night's kiss hadn't shown him her real feelings, then nothing would.

He leaned toward her, an impish smile on his lips. She was struck by his eyes in the candlelight—they were a warm brown, almost a soft caramel color, and they promised many things. "Perhaps I could look enthralled while you tell me what's happened in your life today."

"It might take some acting on your part. My life has hardly been enthralling today. I've stayed in bed most of the day, considering that you must have bribed Dovey to bring me something to make me sleep."

"Dovey isn't bribable. I've tried."

"Oh, you did?" She smiled at him. "We may have to discuss that, Mr. Gill."

He laughed again. "I still want to hear about your day. I'm sure something has happened to you."

"Absolutely nothing."

"What? No proposals. You've had how many so far? Four? One from each of your cousins."

She glanced over at the three playing cards. "Yes. I've turned all of them down." She giggled. "Bentley thinks I won't marry him because I care for Crawford. Pearce really doesn't care, but he wants to know if I will loan him money to build a rocket factory." She fanned herself in the close, warm room.

"Would you like me to open a window for you?"

Shelby shook her head. "Mother doesn't like fresh air. She thinks it gives her aches in her joints." She looked at him and grinned. "This heat is nothing. I suffered all the way across Italy. I could always locate our hotel rooms no matter where we stayed. They were the only ones that were closed and shuttered."

Gill returned her smile. "Then would you like to step outside into the garden for a breath of air?" He lowered his voice. "I promise to behave."

Shelby unlocked the French doors and they went out. The night was warm, but there was a breeze that fluttered tendrils of her hair. The breeze also carried with it the heady scent of the garden flowers; Shelby particularly noted the mignonette, heliotrope, and lavender. Gill stood behind her, and she could smell his scent mixed with that of the flowers. It was intoxicating. She stepped out into the garden path and began walking slowly. The moon turned the garden into silver, dotted with purple flowers.

"Lovely, isn't it?" Gill said, falling into step beside her.

Shelby looked at the garden and back at the house. "Yes. It's difficult for me to believe that anything evil could be here." She paused and looked up at him, wanting him to kiss her again, but not daring to let him know. He looked away from her, and she moved, going on down the path until she was standing in the shadow of a large bush that grew by the side of the house.

He stood so that Shelby was between him and the bush. "Perhaps we should return. I'm having a great deal of difficulty keeping my promise, Miss Falcon," he said, his voice low and husky.

She looked up at him, his face in shadow, his scent filling her. "As you said a moment ago, perhaps we need to practice."

"I do believe you're flirting with me, Miss Falcon." He touched the side of her ear, and ran his fingers down her jaw. "My problem is that this is no game. You do strange things to me, Miss Falcon." He jerked back, tense, and listened. Only then did Shelby hear the crunch of the gravel on the garden path. The footsteps stopped, only to be replaced by other noises. To Shelby's horror, these noises suggested two people engaged in a very passionate kiss.

"Will you marry me?" It was Crawford's voice, husky with emotion. "Please. I can't live without you, Rose. I thought I could survive, but I can't. Please, Rose."

"Yes, yes," Rose answered faintly.

The sound of their kissing began again. Shelby stood on tiptoe and whispered to Gill. "What shall we do? We've got to leave before they discover we've heard."

"Walk only on the grass," Gill whispered back. "Stay close to the house. We'll go around the corner."

They managed to stay near the house for several feet until they were in sight of the front door. Then Shelby tripped over something. There was a terrible squall and squeal as something ran right under her feet and she went crashing down.

"Dick!" Colonel Falcon yelled, hobbling up to Shelby and rolling her over. "Where are you, Dick?"

"I have him," Gill said, handing Dick Turpin to the colonel. "I think he's fine." He bent to help Shelby up. She had landed right in a bush and was scratched and bruised. Her hair had all tumbled down. One shoulder of her emerald green gown had slipped, exposing the top swell of one breast. Gill thought he had never seen anything more alluring, and he had to clench his fists at his sides to keep from touching her.

"Had to bring Dick out for his necessaries," the colonel explained as Gill helped Shelby inside. "What were you two doing out there?"

"Unfortunately, absolutely nothing," Gill said with a sigh.

Fourteen

Shelby was roused the next morning by Dovey shaking her. "Wake up, mum, wake up!"

Shelby groggily sat up in bed. "What is it, Dovey? Has something happened?"

"Oh, has it just, mum. Everything is all at sixes and sevens, and Colonel Falcon is about to have apoplexy. I thought you'd better get dressed and come down as soon as you could."

Shelby was wide-awake now. "I'll be glad to, Dovey, but what happened?"

"I've brought up some coffee and muffins for you, mum. No one should have to face that with no breakfast. I've laid out your clothes." She jerked a tray off the table and set it in front of Shelby. "Oh, I forgot the water." She grabbed the water pitcher from the washstand and ran out the door with it.

"What happened?" Shelby asked the closed door.

She ate her muffins and drank two cups of coffee before Dovey returned. Dovey had forgotten to bring the water pitcher back. "You need to get down there, mum. The colonel is so red in the face that I think he's going to explode."

"Dovey, stop. Just stop and take a deep breath." She paused while Dovey gulped air. "Good. Now what happened?"

Dovey looked at Shelby, her eyes wide. "Why, mum, someone came inside last night and took all the jewels. There's nothing left at all except an empty case!"

Shelby almost choked on her last sip of coffee. She tossed the covers back and almost jumped into the dress Dovey held for her. Dovey put up her hair in record time, and Shelby sped down the stairs to the drawing room.

Dovey had been right. Colonel Falcon did look as if he were going to explode. His face was red and he was shouting. Gill was trying to calm him, but everyone else was just standing back. Hayward was examining the French doors, while Bentley and Pearce were shrinking against the far wall. Crawford was standing beside the fireplace. In the middle of the floor was the paneled oak case, opened. Both the oak panels and the metal panels had been opened in the usual way, so someone must have had a key. The heavy glass had been broken. There was a small rug lying next to the shattered case. Inside the case was nothing at all, not even the velvet on which the jewels had rested.

Gill managed to get a glass of brandy into the colonel's hand. "Drink this," he ordered. "There's nothing to be gained by this. We've got to keep cool heads and plan some strategy."

Colonel Falcon tossed down the brandy. "Good thought, boy. That's what I always said to Biddle when we were on the eve of battle." He took a deep breath. "What have we discovered?" He sat down in his chair, breathing heavily. Shelby came and pulled up a chair beside him. "Your inheritance, girl," he said to her. "It's gone."

Shelby nodded and looked up at Gill. "To repeat Grandfather's question, what have you discovered?"

Gill looked around. "Anything wrong with the French doors, Hayward?"

Hayward shook his head. "Nothing. Not a scratch on them. If our culprit came in this way, he either had a key or they were unlocked."

Shelby had a sinking feeling. "I unlocked them last night when we stepped out for a breath of air, and didn't lock them again. I didn't tell Luke or Thomas to lock them either. I forgot since I didn't come back in that way."

"One of them should have checked," Colonel Falcon said. "That's Thomas's job."

"Yes, but you took Thomas up to the blue room to sit with you last night. He wasn't down here to check," Gill said. "So our culprit could have found the doors unlocked, or"—he paused—"could have been inside all along." He looked at Crawford. "Anything unusual there?"

"No, not that I see. I can't figure out why we didn't hear the crash when the glass was broken. It must have been fairly loud. That glass is thick."

Gill bent and picked up the small, rolled-up rug and felt inside it. He drew out the poker. "I imagine the rug muffled the sound." He looked at the rug and pulled bits of glass from it. "It seems that everything needed was at hand"—he ran his fingers over the metal and oak panels—"including a key to these. That would move this out of the realm of simple burglary." He frowned. "Where could our culprit have gotten a key?"

"From my bedroom." Colonel Falcon said slowly. "I always kept a spare key in the drawer in my bedroom. That's what the intruder was after the other night."

"Then our burglar is either someone in the house or working with someone in the house," Crawford said, looking from one cousin to the other until he included them all.

"Someone in here?" Colonel Falcon looked slowly around the room, his eyes resting on each person in turn. "I don't want the magistrate notified just yet. I want to establish that the thief isn't one of my own family."

Biddle came in, carrying Dick Turpin, and put the dog down on the floor. Dick stopped in front of Hayward and grinned. Hayward sneezed and Dick looked satisfied. He hopped on over to Shelby and whimpered to get up in her lap. She bent and picked him up. "It's amazing. I thought he was going to die, but he's well on the way to getting better, isn't he?" she said to the colonel.

"Can't kill that demmed dog," the colonel said with a touch of pride in his voice. "Now, as for the rest of you, I want you to tell me one by one where you were last night."

The question was futile. Everyone swore he had been in bed all night sound asleep. No one had heard a single thing. Colonel Falcon sent Luke and Thomas up to search the men's rooms; Mrs. McKilley and Dovey were dispatched to search the women's rooms. Nothing was found, but Countess Rimildi did come down the stairs, screeching.

"How dare you?" she demanded, sailing into the drawing room.

"Put it in a box, Daisy," Colonel Falcon said. "This is no time for hysterics."

The countess stopped and looked in horror at the shattered glass and empty case. "They're gone, Mother," Shelby said quietly.

"Your inheritance! Your dowry!" She clutched at her heart and fell to the floor. "Oh, Shelby, I could just die!"

"Not today, Daisy," Colonel Falcon growled. "We don't have time."

Shelby put Dick down on the floor and went to her mother. After looking at her, Shelby decided this was simply another of her mother's spells of the vapors. "You must stay with me, Shelby," the countess moaned as Luke and Thomas carried her out of the room. Shelby debated with herself for a moment, then decided to stay with her grandfather. She sent Dovey to her mother with instructions to come get her if it was necessary. "But only if it's *absolutely* necessary," she cautioned. "You know how Mama is when she's having one of her spells."

"Yes, mum." Dovey's eyes were wide with excitement as she dashed upstairs.

Shelby sat down beside the colonel, and Dick came over to sit beside her. Bentley wandered over and pulled up a chair next to her. Dick began whimpering; then he crawled under Shelby's feet. "Dick, whatever are you doing?" she asked as Dick peered out, showing only his nose and eyes. Shelby reached down and picked him up carefully. He curled up on her lap into a little ball, trembling.

"All this is too much for him," Shelby said, smoothing him gently.

"He's probably acting, hoping he'll get your sympathy. He's enough like the colonel to do that." Bentley put out a finger to scratch Dick between the eyes. Dick snarled at him and curled up tighter against Shelby's arm. "He's as irascible as the colonel, too," Bentley said, quickly moving his hand.

Gill and Crawford came in through the French doors. They had been checking the soft dirt in the garden, hoping to find a footprint. "One of the doors was open when I came down," Colonel Falcon said. "Did you see any sign of entry outside?"

Gill shook his head. "No. There's stone right outside the door, and then gravel on the path. I don't think we'll find any trace unless our thief dropped something." He looked at the colonel. "Do you want to call in a magistrate?" He paused. "Or send to London for a Runner?"

"No magistrate just yet. As for a Runner, let me think on it." Colonel Falcon stood and ran his fingers over the bare wood where the Jewels of Ali had rested on a bed of velvet. "It's the loss of the jewels, of course," he said slowly, "but it's also the thought that someone close to me would do this." He looked around at each of them in turn. "That's what breaks my heart."

There was silence as he left the room. "Do you really think it's one of us?" Pearce asked, looking around with wide eyes.

"Who else?" Hayward said, sitting down and running his fingers through his hair. "It had to be someone in the house who knew that key was kept in the colonel's bedroom." He looked around. "How could someone know that?"

"Everybody here knew the colonel had several keys. I think

he once left one with Luke for some reason. All anyone had to do was go into the colonel's room and get it," Bentley said. "Easy enough."

"Yes," Shelby said, still smoothing Dick Turpin's remaining fur, "if you remember, Hayward, all the rooms on the second floor use the same key. Getting into Grandfather's room would be easy enough for any of us to do."

"And," Pearce added, "we're probably the only ones who would *know* that the same key opened all the doors on that floor."

"And," said Bentley with a smile, "the only ones who had a key that would open every door there."

Hayward looked around slowly at each of them. "I don't know how the rest of you feel, but I want the thief found. I don't think we can go through life without suspecting each other always, and I don't want that. I vote that we convince the colonel to send for a Runner."

"I also vote that way," Crawford said. "And I suggest that none of us leave Wychwood until the thief has been found."

"That won't work, Crawford," Bentley said. "What if he isn't found?"

There was silence in the room. Then Hayward spoke. "In that case, I suppose we'll all spend the rest of our lives wondering just who did this—and being afraid to ask each other into our houses."

Colonel Falcon sent for Dr. Fish during the afternoon, and, on receiving word that his health was improving and his burns were healing nicely, came down and announced that he was going to London first thing in the morning. He was, he told them, going to confer with Bow Street and make a decision about hiring a Runner. He would be back in three days.

Shelby went to see him. "Grandfather, I don't want you to go to London. I don't think you're well enough."

"Nonsense, Dr. Fish said I would do fine." He looked at Dick Turpin nestled on Gill's coat. "I don't want to take Dick with me, though, Shelby. Will you watch him while I'm gone? He likes you better than anyone else here except me."

"You know I'll take care of him." She sat and watched as Biddle packed. As soon as Biddle left the room to get some more things, she turned to her grandfather. "Grandfather, you know someone's tried to harm you, and that's really why I don't want you to go to London. Anything could happen to you there. At least here Gill, Luke, Thomas, and Ranja can guard you."

"I think I'm in more danger in this house than in London," he said with a ghost of a smile. "At any rate, Gill has already discussed this with me. I'm taking Thomas and Ranja with me. Gill has also arranged quarters for me with some army friends of his, so I'll be well guarded."

"I still don't like it," Shelby said.

Colonel Falcon shook his head. "I don't either, girl, but it has to be done. I'm more worried about Dick Turpin than I am me. You take good care of him."

Colonel Falcon left early the next morning. "So much for his being on his deathbed," Countess Rimildi said with feeling. "Now he's gone to London while we're here worrying about being murdered in our beds!" She put a hand to her head. "Do loan me Dovey for today, Shelby. She sat right there and put cool cloths on my head yesterday. I do believe I would have died if she hadn't been there!"

"By all means, do ask her to sit with you, Mother. If you wish, she might also read you a novel. She told me that she could read." Shelby stood and edged toward the door. She had spotted Gill walking across the front toward the side garden.

As soon as the countess was safely on her way to her room, Shelby sped to the drawing room and went out the French doors. Gill was on the path, kneeling down, looking at it closely.

"I keep thinking that I'll see something if I look again," he said, standing, "but there's nothing. I'm beginning to think the fact that the doors were unlocked was just a coincidence."

"That would mean that the thief stayed in the house? That the thief is definitely one of us who just went downstairs, took the jewels, and then went back to bed?"

Gill sat down on the garden bench and looked at the French doors. "I can't think of any other alternative."

Shelby sat beside him. "Do you think Grandfather will be all right in London?"

He smiled down at her. "Actually, I encouraged him to go. He'll be well guarded, and I think he needs to get away from here for a day or two. He's accustomed to action, and this will give him something to do."

"I hadn't considered that." Shelby jumped up. "Dick Turpin! I forgot about him this morning. I'd better go up and check."

"Bring him out here, and we'll go for a short walk." He grinned at her, a touch of the devil on his lips. "After all, we are working on developing a *tendre* for each other."

Shelby collected her bonnet and Dick Turpin and fairly flew down the stairs. Gill was waiting for her on the bench. He was dressed all in black again, and his cravat was endearingly crooked. She longed to reach up and straighten it, but managed to restrain herself.

They walked across the garden and toward the side field, then stopped on a knoll and looked back toward the fire-blackened back field. Gill led Shelby to the shade of a tree, and they sat while Dick Turpin wandered around in the grass, wriggling under a bush or two, sniffing.

"Do you think he's after a rabbit?" Gill asked, laughing.

"Dick could have found anything. I'd better go get him. I don't want him digging until his back leg heals completely. He'll have himself all dirty." She started to get up, but Gill stopped her.

"I'll get him for you." He walked over to the bush where Dick was scratching and picked him up. Dick kept looking back at the bush, but began grinning when Shelby held out her hands to take him.

"I can't believe he's doing so well," Shelby said.

"He's as tough as the colonel," Gill said with a laugh. He looked at her. "Why don't you take off your bonnet here in the shade? I can't see anything except brim."

She laughed and untied the bonnet ribbons. He reached over and helped her remove it; then he hung it over a limb and tied the ribbons. "Now it won't blow away." He looked back at her, a strange half-smile on his lips. Shelby found herself looking at those lips, noticing how chiseled they were, how they turned up slightly at the corners. She tried to keep herself from remembering how they felt pressed against hers. She looked down at the ground and plucked a piece of grass. "Are you worried about going to the Peninsula?" she asked, groping for a topic.

"Yes and no." He paused. "I've never before worried about going to fight, whether in India or Java or, now, the Peninsula. This time, I find I don't want to go. I don't worry about the actual fighting, I just . . ." He let his words trail off.

Shelby looked at him. "Are you worried about your uncle now that your cousin is dying?" She caught herself. "I'm sorry. That was stated baldly, and furthermore, I shouldn't have asked."

"It's quite all right." He hesitated, as though searching for the right words. "Yes, in one way, I'm worried about Uncle Bates. Charles is his only child, but they've been semi-estranged for several years. I hope they make things up before the end." He paused. "Charles is a difficult person, and Uncle Bates has never known how to reach him."

"For his sake, I hope they reconcile." Shelby patted the ground beside her, and Dick Turpin came running up. "What will your uncle do if Charles does die?"

"He'll go on, I'm sure, in much the same way he has for years." He reached down and began to scratch Dick absently on the head. "He's a good man. He has difficulty being close to people, but he's a good man."

"I gather. You said Charles was his only child. Will there be a problem with inheritance?"

Gill took a deep breath. "I'm next in line for both the estate and the title." He gave her a small smile. "I imagine that Uncle Bates will hope I resign from the army and come home. If anything happens to me, there's no one left except a very distant cousin in America."

Shelby's eyes widened. "There's an estate and a title? I had no idea."

Gill nodded. "Hanbury House, seat of Viscount Souter."

"I've been there," Shelby said, "although the Viscount was away at the time. Mama and I stopped near Oxford to visit some friends, and went over there because the Viscount had sent me a present. I wanted to thank him."

"A present?"

Shelby nodded. "It seems that my father had given him a journal of botanical drawings and notes, and the Viscount thought I should have it." She smiled. "It was a wonderful present and a most considerate thought."

Gill smiled back. "That sounds like Uncle Bates. That's what I mean about him being a good man." He hesitated a moment. "What did you think of Hanbury House?"

"It was quite beautiful." She didn't look at Gill. As the heir to Hanbury House, he would be expected to marry well and produce a future viscount. The granddaughter of a mere colonel certainly wouldn't be in his plans. She looked down as Dick Turpin tried wriggling from her lap. She caught him again and turned to Gill. "I believe Dick is getting tired. Shall we go back to the house?"

Gill looked at her strangely and untied her bonnet ribbons from the limb. Rather than handing her bonnet to her, however, he held it while he helped her to her feet. She was still holding on to Dick Turpin. He was a buffer between her and Gill.

"Allow me, Miss Falcon," Gill said, his voice husky. He carefully placed the bonnet on her head, then brushed some tendrils of her hair back inside the brim. He tied the ribbons under her chin, very slowly and deliberately, letting his fingers trail along the ends of the ribbons when he finished. Then he looked into her eyes and, for a wild moment, Shelby thought he was going to kiss her, but instead, he looked away. "Shall we go, Miss Falcon?" he said formally.

They had barely reached the door when Rose came flying out to meet them. "Where have you been!" she cried, wringing her hands together. "I've looked everywhere for you!"

"We were out walking," Shelby said. "Rose, whatever is the matter with you?"

"It's Crawford." She tried to go on, but she burst into tears.

"Let's get her inside," Gill said, taking Rose's shoulders and guiding her to the front steps.

Inside, Shelby put Dick down on the floor as she and Gill half-carried Rose into the drawing room. Gill helped her into a chair while Shelby got a glass of brandy. "Here," Gill said, taking the brandy and holding it to Rose's lips, "sip this."

Rose spluttered as the brandy went down, then wiped her eyes with the back of her hand. "He's been shot!" she cried, grabbing on to Gill's coat. "And they won't let me into the room to see how he is! He may be dead for all I know." She put her hands over her face and began shaking.

"What happened?" Gill asked.

Rose shook her head. "I don't know for sure. He went out riding, and came back just hanging on to his horse. He'd been shot, and there was blood all over. The doctor is up there now."

"I'll go see what's happening," Gill said. "I'll come right back down and tell you." He turned to Shelby. "Will you stay here with her?"

Shelby sat down beside Rose and put her arms around Rose's shoulders. "Oh, I love him, Shelby, I love him so,"

Rose sobbed. "I've been such a fool. Think of all the happiness we've missed."

"It's all right, Rose. You and Crawford can get married and you'll be happy forever."

Rose looked at her, tears in her eyes. "How did you know? We were going to keep it a secret until Crawford could get financing for his next issue."

"I just knew." Shelby certainly wasn't going to tell her that she and Gill had heard the entire episode.

Bentley and Pearce came into the room. "They chased us away from Crawford's room," Pearce said. "I thought I should be allowed to stay since he is my brother, but they said he needed rest. I think he wanted to talk to Gill."

"He'll have a time doing that with all the laudanum Dr. Fish poured into him. Crawford didn't even know his name," Bentley said, sitting down. He looked at Rose and Shelby. "Crying over Crawford?"

Shelby frowned at him. "Hush, Bentley."

Pearce was pacing and fidgeting. "I think I'll go to the village, to the inn. Coming, Bentley?"

"I don't think so. I have some things to do." He stood and looked for a moment at Shelby, then left the room behind Pearce.

It was almost an hour before Gill returned. "I have good news," he said. "Crawford will recover fully. The doctor says he's in a great deal of pain, but there's no question about his recovery."

Rose leaned back, limp. "May I see him? May I talk to him?"

"Not right now. The doctor gave him laudanum so he's sleeping heavily. I would hazard a guess that he won't be able to talk until tomorrow morning."

Shelby took Rose up to her room and put her to bed, giving her a few laudanum drops to help her rest. "If anything happens at all, I'll come get you," she promised Rose. "Everything will work out, you'll see."

She hurried back down to quiz Gill. He was still in the drawing room, talking to Hayward. They stopped speaking when she entered. They were standing next to the shattered glass and open panels of the jewel case. The colonel had ordered that nothing be touched until he decided whether or not to bring in a Runner.

"Do you think this is connected?" Shelby asked bluntly, walking up to them. "I don't recall a hunting accident of any kind around here before."

Gill sighed. "I think it's connected, but we won't know much until tomorrow when we can talk further to Crawford. I hope he can tell us something. Until then, there's nothing we can do except wait. I tried talking to him, but the laudanum Dr. Fish had given him had already taken effect."

"So you got nothing from him?"

Gill shook his head. "No, no name, no circumstances, nothing."

Later in the day, the entire family, except the colonel and Crawford, gathered for supper. Rose was deathly pale and merely shoved food around on her plate. Countess Rimildi tried to engage everyone in conversation, but that invariably died without more than a monosyllable or two. She even suggested cards after supper, but no one was interested. Everyone drifted off one by one at an early hour. Shelby excused herself and waited in the breakfast room until she saw Gill come out of the drawing room. She headed across the hall and intercepted him. "Have you any more news of Crawford?" she asked.

He looked around cautiously. "Would you like to go outside and carry on this conversation?" he asked softly. "You know my feelings about talking in the house."

She nodded and they went out, Dick Turpin right at her

heels. "Has he made you his surrogate parent?" Gill asked with a chuckle.

"I think so." Shelby sighed. "We accidentally left him outside when we came back from our walk this afternoon. I forgot him until almost five and then had to go searching for him. He came running up all covered in dirt. I thought he had been digging for moles, then decided he had been back on the hill, hunting for his rabbit."

Gill laughed softly. "No doubt the gardeners love that." He guided Shelby farther away from the house. They didn't talk until they reached the far edge of the garden where they had been during the morning, Dick Turpin beside them.

"Shall we sit under the tree again or on the garden bench over there?" Shelby asked, nodding toward an open spot. "With the evening damp, I think I prefer the bench." They walked to it, but Dick ran off in the opposite direction and began digging furiously under the bush he had been investigating during the morning.

"Is that a hole over there? It looks as big as Dick. He must have been working there all afternoon." Gill smiled, then looked at Shelby and became serious. "I suppose you want my thoughts on Crawford's accident."

"I thought it was no accident."

"I don't see how it could have been. Judging from the wound, whoever shot him was on the ground, shooting upward. That had to be deliberate. I only hope Crawford saw something."

Shelby hesitated, then blurted out her thoughts. "Do you think he might be harmed tonight? After all, if our culprit thinks Crawford saw something, then he might be in danger. The person would naturally want to silence him."

Gill sighed. "I've thought about that, and I think you're right. I've sent Luke and two men from the stables to stand guard. Two by the door, and one by the window. I've also requested that Mrs. McKilley prepare all his food herself." He paused. "I know you don't want to think it, but it has to be one of the family. But why Crawford? What would the person have to gain there?"

"I've asked that a dozen times today," Shelby said, "and I can think of no reason at all."

"Has anyone mentioned Crawford to you lately? In any manner?" Gill frowned.

Shelby watched Dick Turpin dig under the bush as she thought. The little dog scratched furiously, whining and whimpering as he dug, and she fretted about him getting his leg wound dirty. Gill followed her gaze. "Dick will be fine, I think. I looked at the cut on his leg this evening, and it's healing nicely."

"I just feel responsible for him with Grandfather gone." She looked at him digging furiously. The only part of Dick visible in the moonlight was his hind quarters. "He's going to fall into that hole in a minute," she said absently.

"Crawford?" Gill reminded her.

She sighed. "There's nothing at all that I can think of. Everyone has mentioned that he needed money. Rose has talked about it. That's about all I can remember."

"Who mentioned him within the past day or so?"

Shelby waved her hand in frustration. "We've all talked about each other in some way over the past days. I told Rose that I didn't really care for him, and Bentley asked me if Crawford was the reason I rejected his offer."

"Bentley asked that?" Gill's voice was flat.

Shelby nodded. "It doesn't signify. I told him that Crawford wasn't why I refused him."

"And how did he take that refusal?"

Shelby looked at him, frowning. "Oh, good heavens, Gill. Don't even consider Bentley. I know he's odd, but he's just a child in many ways. He's never grown up at all."

"A selfish child?"

"Just a child." Shelby peered through the gathering gloom

to see Dick Turpin emerge from the hole he had dug. "What has that scamp found? If he comes in here with a mole or a rabbit, I'm going to. . . ." She stopped as the moonlight caught and gleamed on the object in Dick's mouth. She leaned forward and called to Dick to come to her. He obligingly trotted over to her, his prize in his mouth.

"Look, Gill! Oh, good Lord, is that what I think it is?" she asked breathlessly.

Gill stood up and went to Dick, kneeling down beside the dog who dropped his prize and tried to grin. Shelby fell to her knees beside him and picked up the dirty circlet.

"The tiara," she gasped. "Dick has found the Jewels of Ali."

Fifteen

Gill dug carefully in the hole, unearthing the rest of the jewels and their wrapping. "We might find a clue here," he said, pulling the cloth from the hole. "It looks like some kind of coat. We'll take it back to the house where we can see it better. This may be able to tell us something." He glanced at her. "Are all the jewels here?"

"Yes." She looked at the heavy jewels in her hands. "These aren't really worth all the trouble they've caused, are they?"

Gill stood with the coat in his hands and helped her up. "That kind of thing seldom is," he said, taking her elbow. They walked back to Wychwood, Gill carrying the coat and jewels, and Shelby carrying Dick Turpin.

Once inside, they went into the dining room where they could spread out the jewelry out and examine it in the candlelight. Bentley and Pearce saw them come in and followed them. "How did you find them?" Pearce asked, fingering the bracelet. "Is everything here?"

"Dick Turpin found them. I don't know how he knew where to look. He had been sniffing along the ground all the way, and, yes, as far as I know, everything is here." Shelby began spreading the jewels on the table.

"This is great news," Pearce said with a smile. "The others are in the back, playing cards. I'm going back and tell them. They'll be as glad as I am that these things have been found.

Perhaps we can get back to normal." He paused at the door and grinned. "Or at least as normal as this family ever gets." He went out the door, muttering, "Dick Turpin. Who would have thought it?"

Gill looked at Shelby and grinned. "Dick is turning into quite a hero."

Shelby smiled down at Dick, who was sitting on his haunches, looking quizzical. He waved his front paw at her and tried to grin. "All right, Dick," she said with a laugh as she picked him up and held him, "I'll get you a nice piece of ham as a reward. I promise."

By the time Shelby had spread the jewels out and checked to see that all the stones were still in each piece, all the others except Hayward had crowded into the small room. Hayward had gone up to check on Crawford for a moment. He returned as the others were examining the jewels. Pearce was just putting the tiara on his head.

"Lovely, Pearce," Hayward said briefly. "I bring good news as well." He stopped to sneeze and gave Dick Turpin a significant look. Shelby gave him a rueful smile and put Dick back down on the floor. Hayward sneezed again as Dick walked by him. Dick stopped, looked up at Hayward, and shook his fur. Hayward again sneezed, and Dick looked quite satisfied. He went out into the hall and flopped down, putting his nose on his paws and looking at them.

Hayward wiped his nose with his handkerchief. "Now my news—Crawford is awake and asking for something to drink. Perhaps he'll feel like talking to us within a couple of hours. I'm going up and sit with him. I'll let you know if he says anything."

"Good. Luke and the men from the stable are still there, aren't they?" Shelby asked.

Hayward nodded. "I checked the windows as well. I'm sure that no one can get in there."

Gill gave him an approving look. "That's good. I'm hoping

Crawford saw something that may identify the person who shot him." Gill picked up the coat that had wrapped the jewels and spread it out across the table. "There may be a clue here that will help us." He frowned and looked closely at the coat. "Damn," he muttered.

"What is it?" Shelby asked as she stepped closer to him. The others crowded around the table.

Shelby touched the coat and turned over the facings to look at the buttons. "I've seen this coat somewhere," she said, running her fingers down the dirty, damp nap. Parts of the soft fabric had been burned. Suddenly it came to her and her fingers fell limply against the fine wool. "This is yours, isn't it?" she asked, looking at Gill.

"Yes, but. . . ." He frowned and shook his head.

"So you took them," Bentley said flatly. "Do we need to disarm you, Mr. Gill?"

"Of course not." Gill's tone was sharp. "This is the coat I had on the night the carpet burned. I looked at it and saw that it was ruined and must have left it down here somewhere. I didn't think of it again."

"Or," said Bentley slowly, "you needed something to wrap the jewels up in until you could retrieve them and make your escape, and that ruined coat was convenient. It was just your ill luck that Dick Turpin found it." They all looked at Gill, waiting for an answer.

"That's ridiculous," Shelby blurted out. "Mr. Gill and I were alone when we found them. If he had wanted to take them, all he had to do was hit me over the head and run."

"Oh, and what were the two of you doing out alone?"

"Bentley, enough." Hayward pinned his brother with a look. "I'm sure if Shelby and Mr. Gill felt the need to take a turn around the garden for some fresh air, or to walk Dick Turpin, it's none of our concern."

Bentley lifted an eyebrow and looked at Shelby. "First

Crawford, now Mr. Gill. Are you turning fickle on us, Shelby?"

"Bentley." There was a warning note in Hayward's voice. "Enough."

Pearce picked up the necklace and let it run through his fingers. "We'd better send a messenger to London to tell the colonel. He'll be relieved."

"We can do that first thing tomorrow," Gill said, scooping the jewels up and handing them to Shelby. "In the meantime, where can we put them so they'll be safe? I suggest in the room with Crawford since we have guards posted there."

They all agreed, and Gill glanced around for a container. Shelby handed him a silver pitcher, and he put everything except the tiara in it. He hung the tiara across the neck of the pitcher. "Here, Hayward. Take these up when you go."

Hayward took the pitcher and went out, giving Dick Turpin an evil look as he passed him in the hall. Dick grinned at Hayward and wriggled on the floor. He stood up and shook, but Hayward was already out of range. Dick began hopping up the stairs behind him.

Gill looked at the door, then made a decision. "If you'll excuse me, I believe I'll go up and see if Crawford is talking." He took a deep breath. "Might I escort you to your room, Miss Falcon?"

Shelby hesitated, then left with him. As they walked up the stairs, she looked up at him. "Why did you do that? You were rather obvious in wanting to get me away from Bentley and Pearce. Why?"

Gill sidestepped to dodge Dick Turpin on the landing. Dick grinned at him, got nowhere, and began hopping back down the stairs. Gill glanced down the stairs and saw Bentley watching them from the hall. He turned the corner to be out of sight before he answered. "Because," he whispered, "I don't want to leave you alone with anyone I don't trust."

"And you don't trust Pearce and Bentley?" She paused in front of her door and looked at him.

He hesitated. "No."

"Why not? I don't think . . ."

"Shelby," he said patiently, interrupting her, "someone has tried to kill both your grandfather and Crawford. We've agreed that it has to be someone in this house, probably someone in the family. With Crawford getting shot, that eliminates him."

"And Hayward?"

"Just instinct on my part. I don't think he would do it."

"Not even if he needed money? After all, he is supposed to be in worse shape financially than any of the others."

Gill nodded. "I know, but my instincts tell me he didn't do this."

"So," she said slowly, "you think that leaves Pearce or Bentley."

"That's right." Gill frowned and held her arm. "I'm going to see if Crawford is talking yet. Don't come out of your room for anyone. Since all the keys match, there's no locking your door against an intruder, so put a chair under the knob." He turned to leave.

Shelby caught at his sleeve. "Come back and tell me how Crawford is."

"All right." He hesitated. "Crawford may not feel like speaking until the middle of the night. It might look curious if I come knocking on your door."

She smiled at him, and he thought he had never seen anything more lovely. The candlelight in the hall was glinting off her luxuriant auburn hair, and her eyes looked dark and smoky in the shadows. There was laughter in her voice as she answered him. "Perhaps it may seem curious, Gill, but it might be a nice touch. Remember that we're pretending to have affection for each other."

He couldn't help himself. He put his hands on the wall, one on either side of her head, and backed her against it. He didn't

touch her with any part of his body, but he was acutely aware
of her of every contour of her body. He could smell the faint
touch of lavender that always reminded him of Shelby, gardens,
and things promised and unpromised. He looked at her a long
time, as though memorizing every feature, every nuance of
her. Finally he moved one hand and ran his fingers around the
oval of her face. "I have a problem with that, Miss Falcon . . .
Shelby." He hesitated. "I'm no longer pretending." With that,
he moved away, gave her an enigmatic look, and went down
to Crawford's room.

Shelby touched her face where Gill's fingers had moved
over her skin. Had she heard him correctly? In a daze, she
went into her room and shut the door. She went over to the
small chair and sat down, hardly knowing what she was doing.
He cares, she thought to herself. *He cares for me.* She hugged
herself and swayed slightly in the chair.

There was a knock at her door, and she ran to open it. It
was Countess Rimildi. "Shelby, I want to leave this place tomorrow." The countess swept into the room. "Your grandfather
is not dying, so there's no need for us to stay, other than one
small problem." She sat down, frowning. "I just don't like the
way this house feels this visit. You know my intuition is never
wrong."

"We can't leave, Mama. My intuition tells me that something is wrong here as well, but what's the problem you see?"

Countess Rimildi stared at her. "Rose," she said in a mourn-
ful voice. "There's just no reason for us to stay other than
Rose. I can't in good conscience leave her here alone, and she
refuses to leave until Crawford gets better." She lowered her
voice and patted Shelby on the knee. "I don't know how to
say this, Shelby dear, but I completely understand. I'm so
sorry. I do know that you have feelings for Crawford, but it
looks as if he and Rose are going to reconcile." She sighed.
"I expect wedding bells as soon as possible."

"Good," Shelby said.

The countess's eyebrows went up. "I thought you would be devastated, dear. That's why I wanted to break the news myself and console you."

Shelby laughed. "I'm happy for them, Mother. Furthermore, I don't blame Rose for staying, and, as you say, it is our duty to stay here with her. It will probably be only a few days. Hayward said Crawford was much improved." She couldn't resist a glance at the door. If Gill came knocking while her mother was in the room . . . It didn't bear thinking on.

"Why don't you go tell Rose that we'll stay here for a few days with her? I'm sure she's distressed beyond words, and that would mean a great deal to her. She does need our comfort." Shelby stood and tried to steer her mother toward the door.

Countess Rimildi sighed. "You're right, of course, Shelby, but I can't say that I like it. I've never really liked this place, not in the way you do." She frowned. "Bates didn't either, truth be told. He much preferred"—she paused—"actually, he much preferred looking at leaves and flowers to anything else." She sighed again. "I've had my difficulties in life, but I always knew my duty. I'll do it now."

"Wonderful, Mother." Shelby gave her a quick kiss. "I'm sure Rose will be grateful." She opened the door and peered out. No one was in the hall except Bentley, and he was going back down the stairs. Shelby nodded at him, and nudged her mother out into the hall and toward Rose's room.

Shelby closed the door behind the countess and leaned against it, hugging herself. She sat back down, reveling in what Gill had said, wondering again if she had heard him correctly. She couldn't wait until he came to tell her about Crawford so she could talk to him. Should she tell him how she felt? Should she wait for him to say something else? She played a dozen scenes over in her mind.

There was another knock on the door, but it was only Dovey.

Shelby had her lay nightclothes out and then leave. She didn't want anyone around when Gill came back to see her.

Shelby sat waiting, and then waited some more. The clock in the hall struck the hour, then another. She got up and paced, trying to place the feeling that she had forgotten something. "Dick Turpin," she finally said aloud in horror. "I forgot Dick Turpin. And after I promised to take good care of him and watch him." She ran for the door and looked out, but Dick wasn't in the hall or sleeping in front of the colonel's door. She slipped through the quiet to the landing and looked down the stairs. "Dick," she called softly, "where are you? Come here." There was no answer, and no wriggling little dog in sight. Slowly she went down the stairs, looking off to the side, calling softly for Dick.

Candles were still burning in the breakfast room and Shelby peered inside. Pearce and Bentley were there, playing cards at the table. They stopped and looked at her as she entered. "Have you seen Dick Turpin? I seem to have misplaced him."

Pearce shook his head and leaned back in his chair, stretching. "No, I haven't seen him lately. Gill came down for some brandy about an hour ago, and I think Dick went back up the stairs with him. He's probably in the blue bedroom with Gill and Crawford."

"And Hayward," Bentley added with a laugh. "Perhaps you could go up and listen for Hayward sneezing."

Pearce tossed his cards down on the table. "I'll go with you to look. I want to see how Crawford is anyway. I've waited for hours for someone to come down and tell me, but there's been nothing." He stood. "After all, Crawford is my brother, and if anyone deserves to know, I do." He paused at the door. "Coming, Bentley?"

"In a moment." Bentley put his cards down and smiled at Shelby. She felt a touch of fear run down her spine. She hadn't been afraid with both Bentley and Pearce in the room, but after Gill's comments, she was afraid to be alone with either one. She shrugged off her feelings. *This is family,* she told herself. *They won't hurt me.*

"Tell me, Shelby," Bentley said, smiling and walking over to her. "Have you changed your mind?"

"About what, Bentley?"

"About marrying me." He took her arm and drew her closer to him.

She looked up at him. "No, Bentley, I haven't. We wouldn't suit at all. Surely you can see that."

"I can't see it at all, Shelby. I've thought about it. I think we would rub along just right. You'd be there to take care of me, and I could do whatever I wished. We'd have money and the jewels; we'd have Wychwood eventually." He loosened his hold on her arm and let his fingers slide down her arm to clasp her fingers in his.

Shelby took a step back and pulled away. "It wouldn't work, Bentley. We have nothing at all in common, and, while I have affection for you as family, it just isn't enough."

He frowned. "Don't tell me that you're concerned for Crawford? He could quite easily die, and then you'd be wearing the willow. Surely not!"

"Don't even think that, Bentley! And no, I don't consider Crawford as a husband. Mother tells me that he and Rose are reconciling. I'm worried about Crawford because he's a part of my family."

Bentley looked at her strangely. He still held her hand, and brought it up to his chest, looking at it. "Then it must be someone else." He paused. "Neither Hayward nor Pearce, I know, so it must be Gill."

Shelby tried to keep the blush from spreading across her face, but felt the warmth as blood rushed to her face. "Don't be ridiculous, Bentley."

"So I'm right." His voice was hard. "It's Gill. He's not for you, Shelby, and I'll see to that."

"Bentley, there's nothing to discuss." She stepped back,

pulling her hand from his. "I've got to go find Dick. I promised Grandfather that I'd watch him." She paused, her foot on the bottom step. "Are you coming up, Bentley?"

"I have something I need to do first," he said, watching her go up the stairs. He had one arm draped casually over the newel post. "I'll be up in a minute."

Shelby went along the hall, calling softly for Dick. He was nowhere to be found. She knocked on the door to the blue room where Crawford was. Hayward opened the door and Shelby was shocked. His eyes were puffy as though he had been crying. "Crawford!" she said in alarm. "Is Crawford . . . ?" She couldn't finish the sentence.

Hayward shook his head and stood aside so she could enter. Pearce and Gill were by Crawford's bed. Pearce looked dazed. He turned as Shelby came in and looked out the window. "Where are Luke and the other men?" Shelby asked.

"I sent them out." There was a strange note in Crawford's voice. He looked weak and spent. "I wanted to talk to everyone."

There was a long silence as the tension in the room built. Shelby looked from one to the other, but no one said anything else. "I came looking for Dick Turpin," Shelby blurted. "I seem to have misplaced him."

"He isn't here," Hayward said, turning away and mopping at his face with his handkerchief. "I haven't seen him." He paused. "Have you seen Bentley?"

"He's coming up in a moment." Shelby moved toward the bed. "Are you all right, Crawford?"

"As well as can be expected, considering the circumstances." He tried a grin, but it didn't work. Shelby looked up at Gill, but he was looking over her shoulder, and she could almost feel the tension in him. Everyone in the room turned to follow his gaze. Bentley was standing in the doorway.

"What a nice family gathering," he said. He looked over at the dresser on the side wall, where the silver pitcher holding the jewels rested. "And you even have all the jewels here with you. How very convenient."

"It's over, Bentley," Hayward said hoarsely. "Crawford saw you."

Bentley looked at Hayward and smiled. "Saw what?"

"Dammit, man!" Hayward shouted, clenching his fists. "Crawford saw you try to kill him!" He stopped and tried to calm himself, then turned around, his back to Bentley.

"Impossible," Bentley said. "He must have been seeing things."

"He saw things, all right," Gill said quietly. "He saw you stand by the tree at the side of the road and shoot straight at him."

Pearce turned, his face contorted. "Why, Bentley? Why would you do such a thing?"

Bentley frowned as though searching for an answer. "Shelby wouldn't marry me because of Crawford. So I had to get rid of him." He smiled. "It's perfectly simple, isn't it?"

"Did you set the fire as well?" Hayward whispered hoarsely.

Bentley smiled at him. "Of course." He walked over and picked up the pitcher with the jewels. "I'm going to take these with me."

"What do you mean?" Hayward turned. "You're not going anywhere." He took a step toward Bentley, only to have Bentley pull a pistol out and aim it at him.

"I thought someone might try to stop me," Bentley said pleasantly. "Shelby, come over here. You're going with me."

"No." Shelby had never actually looked down the barrel of a pistol, and the thing appeared enormous in Bentley's hand. "I'm not going with you, Bentley." She stared hard at him, hearing Hayward sneeze in the background. "Did you do all those things to Grandfather, Bentley? Why?"

"Why?" He looked at her, surprised. "I needed money and things, and he didn't. It was time for him to go and leave us our inheritances. He certainly doesn't need them." He smiled, tucking the pitcher under one arm. "Come along, Shelby. We can be married, and then we'll go to"—he paused—"France? Italy?"

Shelby stood her ground, and Bentley came toward her. "I suppose I'll just have to kill Mr. Gill, won't I? Shelby, you give me no choice."

"No!" Shelby tried to control herself. "No, Bentley, don't do that. I'll come with you."

He smiled sweetly at her. "That's good. Now come along. We need to get to Dover and make arrangements. I'm not much of a sailor, you know, but I can manage." He handed her the pitcher. "You take that." He looked around. "Good-bye, everyone. We'll write once we're married." He began humming as he backed toward the door. Shelby stood still, and he hooked one arm around her neck and began pulling her backward, humming Mozart in her ear. The gun was next to her shoulder, aimed right at Gill. She didn't dare resist.

Hayward sneezed again, and Dick Turpin scooted into the room. Bentley kicked at him as he sidled past and ran over to Gill. Dick hopped on the small steps by the bed, and looked at Bentley and Shelby. Sensing the fear in the room, his hair bristled and he showed his teeth, this time in anger. He growled low in his throat.

"Stupid dog," Bentley said. "If I had time, I'd shoot you right here." He frowned and yanked Shelby's neck. "Come on."

She cried out as Bentley jerked her neck and pulled her backward. With a growl from deep in his throat, Dick Turpin launched himself at Bentley. The pistol went off as Dick, Shelby, and Bentley all went crashing against the wall. Gill flung himself over the corner of the bed, catching Bentley around the midsection. Hayward sneezed.

Gill and Bentley rolled across the floor as Shelby snatched up the pistol. Dick Turpin danced around, barking, trying to nip Bentley when he had a chance. He ran around and hopped back up on the steps by the bed, where he barked some more. Hayward sneezed.

Pearce ran to help Gill, and they subdued Bentley. Gill stood and pulled Bentley to his feet. "Well," said Bentley, looking around at the others and smiling, "I do suppose that ends this evening's entertainment."

Hayward looked at Bentley. "You're still my brother, Bentley, and I'll do what I can." He sniffled and walked over to Bentley. "Pearce, help me with him, will you? We'll need to stay with him until we decide what to do." The two of them escorted Bentley out of the room as Rose and Countess Rimildi came rushing in.

"Crawford!" Rose ran to the bedside.

"Whatever is going on?" Countess Rimildi asked, her mobcap askew.

Gill took the pistol from Shelby's hand and scooped up Dick Turpin who was still barking. "A pistol accidentally went off, Countess. Nothing else." He smiled at her and went out.

Shelby glanced at the door and then back at her mother. "You'd best stay with Rose, Mother," she said hastily. "I'm sure it wouldn't be seemly for her to be in here alone."

"Heavens, no!" Countess Rimildi pulled up a chair and sat down, her eyes on Crawford and Rose. Shelby slipped out the door.

Gill was sitting wearily on the top step, the pistol dangling from his fingers and Dick Turpin curled up beside him. Shelby picked up Dick and sat down beside Gill. "Are you all right?" she asked, touching his arm.

He turned to look at her. "Yes. And you?"

"I'm fine." She paused. "Bentley. I would never have thought it. I thought Hayward was the one who needed money and might try to take the jewels to get it."

"Hayward had some debts of his own, but he had borrowed what he could to cover Bentley's gambling debts. Evidently, Bentley hasn't been . . . hasn't been quite right for the past two years." He paused. "Hayward has been trying to watch him, but things have been happening."

"What things?"

Gill looked at her. "I'm not sure you want to know details. From what Hayward told us tonight, Bentley has been cruel to animals and some people."

"Cruel? Bentley? I can't imagine it? In what way do you mean?"

He put the pistol down on the step beside him. "Torturing helpless creatures. That's all I want to say."

Shelby shuddered. "That's enough." She hesitated. "What will become of him?"

"We were discussing that when you came in. I think my Uncle Bates can arrange for him to stay with a doctor in Yorkshire who treats this sort of thing."

"An asylum? No, no, Gill. No matter what Bentley has done, he doesn't deserve that."

He looked at her. "I know you're thinking of Bedlam, but this is nothing like that. Dr. Moss takes only three patients at a time, and he treats them well. I don't know if Bentley will ever be able to leave, though."

"Does Hayward agree with this?"

Gill nodded. "Yes. Crawford and Pearce do as well." He ran his fingers through his thick, dark hair, leaving one curl brushing his forehead. "It's over, I suppose." He turned to her and grinned weakly. "And I suppose as well that you won't have to endure any more proposals of marriage for a while. How many were there—one from each? Four proposals?"

"Yes, four. And not one of them heartfelt." She smiled at him, a smile that just lifted the corner of her mouth. She waited for him to say something else, but he was silent, just looking at her.

"Did you mean what you said earlier?" she asked him, her heart pounding in her chest. "About not pretending anymore."

He looked at her for a long moment, everything he had ever

wanted coming together in this face, this perfect woman. "Yes," he said quietly, not daring to touch her, to break the spell.

"Is it hard for you to express your feelings, Gill?" she whispered. "Can you say that you care for me?"

He looked away a moment, then back to her. "It is difficult. Everyone I ever loved has gone away and left me. My parents, my family." He hesitated. "I'm afraid that if . . ." He stopped, unable to go on.

"You've got to learn to tell me," she said, twisting so that they faced each other. "Say the words: *I love you, Shelby.* Say them."

He pulled her to him and buried his face in her hair, running his fingers through the tumble of auburn. "I love you, Shelby," he whispered hoarsely. "You'll never know how much I love you."

She pulled away to look at him, tears shining in her eyes. "I think I do know how much, Gill, because I love you more than I can ever tell you." She smiled at him as tears spilled over. "There's only one thing left, isn't there?"

He smiled back at her as Dick Turpin tried to wriggle between them. "Yes, there is love, and this one is heartfelt." He put his hands on either side of her face and looked at her, a warm, loving smile on his lips. "Will you marry me?"

"My fifth proposal, and my last," Shelby said, laughing and crying at the same time. "Yes, my love, yes."

Hello,

I hope you've enjoyed reading *The Fifth Proposal*. I thoroughly enjoyed writing it, as I enjoy all my Zebra Regencies. I am also pleased to tell you that my newest novella will be in the Regency anthology Zebra will be issuing to commemorate Mother's Day, 2000. I'm very excited to be able to be a part of this Mother's Day anthology.

If you enjoyed *The Fifth Proposal* or any of my other books, or just have a comment, please write to me. A SASE would be greatly appreciated. My address is:

> Juliette Leigh
> Box 295
> Pineola, NC 28662

Or if you prefer, e-mail me at romance@sff.net.

You may also want to take a quick look at my Web page if you're on the Internet. The address is http://www.sff.net/people/romance.

My Web page contains a short biography, some frequently asked questions and answers, and my publication list. *The Fifth Proposal* is my nineteenth publication, so I hope you will want to read some of the others. Since I'm learning about the Internet as I go along, that page is always under construction, but I plan to post any news I may have. I would appreciate your comments on it.

I hope to hear from you soon, and thanks so much for reading *The Fifth Proposal!*

> Happy reading!
> Juliette Leigh

LOOK FOR THESE REGENCY ROMANCES